Art preceding page: artist David A. Aguilar's decorative composite of a planet, star, and galaxy. Here: the artist's image of an alien world and its moon in the heart of the Milky Way galaxy.

NATIONAL GEOGRAPHIC

SPACE

ENCYCLOPEDIA

A TOUR OF OUR SOLAR SYSTEM AND BEYOND

WRITTEN & ILLUSTRATED BY DAVID A. AGUILAR

NATIONAL GEOGRAPHIC

WASHINGTON, D.C.

CONTENTS

Introduction by David A. Aguilar **6**

TOUR OF THE SOLAR SYSTEM

WHAT WE KNOW

TO THE STARS AND BEYOND

ARE WE **ALONE?**

DREAMS OF TOMORROW

In the "To the Stars and Beyond" chapter, when a picture of a constellation, galaxy, or nebula has the binoculars symbol beside it, that means you can use your own binoculars to look for the object in the night sky.

ABOUT THE ILLUSTRATIONS

The art for this book was created by David A. Aguilar on his computer. He began by gathering the best scientific information available. Using that information, he sketched images that were as realistic as possible in his notebook. Then he transferred those sketches to his computer and painted with his mouse, using Adobe Photoshop and building up layer upon layer, until his vision of space appeared. Sometimes he built models of spaceships out of junk plastic found around his house (again using the latest data to guide his hand). Or he made planetary landscapes out of torn pieces of paper towels dipped into watered-down plaster of paris, then photographed them and colored them in Photoshop. In some cases he also incorporated images taken by telescopes and satellites into the art.

Why do we even need artwork in a book about the real world? Sometimes we don't. For example, we have very good photographs of Mars, but there are many other places (such as extrasolar planets) and many perspectives (such as gazing at Jupiter from the surface of Europa) along with possible future events (such as astronauts visiting Uranus's moon Miranda) that we can visualize only by turning scientific data into art. Some of the places and events in these imaginary images will never actually be seen, because no telescope is capable of photographing them.

The photographs in this book were taken by satellites and telescopes, as well as by cameras here on Earth. Most came from NASA, the National Aeronautics and Space Administration.

Growing up in the Santa Clara Valley in California, I lived in a dreamland for anyone in love with nature. Orchards full of quail and pheasant stretched as far as a young person could hike in a day. The white, pink, and blue blossoms of fruit trees filled the air when gentle breezes blew in from the Pacific Ocean. Half an hour away, tide pools and clear cold waters awaited the young underwater explorer. It was a nature lover's paradise.

My bedroom was filled with insect collections, pressed wildflowers, fossils, terrariums, and model airplanes. On the walls were posters and drawings of planets and galaxies, and in the corner stood my trusty three-inch (7.6-cm) reflecting telescope, which I constructed all by myself (photo-illustration at right).

For the mirror of my telescope, I had used two glass casters "borrowed" from my grandmother's four-poster bed. The casters were like small glass cups that people used to put beneath the legs of their beds so that the legs wouldn't scratch the floor. I had ground the casters together with abrasives purchased from a rock shop, then polished them using a mixture of water and jeweler's rouge on top of sticky pitch collected from our cherry tree.

My eyepiece was constructed from two slightly chipped lenses salvaged from the pirate spyglass my brother bought at the county fair. I glued the lenses inside the plastic top of a mouthwash bottle. My cardboard telescope tube came from the trash

bin behind a carpet store, and my mount was made from scrap lumber and a few inexpensive plumbers pipe fittings. A little paint here and there, and I was in business exploring the universe. My telescope worked better than anything Galileo used to make his discoveries. I named it Mable, after my grandmother.

The first thing I looked at was the moon. I saw craters, flat valleys, and mountains everywhere! Seeing the moons of Jupiter and the rings of Saturn opened my eyes and imagination in ways I had never experienced before. Little did I know that my hobby would someday become my career.

Besides telescopes, there was something else that drew me to astronomy. It was the mystery of UFOs. In my young mind the same question kept popping up: What if they are real? What if they really are out there?

Today, I am part of one of the largest astronomical research organizations in the world—the Harvard-Smithsonian Center for Astrophysics. Our observatories are located on mountaintops in Chile, Arizona, and Hawaii and in orbit above our heads in space. When I come to work each morning, I never know what great discovery may await me.

The discoveries astronomers make sometimes change the way we think about ourselves and our place in the universe. In the next 25 years we may know the answers to these really big questions: What caused the big bang? What invisible force is speeding up the expansion of the universe? Are there other universes out there besides our own? What type of life exists on other planets? Are there other "Earth-worlds" out there? And maybe, once and for all, what is this phenomenon we call UFOs all about?

This is why I love astronomy so much. The biggest questions regarding our universe are waiting to be answered. Somewhere out there in the world today are the future scientists who will find the answers to these great questions. Maybe one of them will be you.

DAVID A. AGUILAR

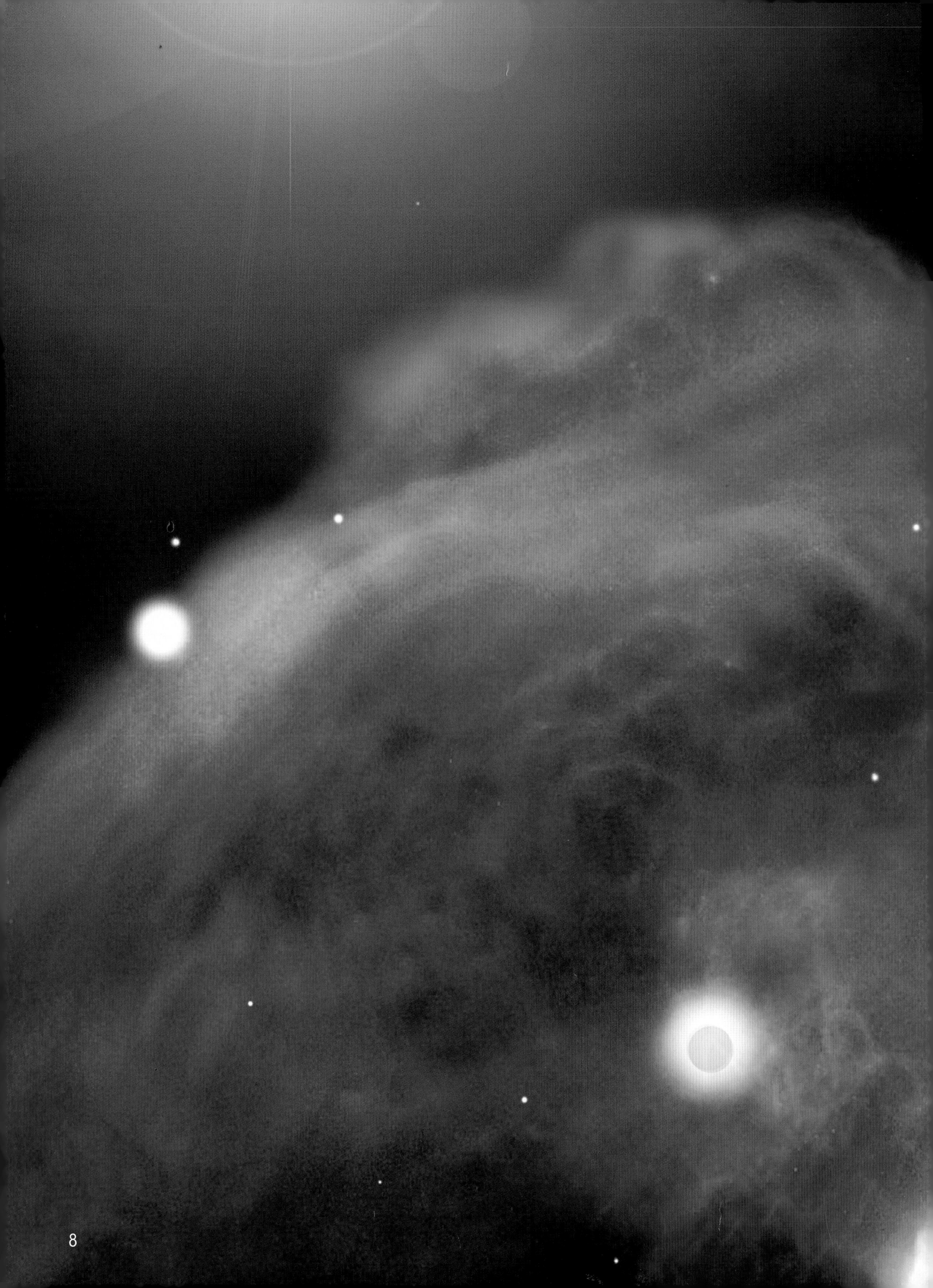

After the big bang that gave rise to our universe, stars began to form from clouds of gas and dust.

THE UNIVERSE BEGAN WITH A BIG BANG

Clear your mind for a minute and try to imagine this: All the things you see in the universe today—all the stars, galaxies, and planets floating around out there—do not exist. Everything that now exists is concentrated in a single, incredibly dense point scientists call a singularity. Then, suddenly, the elements that make the material universe flash into existence. That actually happened about 13.8 billion years ago, in the moment we call the big bang.

For centuries scientists, religious scholars, poets, and philosophers wondered how the universe came to be. Was it always there? Will it always be the same, or will it change? If it had a beginning, will it someday end, or will it go on forever?

These were huge questions. But today, because of our recent observations of space and what it's made of, we think we may have answers to some of them. We know the big bang created not only matter but space itself. We also think in the very distant future stars will run out of fuel and blink out. Once again the universe will become dark.

FACTS ABOUT THE BIG BANG

Big bang happened	13.8 billion years ago
Size of universe at big bang	Infinitely small
Temperature of universe at one second	10 billion °F (5.5 billion °C)
Temperature of universe at 324,000 years	4940°F (2727°C)
First stars form	About 200 million years after big bang
First galaxies form	About 400 million years after big bang

FUN FACT

The very early universe was dense and dark—no light could travel through it. At around 380,000 years, it became transparent, and light could move freely in space. That's why we can see the stars shine! NASA's Spitzer Space Telescope captured the glow of these stars and galaxies in the Ursa Major constellation.

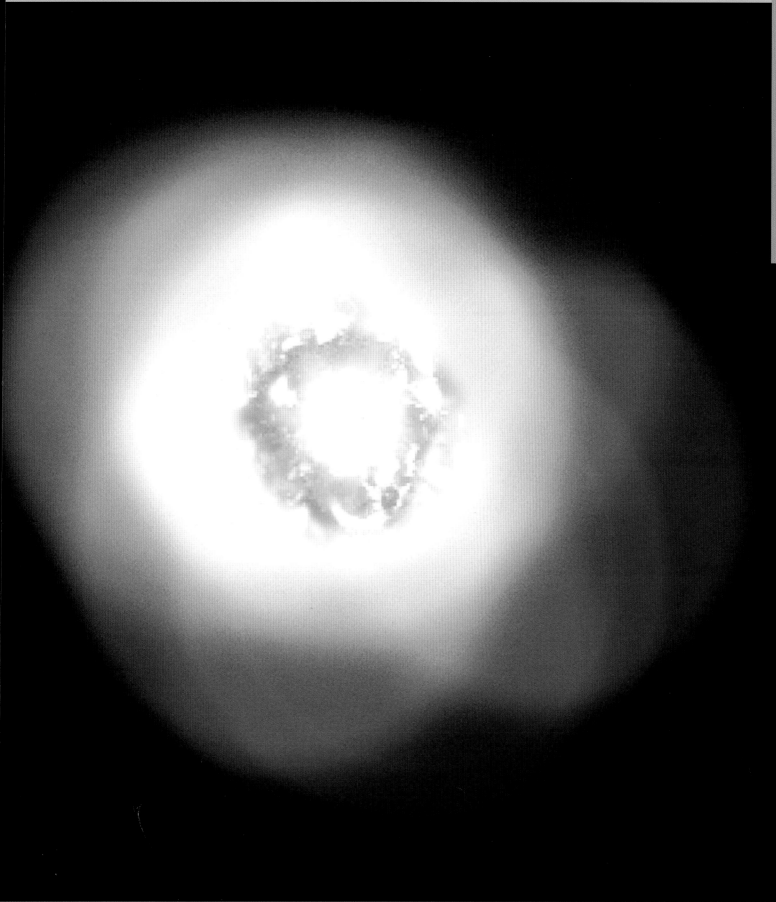

BIG BANG BALLOON

Everything we can see or detect around us in the universe began with the big bang. It wasn't a violent explosion like a stick of dynamite blowing up. Instead, it was a sudden expansion of space, like a giant balloon inflating.

THE MISSING UNIVERSE

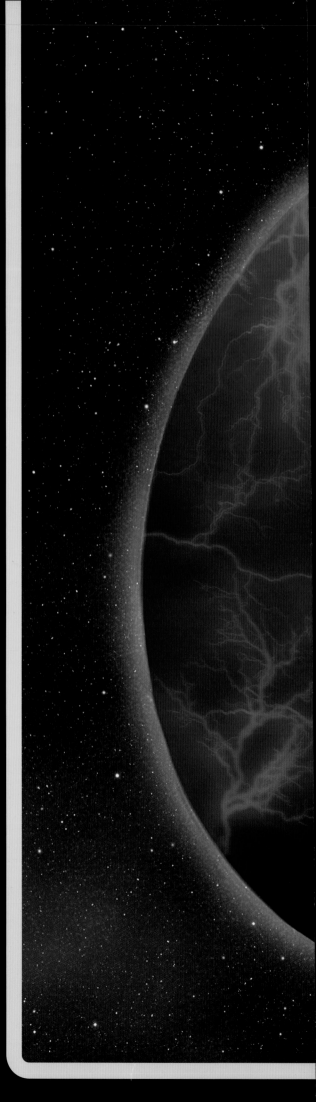

A stronomers have learned that there's a lot more to the universe than what we can see directly. It's like an iceberg. The part of the iceberg that's visible floating above the surface is only one-tenth of the ice. The other nine-tenths lurks underwater, unseen.

In our universe, the gas, stars, and galaxies we can see make up about 5 percent of what is out there. We know there's more we can't see because the unseen "stuff" exerts a gravitational force. It pulls on the stuff we can see. But gravity provides our only clue. The unseen stuff doesn't emit radiation that we can detect, so astronomers call it dark matter.

What is dark matter made of? We don't know. It's not just dark stars or planets or even black holes. It may be vast numbers of tiny particles. We do know that, whatever it is, it makes up about 27 percent of the universe.

Dark Energy

So if regular matter and dark matter together are about 32 percent of the universe, what makes up the other 68 percent? An even more mysterious thing called dark energy. Until the late 1990s, we didn't even know it existed. Then astronomers discovered, to their amazement, that the universe was not only expanding, but speeding up as it expanded.

We still don't know the source of the energy that is powering this speed. Is it some new kind of energy field, or a property of space itself? Or are we completely mistaken about some basic facts of physics and gravity? Will dark energy make physicists rewrite the laws of physics in order to understand the universe? One thing we do know: The universe is much stranger than we ever imagined.

SUPER STARS

In the 1960s and '70s, astronomer Vera Rubin (1928-2016) was studying the way that spiral galaxies (see pages 150-151) spin when she saw a strange thing. The stars on the galaxies' outer edges moved just as fast as ones farther in. They would do that only if the galaxy held a huge amount of unseen mass. Rubin had just confirmed the existence of "dark matter," a mysterious substance that we now know makes up much of the universe.

Vera Rubin had wanted to be an astronomer since she was a girl watching the stars out of her bedroom window. After earning a Ph.D. from Georgetown University in 1954, she was often the only woman astronomer in the room. Working at the Palomar Observatory in California, U.S.A., she saw that they had only a men's restroom, so she taped a skirt over the man's figure on the door to make it a women's restroom, too.

Dr. Rubin was awarded the National Medal of Science in 1993 for her discovery of dark matter. She knew that her discovery had raised more questions than answers. "I'm sorry I know so little," she said. "I'm sorry we all know so little. But that's kind of the fun, isn't it?"

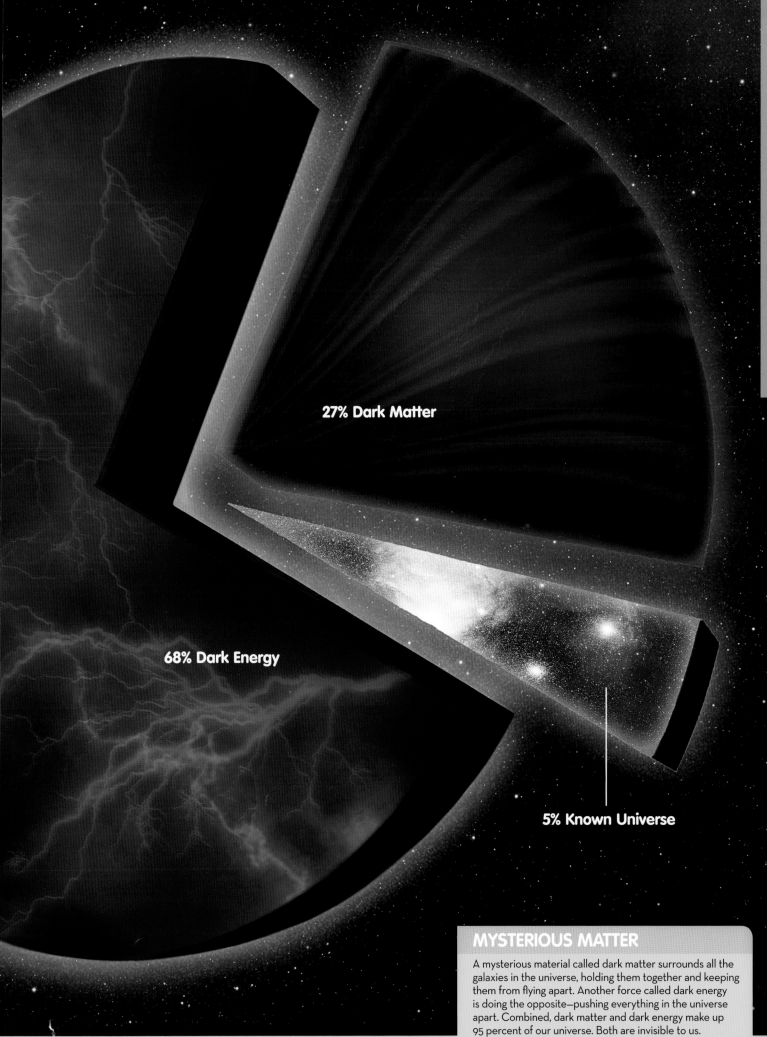

27% Dark Matter

68% Dark Energy

5% Known Universe

MYSTERIOUS MATTER

A mysterious material called dark matter surrounds all the galaxies in the universe, holding them together and keeping them from flying apart. Another force called dark energy is doing the opposite—pushing everything in the universe apart. Combined, dark matter and dark energy make up 95 percent of our universe. Both are invisible to us.

THERE ARE OTHER
SOLAR SYSTEMS

Humans long believed that there were other planets out in space, circling around distant stars. Scientists just never knew where to look for them. In the past 25 years all that has changed. Today, astronomers have confirmed more than 4,100 extrasolar (outside of our solar system) planets, and the number continues to climb. Some astronomers think that there are at least 100 billion planets in our galaxy alone.

These planets come in a variety of sizes, temperatures, and orbits. Many detected so far are giants like Jupiter and Saturn—but this is mostly because these are easier to spot. Big observatories on Earth and orbiting telescopes have also found small, rocky planets, boiling hot planets, iceball planets, systems with seven planets, planets around double stars, planets around red giant stars, and even lonely wandering planets without a star.

The great prize for planet-finders, though, is an Earthlike, Earth-size planet in the "habitable zone." This is an orbit that keeps a planet warm enough to hold liquid water on its surface—and maybe to host life. Scientists are now beginning to identify these Earthlike planets. Will there be life on them? Stay tuned!

FACTS ABOUT EXOPLANETS
(EXTRASOLAR PLANETS)

Total confirmed exoplanets	4,100 and counting
Systems with more than one planet	670 and counting
Giant planets (more than 300 times Earth mass)	1,200 and counting
Hottest exoplanet	KELT-9b, 7821°F (4327°C)
Smallest exoplanet	Kepler 37b, one-third as wide as Earth
Longest year (orbit around its sun)	2MASS J2126-8140, about 1 million years
Shortest year (orbit around its sun)	PSR J1719-1438 b, 2.2 hours

FUN FACT

Ice world OGLE 2005-BLG-390L b (nickname: Hoth) is a freezing cold planet with a surface temperature of minus 364°F (-220°C). The little iceball orbits a star only one-fifth the size of our sun. It's almost three times as far away from its star as Earth is from its own sun.

EARTH-SIZE WORLDS

Extrasolar planets Kepler 62e and f are Earth-size worlds in the habitable zone of a distant sunlike star (at upper left in art). The larger planet (upper right), Kepler 62f, is farthest from the star and covered by ice. Kepler 62e, shown with its rings, is nearer to the star and covered by dense clouds. Both planets may be capable of supporting life.

Q: What do you call a group of icy planets?

A: A polar system!

AN ARTIST AT NASA'S
Jet Propulsion Laboratory (JPL) imagines what it might be like to gaze out at a sunlike star from the exoplanet TRAPPIST-1f, named for the high-powered telescope TRAPPIST (TRAnsiting Planets and PlanetesImals Small Telescope) that found the planet. An exoplanet, short for extrasolar planet, is a world that revolves around another star, just as Earth orbits our sun. If its distance from the star is just right, an exoplanet could have warm Earthlike temperatures, water, and air to support life.

ACCIDENTS HAPPEN

Have you ever caught the bright flash of a meteor streaking across the night sky? It was probably a piece of space debris not much larger than a pencil eraser. Every day, Earth gains about a hundred tons of weight from that kind of debris raining down on it.

Most of it is no bigger than a lemon, but not all. About 180 impact craters have been identified on Earth, created by falling objects larger than a house.

In 1908, in the air above a forest in the Tunguska region of Siberia, something exploded, flattening 80 million trees over an area of 830 square miles (2,150 sq km). Some 50,000 years ago, a meteor hit the desert in what is now northern Arizona, creating the Barringer Crater. It's one mile (1.6 km) in diameter and 570 feet (170 m) deep.

The most dazzling collision, however, came 65 million years ago, when a very large asteroid struck off the eastern coast of Mexico. That spectacular event changed global weather. Some scientists think the change in climate eventually led to the extinction of the dinosaurs.

Jupiter may protect Earth from some comet collisions by snaring these objects before they reach us. However, traveling asteroids and comets are still a danger to our planet. Several space agencies now track these Near-Earth Objects (NEOs), planning for the day when we may have to defend ourselves against the next big impact.

ON JUPITER: BOMBS AWAY!

Telescopes weren't watching Earth when ancient asteroids smashed into it. But in recent years we have seen comets and asteroids smack into the solar system's biggest planet, Jupiter. In 1992, for instance, a comet named Shoemaker-Levy 9 (left) was torn to bits by Jupiter's powerful gravitational field, becoming part of Jupiter's orbit. In July 1994, those orbiting pieces took their revenge. Chunks up to 1.2 miles (2 km) wide rained down into Jupiter's atmosphere like enormous bombs. They caused giant fireballs, and some left dark clouds of debris the size of planets. Another such collision happened in 2009, when an object—maybe an asteroid—plowed into Jupiter with a force thousands of times greater than Earth's Tunguska blast in 1908.

FIREBALL COLLISION

A 5000°F (2760°C) fireball four miles (6.5 km) in diameter slams through our atmosphere (art left), its blinding light a hundred times brighter than the sun. Earth has been slammed by such big asteroids in the past. Now we are actively looking for Near-Earth Objects that might collide with our planet.

SKY-WATCHER
TRACKING SPACE ROCKS

Are we keeping an eye out for unknown asteroids (left) and comets that might zoom close to Earth? You bet! Space agencies and professional and amateur astronomers around the world are finding and tracking Near-Earth Objects (NEOs), as these space visitors are called. Their telescopes search the skies to see if a distant spot is moving. Then they compare that spot to a list of known objects. If it's not on the list already, observers look more closely at it to see if it will pass within 30 million miles (50 million km) of Earth's orbit. If it will, it gets reported and other astronomers join in to track and measure it. They are particularly interested in the big rocks, such as asteroids over 460 feet (140 m) wide. Experts think the solar system has about 15,000 of these. Today, teams of astronomers are tracking more than 7,700 of these NEOs and are adding more to the list every month. None of them, thankfully, are on track to collide with Earth.

SPACE WEATHER

O ur planet has its own atmosphere and its own weather, from calm to stormy. Earth lives in the light of the sun. The sun, too, has weather, and its storms can affect our world.

The sun is constantly giving off both radiation and solar wind. We feel the radiation mostly as life-giving warmth. Our atmosphere blocks most of the dangerous radiation, the kind that can give us cancer if we aren't protected.

Some of the sun's hot outer atmosphere, its corona (opposite), escapes into space in the form of electrically charged particles. This is known as solar wind. The sun sheds millions of tons of its gas this way every second—but because the sun is so huge, this loss doesn't impact it.

When the solar wind reaches Earth, it is usually deflected by our planet's magnetic field. Sometimes its particles enter the magnetic field and create beautiful, shimmering auroras (opposite) in the skies above the North and South Poles.

FACTS ABOUT SPACE WEATHER

Height of Earth's magnetic field from Earth's surface, facing sun	36,000 miles (58,000 km)
Speed of solar wind	1 million miles an hour (1,609,000 km/h)
Travel time of solar wind to Earth	2 to 4 days
Temperature of solar wind around Earth	270,000°F (150,000°C)
Energy in biggest solar flares	As much as in 1 billion hydrogen bombs
Fastest coronal mass ejections	6,700,000 miles an hour (10,800,000 km/h)

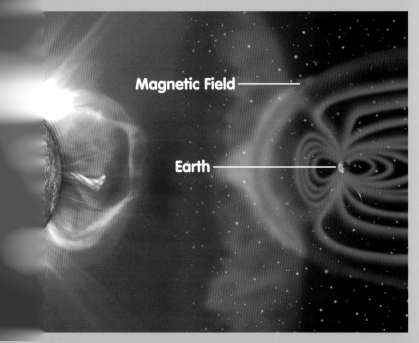

Magnetic Field ————

Earth ————

SOLAR STORMS

While the sun's heat is always steady, its blasts of charged particles can change from hour to hour. Active magnetic regions on the sun sometimes shoot out solar flares (opposite) or clouds of magnetized gas called coronal mass ejections (CMEs). These explosions of solar gases contain high-energy radiation and charged particles.

If these flares or CMEs are aimed toward Earth (and most are not), their charged particles reach our atmosphere in several days (left). The effects of these magnetic solar storms can be serious. Surges in electrical energy can overload transformers on Earth and cause blackouts. A giant solar flare in 1859 knocked out telegraph systems around the world. Another storm in 1989 blacked out electricity for six million people in Canada and also melted power equipment across New Jersey, U.S.A.

Radiation from solar storms can cause our atmosphere to expand temporarily, dragging on satellites. Global positioning system (GPS) signals that guide our machinery can go awry. Flares can be particularly harmful to airplanes and spacecraft. Airplanes caught at high altitudes during a solar storm can be hit with high levels of radiation. Even worse can happen to spacecraft, unprotected by Earth's atmosphere. In 2002, the Mars spacecraft Nozomi, from Japan, was caught in a solar flare and broke down. Its mission had to be canceled. Some agencies now track and predict solar weather. Without advance warning, a big storm like the one in 1859 could shut down technology systems across the planet.

Corona ————

SPACE WEATHER

Most of the radiation and energy directed toward Earth from space is deflected by our magnetic field, resulting in beautiful auroras in the night skies. Satellites in orbit, however, especially communication satellites, can be disrupted and their electronics can be destroyed by these solar events we now call "space weather."

Solar Flare /
Coronal Mass Ejection

Aurora

SEEING INTO SPACE

Since their invention in the 1600s, telescopes have shown that there is more to the universe than meets the eye. By magnifying the light of distant objects, telescopes can reveal previously unseen planets, stars, and galaxies. The first telescopes collected visible light, or light we can see with our eyes. By the 20th century, telescopes could track not only visible light but also all kinds of invisible light, or radiation, such as radio waves, x-rays, and gamma rays.

To collect different types of radiation, astronomers build different kinds of telescopes. And when it comes to size, bigger is usually better. A big mirror or radio dish can collect more radiation than a small one. This gives astronomers more information to work with. So scientists are now building some of the biggest telescopes ever. The well-named Very Large Telescope (VLT), in Chile's Atacama Desert, is actually an array, or grouping, of four big telescopes with mirrors 27 feet (8.2 m) wide. Each telescope can be used by itself, or the four can work together to study the same object.

Joining the VLT in the desert is the collection of radio telescopes known as the Atacama Large Millimeter/submillimeter Array, or ALMA. Signals from its 66 radio dishes are combined by a computer to form one very strong signal. ALMA looks into areas of space too dark for regular telescopes.

When completed, the Giant Magellan Telescope (GMT) will also be located in the Atacama Desert. Its seven mirrors will have a combined working area 80 feet (24.5 m) across.

The Thirty Meter Telescope (TMT) is not yet built. When it is complete on top of Hawaii, U.S.A.'s big mountain, Mauna Kea, its 98-foot (30-m)-wide mirror will pull in visible light as well as invisible infrared light from deep space.

By observing all forms of radiation, astronomers are able to learn more about the universe than they could from studying visible light alone.

SKY-WATCHER
REFLECTING TELESCOPES

The great scientist Isaac Newton was the first person to build a good workable reflecting telescope. These kinds of telescopes collect light using mirrors rather than lenses. The basic design Newton came up with is still used today. In a simple reflecting telescope, light enters the open end of the telescope's tube and travels to a curved mirror at the back of the tube. The light reflects (bounces) off that mirror to a smaller, flat, angled mirror in the middle of the tube. That mirror sends the light through a small lens in an eyepiece at the side of the telescope. The lens focuses the image so you can see it better. The bigger the mirrors in the telescope, the more light it can collect and the more detail you can see. However, the mirrors need to be clean and polished to exactly the right shape and smoothness, or your viewing will be blurry.

TELESCOPE TEAMWORK

Some amateur astronomers still make their own small telescopes by themselves. However, building one of the world's big telescopes is a huge project that takes years and employs hundreds of people. Twelve universities and institutes are contributing to the Giant Magellan Telescope (GMT), for instance. Among other things, their engineers must produce supersensitive mirrors that are polished to within one-millionth of an inch of a precise curving shape. When it's finished, the GMT will pull in images 10 times sharper than those from the Hubble Space Telescope.

TOP OPTICS

Three new major telescope projects will change our views of the universe. The Giant Magellan Telescope (below left) and the Thirty Meter Telescope (below right) will be completed in the 2020s. They will be the largest optical telescopes ever built. Launching in 2021, the James Webb Space Telescope, shown here in orbit, will replace the Hubble Space Telescope. Its sophisticated technologies are designed to serve the United States, Canada, and Europe and to stand the stress of space travel for decades to come.

ASTRONOMY
FROM PREHISTORY TO THE SPACE AGE

People have been astronomers for as long as they have gazed at the skies. In fact, ancient people were excellent, accurate sky-watchers. The light from stars and planets wasn't blocked by electric lights, so they had a clear view of the night sky and knew it well. In the 1600s, telescopes brought a revolution to astronomy. For the first time, astronomers could see distant planets, moons, and stars in detail. In the 20th century, spaceflight took astronomy to a new level. Spacecraft actually visited other worlds. Telescopes were launched into space, to see the universe as never before. Today, uncrewed rovers send news of Mars's makeup, and high-powered telescopes send images of deep space.

30,000 B.C.
MOON PHASES
Early people carve lines on animal bones to track the phases of the moon.

2500 B.C.
STONEHENGE
Stonehenge is built in Britain. The circle of stones marks the rising and setting points of the sun at the summer and winter solstices.

1300 B.C.
CONSTELLATIONS AND PLANETS
Egyptians observe 43 constellations and the five visible planets—Mars, Venus, Mercury, Jupiter, and Saturn.

350 B.C.
SPHERICAL EARTH
Greek scientist Aristotle argues that Earth is a sphere— not flat as believed before—because its shadow on the moon during a lunar eclipse is always a circle.

A.D. 150
EARTH-CENTERED UNIVERSE
Greek astronomer Ptolemy publishes the *Almagest*, an astronomy book that says the universe is centered on Earth.

250 B.C.
EARTH'S CIRCUMFERENCE
Greek mathematician Eratosthenes uses geometry to calculate the circumference of Earth—almost 25,000 miles (40,234 km).

1543
SUN-CENTERED SYSTEM
Polish astronomer Nicolaus Copernicus publishes *De revolutionibus,* which states that Earth and other planets orbit the sun.

A.D. 1054
SUPERNOVA
Chinese astronomers record a supernova that is visible in the daytime; the remains of this explosion can now be seen as the Crab Nebula.

1609
PLANETARY MOTION
German astronomer Johannes Kepler discovers the laws of planetary motion, which describe the shape and speed of planetary orbits.

1609
TELESCOPE
Italian astronomer Galileo Galilei uses a telescope to make important observations of the sun, moon, planets, and stars.

1665-67
GRAVITY
British scientist Isaac Newton discovers the law of universal gravitation.

1781
URANUS
German-born English astronomer William Herschel discovers Uranus, the first planet that had not been known by the ancients.

1846
NEPTUNE
German astronomer Johann Galle discovers the planet Neptune, using calculations by French astronomer Urbain Le Verrier. British mathematician John Couch Adams also predicts Neptune's position.

1912
SCALE OF THE UNIVERSE
U.S. astronomer Henrietta Swan Leavitt catalogs the relative brightness and variability of stars. Her work helps astronomers develop a way to calibrate the scale of the universe.

1915
RELATIVITY
German-born physicist Albert Einstein publishes his general theory of relativity, which explains how space curves around matter.

1923
GALAXIES
U.S. astronomer Edwin Hubble shows that spiral nebulae are galaxies—huge collections of stars far from the Milky Way.

1929
EXPANDING UNIVERSE
Edwin Hubble discovers that galaxies are moving apart because the universe is expanding.

1930
PLUTO
U.S. astronomer Clyde Tombaugh discovers Pluto by spotting a moving speck of light in two photographs of the night sky taken a week apart.

1951
KUIPER BELT
U.S. astronomer Gerard Kuiper proposes the existence of a ring of small, icy bodies orbiting just beyond Neptune, now called the Kuiper belt.

1950
OORT CLOUD
Dutch astronomer Jan Oort says that certain comets come from a band of distant icy objects orbiting the sun, now called the Oort cloud.

1957
SPUTNIK 1
The first human-made satellite, the Soviet Union's Sputnik 1, is launched.

1961

FIRST PEOPLE IN SPACE

Soviet cosmonaut Yuri Gagarin is the first person in space. Astronaut Alan Shepard is the first American in space.

1963

FIRST WOMAN IN SPACE; QUASARS

Soviet cosmonaut Valentina Tereshkova is the first woman in space. Dutch-born U.S. astronomer Maarten Schmidt discovers the first quasar, an extremely bright celestial body.

1965

BIG BANG; MARINER 4

U.S. astronomers Arno Penzias and Robert Wilson use a radio telescope to detect very faint radiation coming from all directions in space. They realize this is radiation left over from the big bang, which helps prove that theory for the formation of the universe. Mariner 4 flies past Mars, sending back pictures of a dry, cratered surface.

1967

PULSARS

British astronomers Jocelyn Bell and Antony Hewish discover pulsars, later shown to be spinning neutron stars sending out beams of radiation.

1958

EXPLORER 1

Explorer 1 is the first satellite successfully launched by the United States.

1969

FIRST PEOPLE ON THE MOON; SOYUZ SPACE STATION

U.S. astronauts Edwin "Buzz" Aldrin and Neil Armstrong become the first people to land on the moon. Soviet spacecraft Soyuz 5 docks with Soyuz 4 to form the first experimental space station.

1976

VIKING LANDERS

U.S. Viking landers safely touch down on the surface of Mars and send back images and information from the planet's surface for several years.

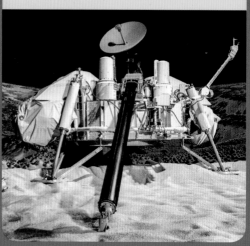

1979

VOYAGERS 1 AND 2

U.S. spacecraft Voyagers 1 and 2 reach Jupiter, and then they use the planet's gravity and motion to become like rocks in a slingshot. This maneuver, called a swing-by, pings them further into space, toward the more-distant planets.

1972

LAST MOON LANDING

Apollo 17 is the last Apollo mission to the moon.

1981

SPACE SHUTTLE LAUNCHED

U.S. space shuttle *Columbia* is launched, successfully making the first flight of a reusable shuttle.

1986
CHALLENGER DISASTER; MIR 1
The space shuttle *Challenger* explodes 73 seconds after launch, killing the crew. Soviets launch the space station Mir 1.

1989
COBE
The Cosmic Background Explorer (COBE) satellite is launched. It detects microwave radiation in the universe that confirms modern theories about the big bang.

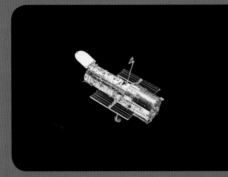

1990
MAGELLAN; HUBBLE SPACE TELESCOPE
U.S. spacecraft Magellan begins radar mapping of Venus. The Hubble Space Telescope (left) is launched. In the years to come, it produces stunning images of distant stars and galaxies.

1992
KUIPER BELT OBJECT
Astronomers discover a reddish, planetlike object circling the sun beyond the orbit of Pluto, confirming the existence of the Kuiper belt.

1995
PLANETS ORBITING OTHER STARS
Jupiter-size planets are discovered orbiting sunlike stars near our solar system in the Milky Way.

2003
COLUMBIA DISASTER
After 27 missions, the space shuttle *Columbia* breaks up during reentry into Earth's atmosphere, killing all aboard.

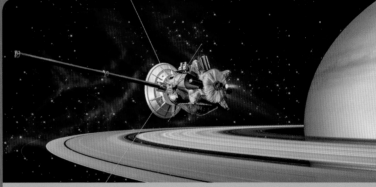

2004
MARS ROVERS; CASSINI
U.S. rovers Spirit and Opportunity reach Mars and begin collecting information about the existence of water. The U.S. Cassini spacecraft (above) goes into orbit around Saturn, sending back images of the planet, its rings, and its large moon Titan.

2005
ERIS
Eris, a planetlike object bigger than Pluto, is first seen orbiting the sun more than six billion miles (10 billion km) away, far past Pluto.

2006
PLUTO DEMOTED
Members of the International Astronomical Union vote to change the way planets are classified. Pluto is no longer considered a planet but officially becomes a dwarf planet, along with Eris and Ceres (formerly the solar system's biggest asteroid).

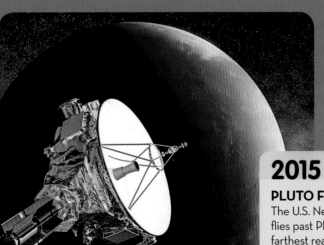

2012
CURIOSITY ROVER
NASA launches the Curiosity rover in November 2011, and it lands on the Gale Crater on Mars in August 2012. Its goal is to study the crater's climate and geology to determine if it has ever supported microbial life.

2015
PLUTO FLYBY
The U.S. New Horizons spacecraft flies past Pluto on its way to the farthest reaches of the solar system.

2021
JAMES WEBB SPACE TELESCOPE
The James Webb telescope will be launched to replace the Hubble Space Telescope.

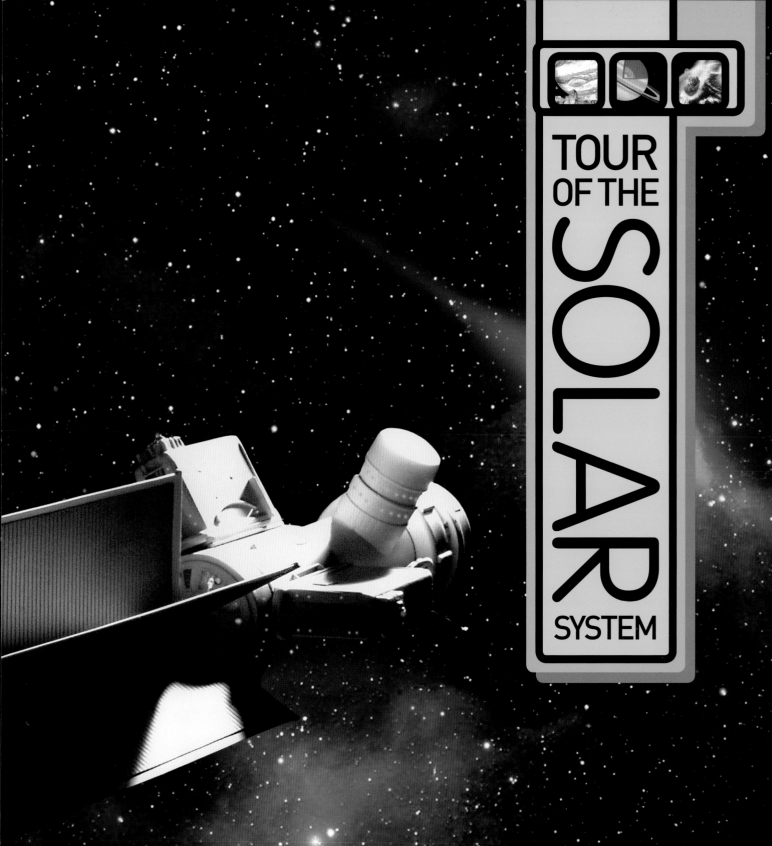

TOUR OF THE SOLAR SYSTEM

As our spaceship passes Neptune, the sunlight is bright, even though the sun is nearly three billion miles (4.8 billion km) away.

OUR NEW SOLAR SYSTEM

The solar system is made up of planets, asteroids, and comets orbiting around a star we call the sun. Our star system formed 4.6 billion years ago from a nebular cloud—a large, spinning cloud of gas and dust. Today, astronomers divide the solar system into three different categories of planets, based on their size and density. Orbiting closest to the sun are the small, dense, rocky worlds of Mercury, Venus, Earth, and Mars. If they were dropped into a gigantic tub of water, they would sink. We call them the terrestrial planets—a word taken from the Latin word *terra*, which means "land."

Beyond the terrestrial planets lies the asteroid belt, filled with small rocky asteroids and our fifth planet, Ceres. It's a dwarf planet, a category established in 2006 by the International Astronomical Union.

Next come the gas giants—Jupiter, Saturn, Uranus, and Neptune. They're large, surrounded by rings and multiple moons, and made out of gases. Astronomers call them the Jovian planets, after the Roman god Jove, which is another name for Jupiter.

Past the gas giant planets, extending far out into space, is the Kuiper belt, an area filled with comets and other galactic debris. Also orbiting the sun in the Kuiper belt are Pluto and our 13th planet, Eris. Like Ceres in the asteroid belt, Pluto and Eris are now classified as dwarf planets. They're made of a mixture of ice and rock. Following Pluto and Eris are our newest dwarf planets, Haumea and Makemake. Astronomers believe that other possible dwarf planets, perhaps bigger than the ones we know now, wait for discovery in the far reaches of the solar system.

Mercury · Venus · Earth · Mars · Ceres · (Jupiter)

FACTS ABOUT THE SOLAR SYSTEM

Distance to end of sun's gravitational pull	2 light-years
Planets	8
Dwarf planets	5
Moons	210
Asteroids	More than 715,000
Biggest planet	Jupiter, 11 times bigger than Earth
Smallest dwarf planet	Ceres, 13 times smaller than Earth

FUN FACT

The word "planet" comes from the Greek word for "wanderer." In early history, sky-watchers used the term "planet" for any heavenly body that wandered across the sky, unlike the fixed stars. This included the sun, moon, Mercury, Venus, Mars, Jupiter, and Saturn.

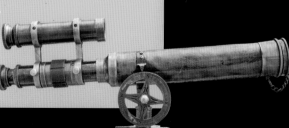

OUR HOME PLANETS

This artwork shows the 13 planets and dwarf planets that astronomers now recognize in our solar system. The relative sizes of the planets are also shown, but not the relative distances between them or their true placements as they orbit the sun. Many of the planets, except the ones far from the sun, can be seen in the night sky without a telescope.

Jupiter

Saturn

Uranus

Neptune

Pluto

Haumea

Makemake

Eris

SUPER STARS

We now take it for granted that Earth and the other planets orbit the sun, but this was not common knowledge until the Polish astronomer Nicolaus Copernicus (1473-1543) pointed it out in his 1543 book, *De revolutionibus (Six Books Concerning the Revolutions of the Heavenly Orbs)*.

Copernicus was the youngest of four children born to a wealthy merchant. He was raised by his uncle, a bishop, and went on to study law, medicine, mathematics, and astronomy in Poland and Italy. While in Italy, he lived with a mathematics professor who encouraged him to question the accepted idea that Earth was the center of the universe, and that all other bodies, including the sun, revolved around it.

After studying the old models of the universe, Copernicus realized they made no sense. He later wrote that previous astronomers "are just like someone taking from different places hands, feet, head, and the other limbs ... not matching one another—so that such parts would produce a monster rather than a man." His book reorganized the six known planets and put the sun at their center. It was not published until shortly before Copernicus's death, and its theories were not widely accepted until the 1600s.

THE GRAND TOUR

Heat Radiators

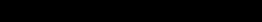

Combustion Chamber   **Fusion Reactor**

Longer than most luxury cruise ships traveling Earth's oceans, our imaginary voyager, Stella Nova, which means "new star," will take us to the dwarf planet Eris in the farthest reaches of the solar system. Our crew consists of a captain, a chief pilot and navigator, a flight engineer, a medical doctor, two scientists, a payload specialist, and two lucky guests. The total number of crew members isn't much more than the number of astronauts who typically crew the International Space Station.

This will be mostly a sightseeing and research tour, so we'll spend a lot of time simply observing. Much of what needs to be done will be done by the computers on board the ship. Even the flight plan is locked in, so Stella Nova will more or less fly itself. That's good, because whatever we try to do, from work to exercise, we'll have to do in zero gravity, which means we'll be floating through Stella Nova as we speed through space.

Moving Fast

Our journey to the most distant planet now known will take only months instead of years because our spaceship is powered by nuclear fusion. The nuclear reactor on board fuses deuterium, also called heavy hydrogen, and helium-3. This allows us to travel incredibly fast—at one percent the speed of light. Light travels at about 186,000 miles a second (300,000 km/s), so we'll be zooming along at more than 600 million miles an hour (966 million km/h). At that speed we can journey out to Eris and be back on Earth in just 60 days. By comparison, spacecraft to the International Space Station poke along at 17,500 miles an hour (28,164 km/h), so the same trip, without any stops, would take more than 70 years to complete.

Although the idea of a fusion-powered ship is already scientifically possible, building one isn't practical yet. We still need to develop the technology to contain the heat and radiation that fusion would generate. Scientists are working on this challenge right now.

Crew Living Quarters and Recreation Area

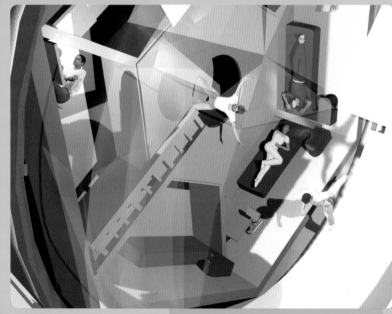

SHIP LOG DAY 2: Approaching Uranus, landing on its moon Miranda

READING THE SHIP'S LOG

Check the ship log entries throughout the chapter. They will tell you what day it is on our trip and what our activities will be. The arcs above each log entry represent the planetary orbits. The red line is the orbit of the object we are approaching. The yellow half-circle is the sun.

FUN FACT

Light speed, or "warp speed," just isn't possible for a spaceship. Physics tells us that a ship would need an infinite amount of energy to travel at the speed of light.

THE STELLA NOVA

The Stella Nova is divided into four different sections: The front part contains the navigation and control area, along with the crew's living quarters and recreation area. All this is located as far away as possible from the ship's engines, which emit intense heat and radiation. Behind the living area is a section with rectangular structures jutting out. This is where the tanks of deuterium fuel are stored.

Next come the long, flat heat radiators, which make up the reactor. It gets rid of heat created by the fusion engine at the back of the ship. Beyond the reactor, the bell-shaped combustion chamber emits the glowing plasma tail exhaust coming from the engine.

Deuterium Fuel Tanks

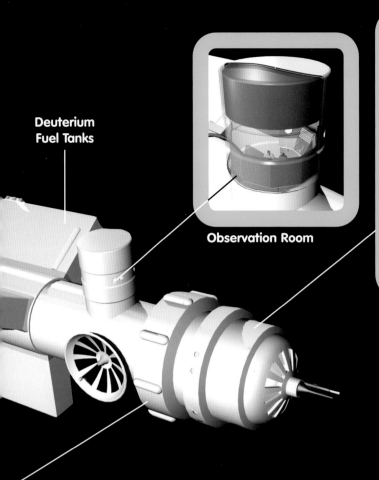

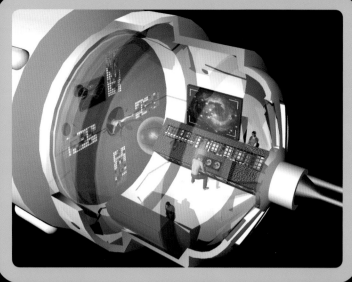

Observation Room

Navigation and Control Area

GRAVITY MEANS SPEED!

Our flight will take us in toward the sun before we zoom out to the planets beyond Earth. We planned it that way to take advantage of something called "gravitational assist." This is how it works: We aim the ship at a particular angle when approaching a planet or the sun. Gravity pulls us into that object's orbit, so we both accelerate and save on fuel. Passing the planet, we spin out of its orbit and shoot into space as if hurled by a giant slingshot. Many space probes already use this method to speed along.

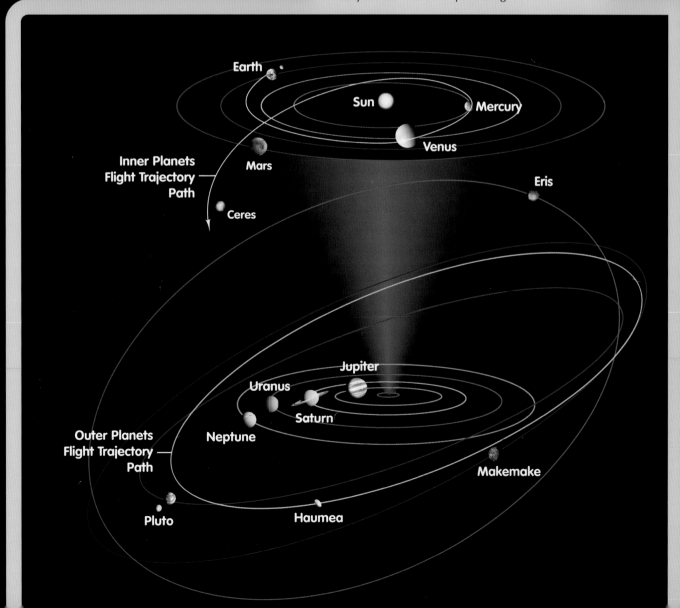

Earth

Sun

Mercury

Venus

Inner Planets Flight Trajectory Path

Mars

Eris

Ceres

Jupiter

Uranus

Saturn

Neptune

Outer Planets Flight Trajectory Path

Makemake

Pluto

Haumea

VENUS

Shining like a brilliant jewel in space, Venus has been called Earth's sister planet. Despite the fact that humans like to associate it with things of beauty, Venus has an eerie red landscape with thick clouds that choke out the sunlight.

Slightly smaller than Earth, Venus has a chemical composition similar to Earth's. In the past it may have been covered by oceans and may have had a moon. But today Venus is one of the most inhospitable planets in the solar system.

Venus is blanketed in a cloud layer of carbon dioxide 40 miles (64 km) thick, the densest atmosphere of any planet in the solar system. It is 90 times denser than Earth's atmosphere. Anyone venturing out onto the surface would be crushed like a paper cup—or toasted.

Venus's surface temperatures reach 864°F (462°C)—hot enough to melt lead. At the top of its clouds, winds roar at more than 200 miles an hour (320 km/h). On the surface, though, the wind hardly blows. But the air has so much density that even a gentle breeze would push you along like a large ocean wave.

FACTS ABOUT VENUS

Average distance from the sun	67,238,251 miles (108,209,475 km)
Position from the sun in orbit	Second
Equatorial diameter	7,521 miles (12,103 km)
Mass (Earth = 1)	0.815
Density (water = 1)	5.24
Length of day	243 Earth days
Length of year	225 Earth days
Average surface temperature	864°F (462°C)
Known moons	0

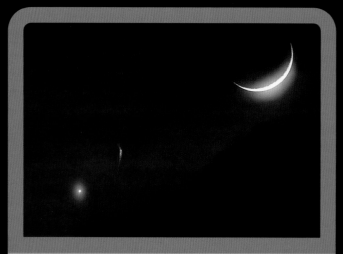

Earth

Venus

SKY-WATCHER
SPOTTING VENUS

Beautiful Venus is the easiest planet to spot in the night sky. Look for a white, brilliant, starlike object, the brightest light in the night sky other than the moon. Venus looks so bright because the planet is close to Earth and because its thick clouds reflect sunlight. In fact, you don't have to wait for a fully dark sky to see it. The best times to view Venus are just before sunrise in the eastern sky or just after sunset in the western sky. (This is why Venus used to be called the "morning star" or "evening star," even though it is a planet.) It will slowly move from being a morning sight to an evening one during the year as it orbits the sun. Several astronomy websites give updates.

You don't need a telescope or binoculars to enjoy this gorgeous planet. However, a good set of binoculars or a home telescope will allow you to see its changing phases (see page 37). These scopes won't show you any detail on the planet's surface, though, because that is hidden beneath its blanket of clouds.

LOL!
Q: Why is Venus acting so crabby?
A: She's been under a lot of pressure lately.

GLOWING VENUS

As our spaceship approaches Venus (art below), the planet's golden crescent shines brilliantly because its clouds reflect sunlight into space. Beyond Venus, the stars of the Pleiades constellation, also called the Seven Sisters, sparkle in the sky.

Until the late 1950s, scientists believed Venus was a world covered by swamps and lush tropical jungles. Today, we know it doesn't look like that at all. Venus is one of the driest places in the solar system, with no trace of water. No need for weather predicting here. As far as astronomers can tell, rain never occurs. Falling droplets of sulfuric acid evaporate before they reach the ground. The temperature doesn't change between day and night. It is the same forecast all the time.

Venus's surface is pocked by large meteor craters that range in size from 1.5 miles to 170 miles (2.4 km to 270 km) across. There are no small craters because the thick atmosphere causes smaller meteorites to burn up before hitting the ground. Two large, flat highland areas may have been left behind from an earlier time, when there were possibly ancient oceans on Venus. One area in the northern hemisphere, Ishtar Terra, is about the size of Australia. Along the equator, Aphrodite Terra is about the size of South America.

A Volcanic World

Volcanoes of every size and type rise from the planet's vast plains, and much of Venus is covered by lava. Almost 170 of these volcanoes are more than 60 miles (97 km) wide.

The tremendous heat on Venus was the result of volcanic eruptions that released carbon dioxide into the atmosphere, creating the greenhouse effect. Scientists think that, if oceans did exist on Venus, rising temperatures caused the ancient oceans to evaporate.

Some day, hundreds of millions of years from now, when the volcanic eruptions are far in the past, Venus will begin to cool, and oceans may form again. They will help speed up the removal of carbon dioxide from the atmosphere by naturally dissolving it into the seawater, just as oceans do here on Earth. Venus may then be more Earthlike and become our true twin sister.

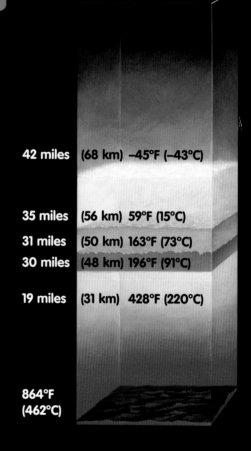

42 miles	(68 km)	−45°F (−43°C)
35 miles	(56 km)	59°F (15°C)
31 miles	(50 km)	163°F (73°C)
30 miles	(48 km)	196°F (91°C)
19 miles	(31 km)	428°F (220°C)
864°F (462°C)		

CLOUD COVER

Clouds form a thick blanket around Venus (art above), up to 42 miles (68 km) above its surface, reflecting sunlight back into space and keeping the planet much cooler than it would be without them. But the high concentration of carbon dioxide in the atmosphere also traps heat, causing the greenhouse effect. Scientists are now concerned about the growing concentration of carbon dioxide in Earth's own atmosphere.

VOLCANOLAND

The landscape of Venus is 80 percent volcanic plains covered by strange domelike structures that are the result of molten rock bulging out and then hardening. The shield volcano known as Maat Mons (radar-made image below) has a peak 5 miles (8 km) high.

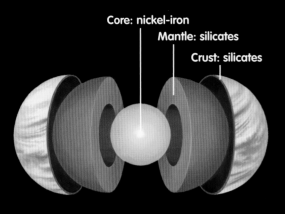

Core: nickel-iron
Mantle: silicates
Crust: silicates

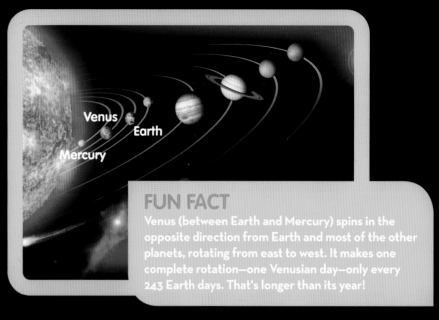

Venus
Earth
Mercury

ANCIENT LAVA

Like Earth, Venus has a nickel-iron core surrounded by a molten-rock mantle and crust. As this mantle of molten rock pushed up, it flowed out of volcanoes in the form of lava. The oldest surface features on Venus are about 800 million years old.

FUN FACT

Venus (between Earth and Mercury) spins in the opposite direction from Earth and most of the other planets, rotating from east to west. It makes one complete rotation—one Venusian day—only every 243 Earth days. That's longer than its year!

SKY-WATCHER
PHASES OF VENUS

Viewed from Earth, Venus goes through phase changes (art left), just like the moon. When it is farthest away from us in its orbit, it looks smallest in size but is fully illuminated by the sun. In shape it resembles a full moon. As it draws nearer to Earth, its size grows larger but its phase now resembles a thin crescent, so it looks dimmer to us.

When the astronomer Galileo first observed Venus in 1610, it was added proof that not everything in the heavens circled around Earth, as many believed. Galileo's observation was important evidence for the theory that Earth—and all the other planets—circled around the sun.

You can easily watch Venus change phases over a period of weeks with a small telescope that has 40x magnification, meaning through it, objects will appear 40 times closer. It may appear slightly distorted, with rings of yellow and purple around it, because our thick atmosphere distorts light from Venus.

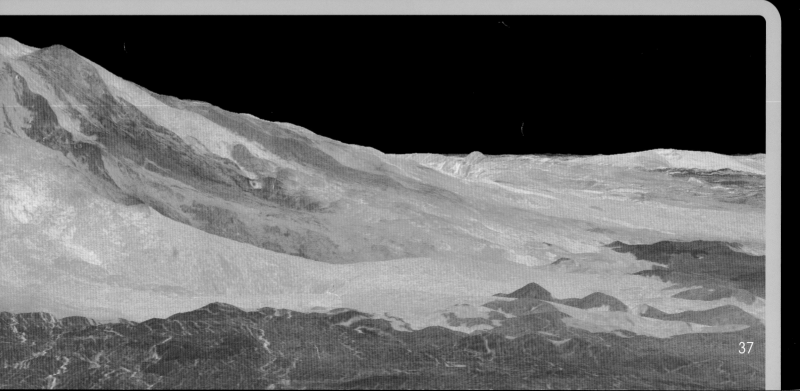

MERCURY

The next planet on our tour is Mercury, the innermost and smallest of the rocky planets. Because it orbits so close to the sun, this planet is usually lost in the sun's glare and difficult to see from Earth. The terrain is scarred with craters, high ragged walls, and old volcanoes. The rims of barely visible "ghost craters" are buried under volcanic rock from a time when lava flooded the surface.

Mercury's axis doesn't tilt, so the sun shines directly on the equator, making it sizzling hot during the day and freezing cold at night. Temperatures can range from 801°F (427°C) on the sunlit side to minus 279°F (-173°C) on the night side. Even while the sun scorches the equator, water ice fills permanently shadowed craters at both poles.

Mercury speeds around the sun once every 88 Earth days, but one day on Mercury is 59 Earth days long! Rotating three times on its axis for every two orbits around the sun, Mercury also has bizarre sunrises and sunsets. If you were standing on Mercury's equator, you would see the sun rise and set in different ways, depending on where you were. At some places, the sun would rise toward its high point in the sky, then stop and reverse direction, seeming to set. Then it would stop and rise again, getting smaller as it finally set in the west.

SHIP LOG 17 HOURS: Landing on Mercury, replace seismic monitors

FACTS ABOUT MERCURY

Average distance from the sun	35,983,125 miles (57,909,227 km)
Position from the sun in orbit	First
Equatorial diameter	3,032 miles (4,879 km)
Mass (Earth = 1)	0.055
Density (water = 1)	5.43
Length of day	59 Earth days
Length of year	88 Earth days
Average surface temperature	-279°F (-173°C) to 801°F (427°C)
Known moons	0

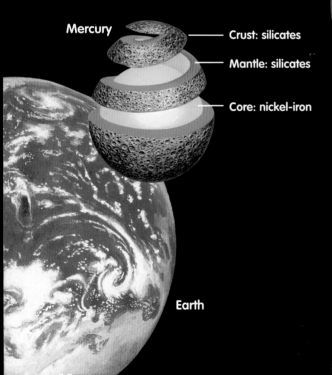

Mercury

Crust: silicates

Mantle: silicates

Core: nickel-iron

Earth

SUPER STARS

The great physicist Albert Einstein (1879-1955) changed the way people think about time, space, and the universe. Born in Germany, Einstein was brilliant at math and physics but didn't have much luck at first finding jobs as a scientist. Even so, while working as a clerk in a Swiss patent office he began to publish a series of groundbreaking scientific papers that explained light and energy in new ways. In 1915, he published his general theory of relativity, which said that space and time were like a fabric that would bend around very massive objects. One proof of this: Mercury's orbit. Traditional physics, from the age of Isaac Newton, couldn't explain how Mercury's orbit shifted from year to year as the planet circled the sun. The theory of relativity gave the answer. Because Mercury is so close to the massive sun, Mercury's orbital motion is distorted slightly by the sun's gravity. Einstein was right.

MEGA CRATER

One day, as imagined here, astronauts may explore Mercury's Caloris Basin, one of the largest craters in the solar system. Its diameter stretches 960 miles (1,550 km). It was created 400 million years ago, when a giant asteroid, with the impact of a trillion hydrogen bombs, slammed into the planet.

THE SUN

The sun is a middle-aged star, about 4.6 billion years old. As the anchor that holds our solar system together, it provides the energy necessary for life to flourish on Earth. It accounts for 99 percent of the matter in the solar system. The rest of the planets, moons, asteroids, and comets added together amount to the remaining one percent.

Even though a million Earths could fit inside it, the sun is still considered an average-size star. Betelgeuse (say BET-el-jooz), the star on the shoulder of Orion in that constellation, is roughly 1,000 times larger. Like other stars, the sun is a giant ball of hydrogen gas radiating heat and light through the process of nuclear fusion. Unlike nuclear fission, in which atoms are split apart and create deadly radiation, fusion rams atoms together, producing cleaner and hotter reactions. Through fusion, the sun converts about four million tons of matter to energy every second.

Also like other stars, the sun revolves around its galaxy. Located halfway out in one of the arms of the Milky Way galaxy, the sun takes 225 to 250 million years to complete one revolution around the galaxy's center.

SHIP LOG DAY 2: Flyby of sun, use gravitational assist to accelerate

FACTS ABOUT THE SUN

Equatorial diameter	864,337 miles (1,391,016 km)
Rotation at equator	26.8 days
Temperature at surface	10,000°F (5500°C)
Temperature at core	27,000,000°F (15,000,000°C)
Mass (Earth = 1)	333,060
Density (water = 1)	0.256
Kind of star	Yellow G2
Age	4.6 billion years

SOLAR EXPLOSION

Traveling millions of miles across space, a gigantic solar flare unleashes more energy than all the atomic bombs ever exploded on Earth combined.

FUN FACT

It takes 170,000 years for energy to travel from the sun's core to its outer surface.

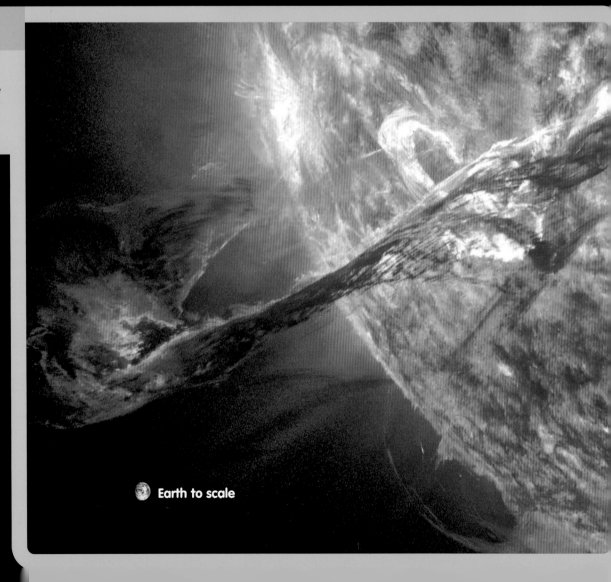

🌍 **Earth to scale**

CLOSE CALL!

As our ship passes within a safe distance of the sun, a giant solar flare erupts (art below).

INSIDE THE SUN

The sun is composed of about 92.1 percent hydrogen, 7.8 percent helium, and 0.1 percent trace elements like iron, carbon, lead, and uranium. These trace elements provide us with an amazing insight into the history of our star. They're the heavier elements that are produced when stars explode. By studying these trace elements in the sun, scientists know they were forged from the materials that came together in two previous star explosions. The sun and all the elements that are found in it and on Earth and in our bodies were recycled from those two exploding stars.

When viewed in space by astronauts, our sun burns white in color. When we see it from Earth, through our atmosphere, it looks like a yellow star. When astronomers study the sun's surface features, they see a much more complex structure than just a big, bright ball of gas. Most obvious are the sunspots. These blotches are slightly cooler areas that appear darker against the hotter background. The surface of the sun averages about 10,000°F (5500°C); the sunspots average about 6000°F (3320°C). Out of these sunspots shoot loops, or prominences, of superhot gas. These prominences follow invisible magnetic lines that connect the sunspots together. The loops extend for hundreds of miles above the photosphere, or visible surface of the sun. Solar flares, explosions of charged particles, sometimes erupt from the sun's surface into the farthest reaches of space. They create beautiful aurora displays on Earth, Jupiter, Saturn, and even on distant Uranus and Neptune.

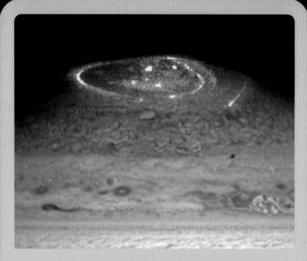

FUN FACT

Aurora displays on Jupiter are more spectacular than those we see on Earth. After viewing photographs from the Hubble Space Telescope, one scientist said, "It looks like Jupiter is throwing a fireworks party!" The auroras are bigger, too—the size of our entire Earth! This NASA photograph combines an image of Jupiter and the aurora so you can see where it happens.

CROWNING GLORY

In this satellite photograph, the wispy streamers of gas in the sun's corona (which means "crown") are visible, extending millions of miles into space. On Earth, the corona is visible only during a total eclipse of the sun.

Solar Prominences

Corona

Chromosphere

Photosphere

Core

Radiative Zone

Solar Flare

Convective Zone

Sunspots

HOT TO THE CORE

Above the sun's visible surface, or photosphere, is the chromosphere (art above)—a layer about a thousand miles (1,609 km) thick. Surrounding this is the corona, or crown. Scientists have discovered that the sun's corona is thousands of times hotter than its surface because the corona is heated by an extremely hot gas called magnetic plasma.

SUPER STARS

English physicist Arthur Eddington (1882-1944) was the person who finally explained what makes the sun so hot. Eddington was the son of a schoolteacher and was fairly poor as a child, but he was brilliant at math and astronomy, and he became a professor of astronomy at Cambridge University in 1913. As a Quaker, Eddington took a stand against war and refused to serve in the military when World War I broke out, despite much public pressure. During the war, he began to read Albert Einstein's papers on relativity. Eddington was a clear, often funny writer; he became famous as an explainer of Einstein's complicated theories and physics in general. In the early 20th century, scientists still didn't know how a star, such as our sun, could give off so much energy for so long without running out of fuel. It was Eddington who correctly suggested that in the superdense heart of a star, matter was crushed into huge amounts of energy that was then released. His discovery formed the basis of our modern understanding of our sun and its fellow stars. Eddington won a number of awards in his lifetime and was knighted, becoming Sir Arthur Eddington, in 1930.

LOL!

I was up all night wondering where the sun had gone—and then it dawned on me.

SOLAR CYCLES

We know the sun makes life possible here on Earth. We couldn't survive without it. But it causes problems, too.

On October 28, 2003, we found out just how serious those problems can be. A huge solar flare shot highly charged energetic particles right at Earth, like bullets. Airplanes had to stop flying over the North and South Poles because passengers would have been exposed to increased radiation. A power blackout occurred in Sweden, and some satellites in orbit around the planet were damaged. Many other satellites, including the Hubble Space Telescope, had to be shut down and put into "safe" mode, to protect their delicate electronics.

As humans depend more and more on new technologies, they also face the prospect of overloaded power grids, a shutdown of electronic communications, and massive power blackouts caused by solar flares. Space travelers especially need to take extra precautions when one of these solar events occurs.

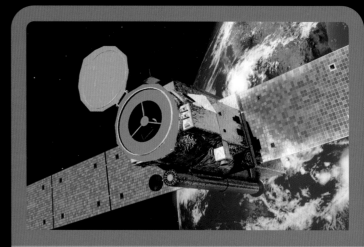

SKY-WATCHER
THE HINODE MISSION

The sun releases enormous amounts of magnetism from its surface into its corona, the thin hot gas that surrounds it. People still don't understand just how these magnetic fields affect solar weather. So scientists from the Japan Aerospace Exploration Agency, working with others around the world, launched the Hinode spacecraft in 2006 to study the sun's active surface. Hinode orbits Earth about 370 miles (600 km) high. It carries three telescopes that study the sun in three different wavelengths of light. One looks at the sun in visible light (the kind we normally see). The two others study x-rays and ultraviolet light, which we can't see with our own eyes. The information these telescopes collect is helping us understand how solar storms erupt, why the corona is so hot, and other mysteries of the sun.

11-YEAR REVERSAL

The sun's huge magnetic field reverses direction every 11 years (below). Sunspots, slightly cooler areas on the photosphere (bottom), respond to these cycle changes by growing and shrinking in number and size. The largest sunspots are almost twice the size of Earth.

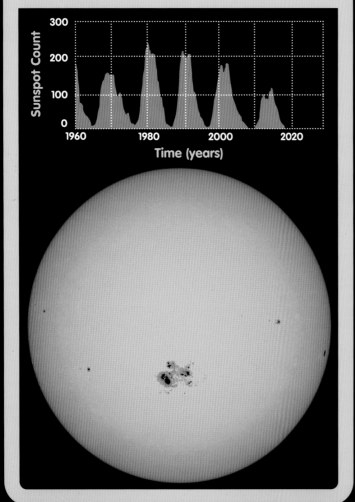

ON THE EDGE

If a solar flare eruption is powerful enough, it can disrupt electronics across Earth.

AURORA BOREALIS

On dark nights, the northern sky lights up with shimmering waves of green and red. Called the aurora borealis, they are caused by charged particles in the solar winds colliding with atmospheric particles high above Earth.

FUN FACT

In 1859, a solar storm caused such bright auroras across Earth's night sky that people woke up and thought it was morning.

MARS

N
ow we're coming to the planet nearest to Earth. Mars is about half the size of Earth, and it has some of the most spectacular scenery in the solar system. Its soaring canyons would stretch across North America, and its skyscraping volcanoes overlook jumbled plains that may once have been shallow seas.

Mars also boasts polar ice caps, majestic sand dunes, impact craters formed millions of years ago, and dust devils that whirl around like small tornadoes. In the 19th century, astronomers began to think Martian engineers might have designed canals to crisscross the planet and bring water from the poles to Martian cities. That idea vanished when spacecraft reached Mars, but scientists still wonder if the planet could be capable of supporting microscopic life.

Liquid water is necessary for life on Earth. The atmosphere on Mars is so thin and the temperatures so cold that liquid water cannot exist on the surface. It would quickly freeze or evaporate. That's why there are no oceans. But there are signs that underground water might occasionally flow up to the surface. Mars might well have hidden wet habitats that are capable of supporting life.

FACTS ABOUT MARS

Average distance from the sun	141,637,725 miles (227,943,824 km)
Position from the sun in orbit	Fourth
Equatorial diameter	4,220 miles (6,792 km)
Mass (Earth = 1)	0.107
Density (water = 1)	3.93
Length of day	24.6 Earth hours
Length of year	1.88 Earth years
Surface temperatures	-243°F (-153°C) to 68°F (20°C)
Known moons	2

Earth

Mars

FUN FACT

Earth's entire Grand Canyon could fit into one of the side cracks of Mars's huge canyon, Valles Marineris.

FRIGID PHOBOS

Mars looms like a great red sphere over the barren terrain of its largest moon, Phobos (art above), which orbits very close to the planet. Astronauts like those imagined here would have to be prepared for frigid nights.

EXPLORING MARS

An orange beacon in the night skies, Mars grows brighter and dimmer on a two-year cycle, as it moves closer to, then farther away from, Earth. It owes its distinctive color to iron oxide in the soil. Like a piece of metal left outside, Mars has rusted. Although there are no thunderstorms here, weather is extremely unpredictable. Out of nowhere, blinding dust storms can blow up and blanket the landscape for months.

Temperature swings are also enormous. At the Equator, noontime highs can reach 68°F (20°C), then at night dip to minus 100°F (-73°C). Mars's two moons, Phobos and Deimos, might be captured asteroids. Unlike our moon, these two tiny space rocks zip across the night sky.

Missions to Mars

Dozens of spacecraft have flown by, orbited, or landed on Mars over the past 50 years or so. Recently, robotic rovers have sent back pictures and scientific information directly from Mars's desertlike surface. NASA's Curiosity rover, which landed on Mars in 2012, has been studying Martian soil. Scooping up sand with its robotic arm, it has found traces of an ancient streambed and—possibly—of molecules that may mean that Mars could once have hosted living organisms. Curiosity will keep looking for signs of life as it trundles along at about 98 feet an hour (30 m/h).

KING OF CANYONS

Mars has the longest canyon in the solar system, Valles Marineris, seen as a dark slash around the planet's middle in the photo below. Measuring more than 3,100 miles (4,990 km) long, this huge system of valleys is some 120 miles (193 km) wide and 4 miles (6 km) deep. It was not carved by water but by the cooling and wrinkling of the landscape over time.

ROVER SELFIE

During its Mars travels, NASA's Curiosity rover snapped this selfie in August 2015. Here, the rover sits atop a mound, where it is about to drill into a rock called "Buckskin." Curiosity has already discovered evidence that there may be dried streambeds on the planet.

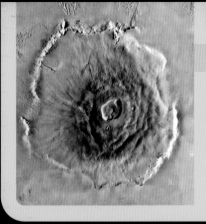

MASSIVE MONS

Mars has gigantic volcanoes on its surface that grow a hundred times larger than they can on Earth. Soaring 14 miles (22 km) high, Olympus Mons is the largest of four enormous volcanoes located near Mars's equator. Olympus Mons is a shield volcano, meaning it rises from the surface of the planet. The crater measures 53 miles (85 km) across, and the total area of the volcano is about the same as the U.S. state of New Mexico.

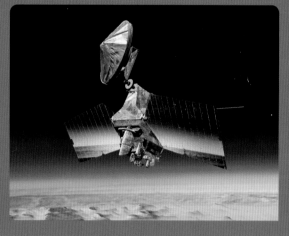

ROBOT IN ACTION

A close-up of the Mars Curiosity rover shows what this robot looks like in action. The size of a car, the rover was sent to Mars from Cape Canaveral, Florida, U.S.A., in November 2011 and landed on the planet in August 2012. As of 2020, Curiosity was exploring Gale Crater and beginning a climb up the slopes of Mount Sharp.

Mantle: silicates

Core: iron sulfide

Crust: silicates

LOW GRAVITY

Mars is smaller than Earth, with less rock and iron, so the planet has only a tenth the mass of Earth and weaker surface gravity, about a third of what we experience on Earth.

SKY-WATCHER
RECON MISSIONS

Space agencies have sent all kinds of spacecraft to Mars. Some have flown past without stopping. Some stay high above the planet in orbit, while others land on the surface. Missions to the red planet fall into four basic types:

Flybys: These spacecraft fly past Mars and observe it but don't go into orbit or land. Mariner 4 flew past Mars in 1965 and took the first detailed pictures of the planet.

Orbiters: Orbiters go into orbit around the planet, observing it from the sky. The Mars Reconnaissance Orbiter (art above) is there now, studying the planet's weather and surface.

Landers: Landers touch down on the planet and stay in one place, taking measurements around them. The Viking 1 and Viking 2 landers in 1976 tested the soil for signs of life.

Rovers: Rovers are little wheeled vehicles that land on the surface and then travel around, conducting scientific experiments using robotic arms. The Curiosity rover has traveled more than 13 miles (21 km) across Mars since it landed in 2012.

CERES AND THE ASTEROID BELT

Ceres is the closest dwarf planet to Earth. Astronomers have known about Ceres since 1801. When it was first discovered, they thought it might be the "missing planet" that many astronomers believed orbited between Mars and Jupiter. For the next half a century, it was called a planet. But then more and more large rocks, called asteroids, were discovered in that region of space. So Ceres was reclassified as an asteroid, and there it remained until its status was changed again, to dwarf planet.

About 592 miles (953 km) in diameter, much smaller than our moon, Ceres is in the heart of the asteroid belt. Its mass is almost a third of the entire mass of the millions of asteroids in the belt. In 2015, scientists got their first close-up look at the dwarf planet when the Dawn space probe arrived and went into orbit around it. Based on information from the probe, we now think that Ceres may have a thick layer of water ice just under its surface.

Asteroids come in all shapes and sizes, but all of them orbit the sun. Collisions between them happen a lot, but these relics of the early solar system aren't crammed together as they're sometimes shown in science fiction movies.

Occasionally, the influence of Jupiter's gravity can nudge an asteroid out of orbit, sending it in toward the sun. When that happens, the asteroid can strike one of the terrestrial planets.

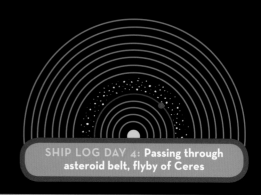

SHIP LOG DAY 4: Passing through asteroid belt, flyby of Ceres

FACTS ABOUT CERES

Average distance from the sun	257,055,204 miles (413,690,250 km)
Position from the sun in orbit	Fifth
Equatorial diameter	592 miles (953 km)
Mass (Earth = 1)	0.00016
Density (water = 1)	2.09
Length of day	9 Earth hours
Length of year	4.6 Earth years
Average surface temperature	-159°F (-106°C)
Known moons	0

Earth

Ceres

CERES LOOK-ALIKES

On Earth you can visit places that look like Ceres—likely because Ceres and Earth formed from similar materials and processes. Using photographs from the spacecraft Dawn, scientists compared Ceres's Occator Crater to this one, called Searles Crater, in California, U.S.A.'s Mojave Desert.

FUN FACT
Most asteroids tumble around as they orbit the sun. Some even orbit each other.

ROCKY CERES

Ceres lies deep inside the asteroid belt between the planets Mars and Jupiter, and is by far the largest object found here. Ceres and more than 200,000 other rocky objects called asteroids are the debris left over from the formation of the solar system.

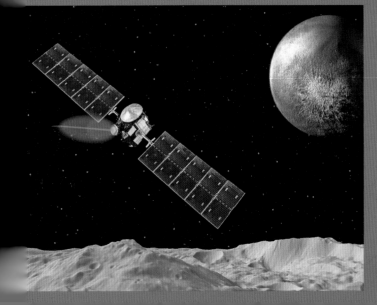

SKY-WATCHER
THE DAWN MISSION

In 2007, the space probe Dawn left Earth to dive into the asteroid belt. Its first visit was to the big asteroid Vesta, which it orbited for more than a year before taking aim at the dwarf planet Ceres. In 2015, the probe reached Ceres and went into a looping orbit around it, sometimes close to the little world and sometimes high up. Dawn took the first good pictures of Ceres's rocky landscape, covered with countless little craters. Its instruments also measured the dwarf planet's density, its structure, and the chemicals that cover its surface.

Dawn moves through space thanks to a futuristic ion propulsion system that uses xenon gas instead of liquid fuel. This is how it works: The ion thrusters accelerate the probe slowly—it takes four days just to get from 0 to 60 miles an hour (0 to 96.5 km/h)—but they keep going for years at a time. After it runs out of gas, Dawn will keep circling Ceres for at least 20 years.

JUPITER

Can you imagine a planet with no ground to walk on? Or a world where a red hurricane three times the size of Earth has been raging for centuries? What about a planet where ferocious winds rip through the skies at 400 miles an hour (640 km/h), brilliant bolts of lightning blast across the sky, and auroras dance around the poles?

That planet, Jupiter, is coming up next on our tour. The largest planet in the solar system, Jupiter is so big that all the other planets, including Saturn, could easily fit inside it and still have room to spare. With at least 79 moons circling around it, Jupiter is almost a miniature solar system by itself.

Looking at Jupiter through telescopes, we can see only the tops of its clouds. In essence, we're looking at the outside of a gigantic slushy snowball. In 2016, the Juno spacecraft went into orbit around Jupiter. Scientists hope to learn more now about what is happening under the giant planet's storm clouds.

Some people have called Jupiter a failed star. They have said that if Jupiter had been just a little bit bigger when it formed, nuclear fires would have ignited deep inside it, radiating heat and light just like our sun. Scientists now believe that it would have needed 80 times more mass to become even a dim, cool star.

SHIP LOG DAY 5: **Approaching Jupiter, landing on its moon Europa**

FACTS ABOUT JUPITER

Average distance from the sun	483,638,564 miles (778,340,821 km)
Position from the sun in orbit	Sixth
Equatorial diameter	86,880 miles (139,800 km)
Mass (Earth = 1)	318
Density (water = 1)	1.3
Length of day	9.9 Earth hours
Length of year	11.9 Earth years
Average surface temperature	–234°F (–148°C)
Known moons	At least 79

Jupiter

Earth

THE TERMINATOR

Cameras on the NASA spacecraft Juno took this lively, colorful image of storm clouds in the atmosphere covering Jupiter's northern hemisphere. In the upper-right corner, you can see an area called "the terminator," where daylight is gradually fading into night.

GREAT RED SPOT

Standing on the frozen surface of Jupiter's moon Europa, space travelers (imagined in art) could peer into the Great Red Spot. This churning hurricane, almost three times the size of Earth, looks like a cosmic eye staring from the candy-striped world of Jupiter.

STORMY PLANET

Days are very short on Jupiter. It spins so quickly on its axis that it makes one complete rotation every 9.9 Earth hours. Because it rotates so fast, it is not perfectly round. Egg-shaped, it bulges out around its equator like a spinning water balloon.

Composed of 90 percent hydrogen and almost 10 percent helium, its atmosphere would be poisonous for us to breathe. Here, little has changed since the planet formed 4.6 billion years ago.

Looking at Jupiter through a small telescope, we can easily see the two main features—the colored bands of clouds and the Great Red Spot. The white clouds are made of smelly frozen ammonia ice. The darker-colored layers of brown, orange, and red are made of ammonium hydrosulfide. They would smell really bad, too, like rotten eggs. As Jupiter spins on its axis, the clouds are pulled into stripes and bands by fast-moving jet streams. The white bands around the equator rotate faster than the darker ones. Where the edges of the bands meet, they tear and pull at each other.

Jupiter has rings like Saturn, but they're too thin and faint to be seen from Earth. The rings are made of rocky material ejected from the planet's smaller moons.

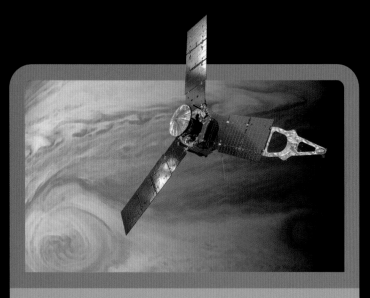

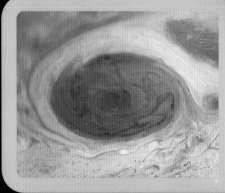

FUN FACT
Winds at the outer edges of the Great Red Spot can reach a ferocious 423 miles an hour (680 km/h).

SKY-WATCHER
THE JUNO MISSION

After being launched in 2011, the Juno spacecraft reached Jupiter in 2016. When it got there, rockets on the spacecraft sent it spinning, a motion that makes it easier to control and to point at regions it needs to measure and photograph. Juno orbits the huge planet from pole to pole, avoiding Jupiter's strongest and most destructive radiation belts. It's loaded with scientific instruments for measuring gravity, magnetism, and gases, as well as with a color camera that has sent back pictures of crazy-looking storms at Jupiter's poles. Long solar panels capture the distant sunlight to keep the spacecraft powered up.

Scientists hope that Juno will reveal some of the mysteries of Jupiter's atmosphere and structure. That information, in turn, may tell us more about how that planet and others were first formed in the solar system. When Juno's mission is over, the spacecraft will end its life dramatically. To avoid having the dead craft collide with one of Jupiter's moons and break up into space debris, controllers will instead send it crashing into Jupiter's stormy atmosphere to vanish forever.

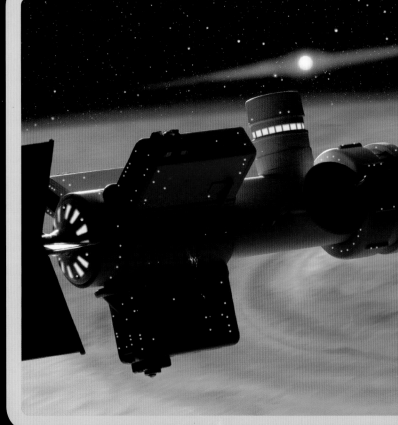

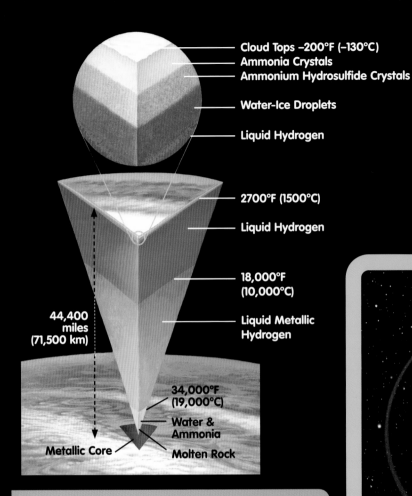

Cloud Tops –200°F (–130°C)
Ammonia Crystals
Ammonium Hydrosulfide Crystals

Water-Ice Droplets

Liquid Hydrogen

2700°F (1500°C)

Liquid Hydrogen

18,000°F
(10,000°C)

Liquid Metallic
Hydrogen

44,400
miles
(71,500 km)

34,000°F
(19,000°C)

Water &
Ammonia

Metallic Core

Molten Rock

MEGA MAGNET

Because of Jupiter's rapid rotation and solid metallic core, it generates the strongest planetary magnetic field in the solar system. The magnetic field, in turn, causes magnificent auroral displays that illuminate the northern and southern poles (art below).

UNDER PRESSURE

Jupiter's visible clouds are separated into three different layers (pull-out at top of art). Pressure and temperature increase the lower down the clouds are. At the lowest level, the atmosphere liquefies into a warm slush. Below the atmosphere (red and orange sections of art), hydrogen gas is compressed into a liquid and then a liquid metal. At the center of Jupiter lies a solid core.

COLORFUL STORMS

The Great Red Spot (art below) is at least 350 years old, maybe older. Cyclonic storms like this are common on the gas giant planets and appear in a variety of colors. As we fly toward the Great Red Spot, we can see the moons Io (foreground) and Callisto (background).

GALILEO'S MOONS

Jupiter has at least 79 moons. The four largest can be seen through a pair of binoculars. They're called the Galilean moons because they were discovered by the astronomer Galileo Galilei in 1610.

The first Galilean moon, Io, is located closest to Jupiter. Almost the size of our moon, it's the most geologically active body in the solar system. Jupiter's gravitational pull bends and stretches Io like taffy, causing intense heating inside the moon. That causes volcanoes to erupt constantly on its surface.

Callisto is one of the most heavily cratered moons in the solar system. Its icy surface may be covering a salty ocean. If that ocean is liquid, Callisto would be a candidate for another object in our solar system, besides Earth, possibly supporting life. But scientists suspect Callisto's ocean is frozen solid.

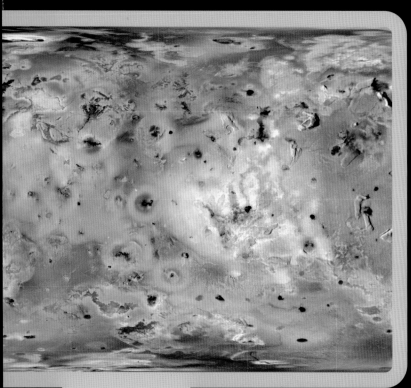

FUN FACT
Pulled by Jupiter's gravity, Io's solid surface can bulge in and out as much as 330 feet (100 m).

LOL!
Q: Why does Jupiter have a werewolf problem?

A: Because it has 79 moons!

SKY-WATCHER
FINDING THE GALILEAN MOONS

When Renaissance astronomer Galileo discovered Jupiter's moons, he gave each one a number instead of a name. But as more and more moons were discovered, the numbering system became a cumbersome way to refer to them. Finally, in the mid-1800s, the numbers were dropped, and the four Galilean moons were named after the girlfriends of the Greek god Zeus (known as Jupiter to the Romans).

All four Galilean moons (above) are easily spotted with a pair of binoculars because they form a straight line on either side of Jupiter. Io is the closest, followed by Europa, the second. Ganymede, the third, is the largest moon in the entire solar system. Callisto, the last of the four, is one of the most heavily cratered moons in the solar system.

If you have a pair of binoculars or a small telescope, go out on a clear night, find Jupiter, and look for the Galilean moons. (You can find out where Jupiter will be in your night sky by looking it up online with an adult.) The moons change position from night to night, but when all four are lined up, you'll see them as four bright points of light.

PIZZA MOON

The surface of Io looks like a pizza. The colors are layers of sulfur and lava that are constantly being sprayed out from very active volcanoes, including the one in the photograph on the right.

CALLISTO

The heavily cratered surface of Callisto was formed a long time ago—maybe four billion years in the past. Callisto seems to be frozen solid, though it may have some water hidden under its surface of thick ice.

ICY OCEANS

The Galilean moon Ganymede is the largest moon in the solar system. If it circled the sun, it would be considered a planet and would be the eighth largest in the solar system.

The darker regions of Ganymede are its original icy surfaces that have been covered with meteorites and dust. This Jovian moon appears to be frozen solid, but it could have liquid oceans under the ice. Astronomers don't know yet.

Europa is slightly smaller than Io. It has an icy surface that covers a hidden saltwater ocean. Water was important for life to begin here on Earth, and Europa may have even more water than Earth. This means that Europa is an excellent place to look for life in the solar system. But drilling through 10 to 16 miles (16–25 km) of ice that covers these oceans will be a challenge. Explorers will also have to protect themselves from the deadly radiation that rains down from Jupiter.

When Galileo discovered these moons, most people still believed that Earth was the center of the solar system. They thought that all the heavenly bodies revolved around Earth. These four moons of Jupiter provided the first real evidence that there was something in outer space that did not revolve around Earth.

SUPER STARS

When Italian astronomer Galileo Galilei (1564-1642) discovered Jupiter's moons Io, Europa, Ganymede, and Callisto in 1610, he called the four together the Medicean stars, in honor of his patron, Cosimo II de' Medici, the Grand Duke of Tuscany, who funded Galileo's work. Galileo was hoping that, by conferring this honor on his patron, the grand duke would give him more money, to fund his future research. It worked—Galileo also won a post as the duke's mathematician and natural philosopher.

Galileo was a brilliant scientist who made discoveries not only in astronomy but also in basic physics and in scientific theory in general. Born in Pisa, Italy, he later dropped objects from the Leaning Tower of Pisa to show that two objects of different weights would fall at the same rate. Using telescopes he had made himself, he observed not just Jupiter's moons but the surface of Earth's moon and many new stars. His observations that the sun, not Earth, was the center of the solar system got him into trouble with the Catholic Church, but he continued to work on new scientific studies until his death.

MYSTERIOUS WATERS

Monitoring a drilling rig, future astronauts (imagined in art) bore down through the 16 miles (25 km) of ice covering the surface of Europa. The challenge is keeping the freshly drilled hole from immediately freezing over, so that a robotic probe can be inserted through the hole to explore the mysterious dark waters below.

ICY EUROPA

The face of Europa is deceptive. Its icy surface looks like a mosaic of giant cracks. However, there is much more to this moon than meets the eye. Underneath all the ice is a saltwater ocean that may be more than 60 miles (97 km) deep.

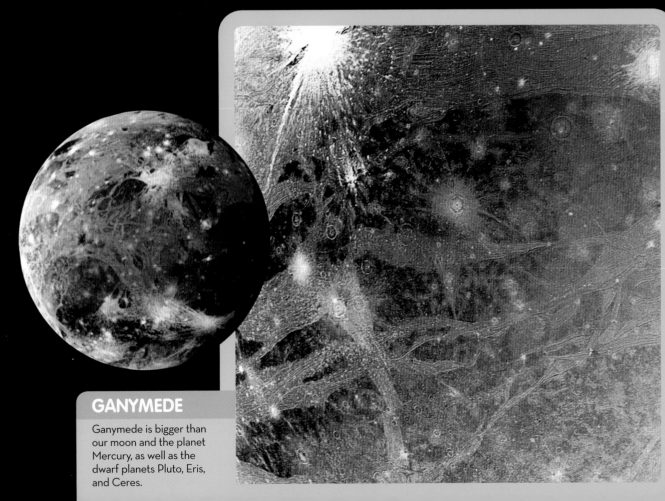

GANYMEDE

Ganymede is bigger than our moon and the planet Mercury, as well as the dwarf planets Pluto, Eris, and Ceres.

SATURN

W hen people first see Saturn through a telescope, they usually gasp in wonder. As our spaceship gets close to the seventh planet, we can see its beauty close up. No other planet in the solar system has the visual splendor of Saturn.

When Galileo pointed his own crude telescope toward it in 1610, the telescope was not good enough to separate the rings from the rest of the disk. So he thought he'd found a "triple-bodied" planet.

Today, we know all four gas giant planets have rings, but Saturn's are the only ones visible by telescope from Earth. Surrounded by a brilliant halo of ice and dust, Saturn seems to mimic the formation of the early solar system. The diameters of its rings together span some 175,000 miles (282,000 km), about three-quarters of the distance from our moon to Earth. Traveling at the speed of a jet, it would take 10 days and nights to cross Saturn's rings. As amazing as this is, even more astounding is the fact that some rings have areas that are more than two miles (3 km) thick.

SHIP LOG DAY 8: **Approaching Saturn, orbiting its moon Mimas**

FACTS ABOUT SATURN

Average distance from the sun	886,489,415 miles (1,426,666,422 km)
Position from the sun in orbit	Seventh
Equatorial diameter	72,367 miles (116,464 km)
Mass (Earth = 1)	95
Density (water = 1)	0.69
Length of day	10.7 Earth hours
Length of year	30 Earth years
Average surface temperature	–288°F (–178°C)
Known moons	At least 82

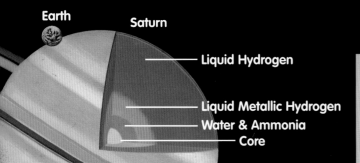

Earth

Saturn

— Liquid Hydrogen

— Liquid Metallic Hydrogen

— Water & Ammonia

— Core

FUN FACT

Because Saturn is less dense than water, it would float if you could find a body of water big enough to hold it.

DELICATE RINGS

If you were standing in the giant Herschel Crater on Saturn's moon Mimas (art below), the planet would fill the sky. From this viewpoint, it's easy to see how thin the planet's rings actually are.

RINGED WORLD

Like Jupiter, Saturn has no surface to walk on. Its slushy atmosphere is mostly liquid hydrogen and helium, driven by gale-force winds into pale, colored bands and stripes. Occasionally, large white, oval-shaped storms appear, similar to the Great Red Spot on Jupiter.

Saturn spins very quickly on its axis, completing a rotation every 10 hours and 40 minutes. But it takes almost 30 years to make one orbit around the sun. Its magnetic field is about 600 times stronger than Earth's, producing aurora fireworks that change hourly.

Saturn's rings reflect back 70 percent of the light from the sun and are sometimes even brighter than the planet. Ring names are assigned letters alphabetically in order of their discovery. Right now, they have names that go from A through G. The rings may have formed within the past 50 to 100 million years, either from the breakup of an icy moon or a captured asteroid. Astronomers think the object would have been about 240 miles (386 km) in diameter. The particles from this captured body are still gravitationally attracted to one another, as if the body were trying to reassemble itself.

The rings consist of thousands of closely spaced bands, called ringlets, with gaps in between them. The largest gap, the Cassini Division, is about 3,000 miles (4,700 km) wide and visible from Earth through a telescope. The rings change over time, and every 15 years, when they face Earth edge-on, they disappear from our view. Early astronomers questioned their own reasoning when they noticed that the rings vanished, only to reappear a few years later. The next time the rings disappear will be in 2023.

SUPER STARS

Dutch scientist Christiaan Huygens (1629-1695) was born in an age when it wasn't uncommon for one person to make major breakthroughs in many different fields. Huygens came from a wealthy family and was educated in languages, mathematics, and law. He went on to make key discoveries about the workings of light, telescopes, pendulums, and the planets, among other subjects. Astronomers remember him best for two things: for discovering Saturn's moon Titan and for determining that Saturn is surrounded by rings.

Huygens designed his own telescopes, and in 1655, "drawn by an urgent longing to see these wonders of heaven," he wrote, he pointed one of them at Saturn. He realized that the blobby "arms" that seemed to stick out of each side of the planet were in fact "a thin, flat ring, nowhere touching." To those who argued that such a ringed planet had never been seen before and was unlikely, he noted: "[It] is less surprising that such a body should have assigned to it a shape of this kind than that it should have some absurd and quite unbeautiful shape."

Huygens also spotted Saturn's large moon Titan, correctly measuring its orbit around Saturn at 16 days. When the European Space Agency designed a space probe to drop onto the surface of Titan in 2005, they named it after the Dutch astronomer.

THE E RING

This remarkable photograph of Saturn was taken by the Cassini spacecraft as it passed along the shadowed back side of the ringed planet. From this angle, with the sun hidden, a wonder never before seen came into view—the E ring, the faint one farthest out in the photograph. It is invisible to telescopes on Earth.

MYSTERIOUS MOONS

Like Jupiter, Saturn has a fascinating array of moons—at least 82 of them. The precise number is uncertain, and most are quite small and oddly shaped. Still, seven are massive enough to have formed into spheres under the influence of their own gravity.

Titan, the second largest moon in the solar system after Jupiter's Ganymede, is bigger in diameter than Mercury and any of the known dwarf planets. It's the only moon in the solar system with a substantial atmosphere. Underneath Titan's dense orange blanket of clouds is a primordial world brimming with mysteries. Because the atmosphere is so thick and the gravity so low, humans could fly through it by attaching wings to their arms and flapping them up and down like butterflies. The moon's surface holds dark lakes of liquid methane with drainage channels rimming the shorelines. Scientists believe the early atmosphere on Earth was very similar to the atmosphere on Titan today. If that is so, Titan is one of the objects in the solar system, along with Earth, Mars, Jupiter's Europa, and Saturn's Enceladus, that may harbor life.

Mimas, about 246 miles (396 km) in diameter, is composed mostly of frozen ice and some rock. It sports one of the biggest black eyes in the solar system—a crater that is almost 80 miles (130 km) in diameter. The crater is named Herschel for Sir William Herschel, who discovered Mimas in 1789.

HAZY TITAN

A photograph taken by the Huygens lander shows Titan cloaked in a thick orange atmospheric haze; the small rocks in the foreground are only a few inches in size.

FUN FACT

Fed by a subsurface ocean, huge geysers of liquid water shoot out of Saturn's moon Enceladus at 800 miles an hour (1,290 km/h). This art includes the Cassini spacecraft above.

TITAN

The largest and most intriguing of Saturn's moons, Titan is nearly half the size of Earth.

MIMAS

The huge crater on Mimas was caused by a collision with a giant piece of space debris that almost destroyed the moon sometime in the distant past.

DIONE

Dione's surface markings resemble the dark marks on our moon and were probably caused by water flooding the surface and then quickly freezing.

SKY-WATCHER

THE CASSINI MISSION

During its 20-year mission, the Cassini spacecraft and its probe, Huygens, greatly advanced our knowledge of Saturn, its rings, and its moons. It also sent us some gorgeous pictures of the ringed planet.

NASA (National Aeronautics and Space Administration), the European Space Agency, the Italian Space Agency, and others worked together to build and launch the spacecraft in 1997. The mission actually had two craft: the Cassini orbiter and the Huygens lander. After entering Saturn's orbit in 2004, the lander left the orbiter and dropped through a thick atmosphere onto the surface of Saturn's moon Titan. It was the first spacecraft to land on a moon other than Earth's own, and it sent back amazing images of a frozen, smoggy landscape. The Cassini spacecraft stayed in orbit around Saturn for another 13 years. It got close-up views of Saturn's astounding moons, discovered seven new moons, measured the planet's rings, and made many other discoveries. To end its mission without smashing into the moons, in 2017 controllers sent the craft weaving through Saturn's rings before it crashed into the atmosphere in what the scientists called "the grand finale."

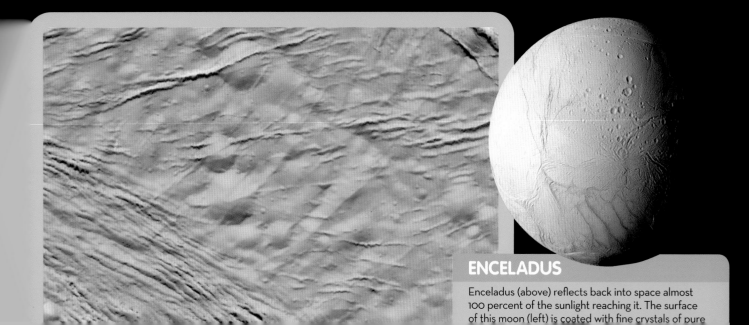

ENCELADUS

Enceladus (above) reflects back into space almost 100 percent of the sunlight reaching it. The surface of this moon (left) is coated with fine crystals of pure

URANUS

As we approach Uranus, it glows like an aquamarine gem in the outer reaches of our solar system.

Like Neptune, this planet is an icy giant. Neither one has a solid surface. Uranus's blue-green color is caused by the absorption of red wavelengths of distant sunlight entering its frosty atmosphere. Methane gas reflects the blue and green wavelengths back into space.

Unlike any other planet, Uranus has a 98-degree tilt to its axis. Hit by something gigantic long ago, it almost lies on its side! Right now, its north pole faces the sun, while the south pole faces away into space. This brings 42 years of constant sunlight to one side of the planet, followed by 42 years of complete darkness.

Since Uranus is tipped over on its side, its 13 thin, wispy rings are also tipped because they follow the planet's equator.

Of all the planets, Uranus may boast the greatest literary roots. Its 27 known moons are named mostly after characters from the works of William Shakespeare, the great English playwright. Two of its largest moons, Oberon and Titania, are named for the king and queen of the fairies.

SHIP LOG DAY 11: **Approaching Uranus, landing on its moon Miranda**

FACTS ABOUT URANUS

Average distance from the sun	1,783,744,300 miles (2,870,658,186 km)
Position from the sun in orbit	Eighth
Equatorial diameter	31,518 miles (50,724 km)
Mass (Earth = 1)	15
Density (water = 1)	1.27
Length of day	17.2 Earth hours
Length of year	84 Earth years
Average surface temperature	-357°F (-216°C)
Known moons	27

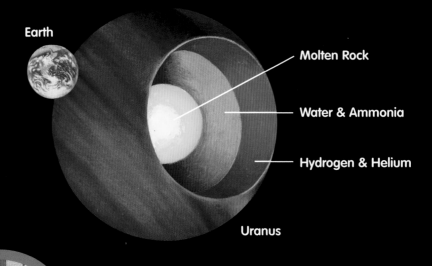

Earth

Molten Rock

Water & Ammonia

Hydrogen & Helium

Uranus

FUN FACT

Uranus stinks! Scientists studying light from Uranus's atmosphere found out that its clouds hold hydrogen sulfide. This nasty gas smells like rotten eggs. It's also poisonous and catches on fire easily. Luckily, any astronauts visiting the planet would already be wearing space suits.

SUPER STARS

William and Caroline Herschel were pioneering astronomers who showed that a brother and sister, working together, can make a great scientific team. Born in Hanover, Germany, William (1738-1822) moved to England to teach music but soon developed a passion for astronomy and telescopes. His younger sister Caroline (1750-1848) joined him there and took up telescope-making and astronomy herself. One night in 1781, as William studied the sky with a 39-foot (12-m) telescope of his own making, he saw what he later described as "a curious either nebulous Star or perhaps a Comet." And yet over the nights, his "star" moved slowly across the sky. He realized it was in fact a planet (later named Uranus), the first to be discovered since ancient times.

William won great fame for his discovery. Meanwhile, Caroline began to discover some actual comets herself. Eventually, she found eight altogether, as well as several nebulae (star-forming gas clouds). She and William both worked on making a catalog of heavenly objects. The catalog she published after William's death won her the Royal Astronomical Society's gold medal, which honors important contributions to astronomy.

MIRANDA

Astronauts visiting Uranus's moon Miranda (imagined in art) would clearly see the way the planet spins tipped over on its axis and surrounded by rings. The surface of Miranda would probably be slippery to walk on because of the ice and snow that scientists think erupt from its water volcanoes.

NEPTUNE

We're nearing the pale blue, icy world of Neptune. It has the wildest weather of any planet in the solar system, with winds that blow at speeds over 1,200 miles an hour (2,000 km/h).

Like the other Jovian planets, Neptune doesn't have a surface to walk on. Although the clouds surrounding it are very cold, minus 350°F (–212°C), its rocky iron core is about the same temperature as the sun's surface. This internal heat causes the planet's violent winds and hurricanes. Dark spots, or storms, similar to Jupiter's Great Red Spot dot its surface. The largest, called the Great Dark Spot, is no longer seen, but it was bigger than Earth. Astronomers call one of the lighter-colored spots Scooter because this small, fast-moving storm seems to chase other storms around. Six rings surround the planet.

Neptune was detected by mathematical calculation rather than by observation in 1846. Astronomers realized something very large was affecting the orbit of Uranus. That something was Neptune, even though it lies a billion miles (1.6 billion km) farther out in space.

Since its discovery more than 170 years ago, Neptune has completed only one full orbit of the sun!

SHIP LOG DAY 17: **Approaching Neptune, close flyby of its moon Triton**

FACTS ABOUT NEPTUNE

Average distance from the sun	2,795,173,960 miles (4,498,396,441 km)
Position from the sun in orbit	Ninth
Equatorial diameter	30,599 miles (49,244 km)
Mass (Earth = 1)	17
Density (water = 1)	1.64
Length of day	16.1 Earth hours
Length of year	164.8 Earth years
Average surface temperature	–353°F (–214°C)
Known moons	14

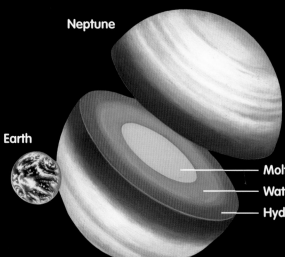

Neptune

Earth

- Molten Rock
- Water & Ammonia
- Hydrogen & Helium

PLANET NINE

Is Neptune really the last full-size planet in our solar system? Maybe not. The orbits of some objects in the Kuiper belt, a ring of small, rocky worlds past Neptune, seem to be influenced by the gravity of a large object. A huge object, in fact—a planet the size of Neptune. This far-distant world might be about 56 billion miles (90 billion km) from Earth, with an orbit that takes 20,000 Earth years. We haven't seen it yet and aren't positive it exists, but hopeful astronomers are already calling it Planet Nine.

TRITON CHALLENGE

Neptune's blue methane clouds help illuminate the frozen surface of its largest moon, Triton (art below). Astronauts here would have to be careful of the surface gashes, craters, and large frozen lakes caused by erupting water volcanoes.

KUIPER BELT

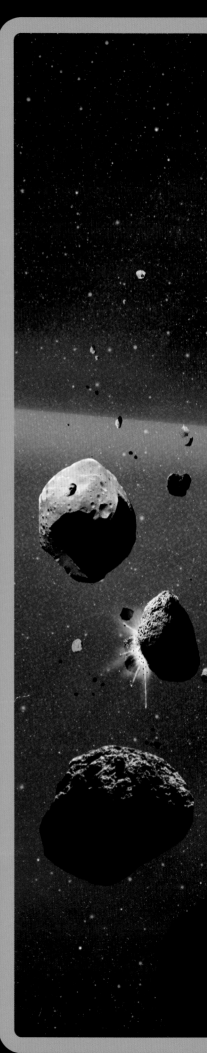

A huge concentration of galactic debris and assorted planetary leftovers makes up a faraway region known as the Kuiper (rhymes with *viper*) belt. It extends from the orbit of Neptune to hundreds of millions of miles beyond the dwarf planet Pluto.

Astronomers believe that after the gas giant planets—so-called because they're made mostly of gases—had taken shape during the formation of the solar system, gravitational interactions between Jupiter and Saturn may have ejected this galactic debris far out into space.

Today, the dwarf planets Pluto, Haumea, Makemake, and Eris, as well as their moons, are all considered members of the Kuiper belt. So are Halley's comet and the other "short-period" comets that make regular trips around the sun every 200 years or more. So far, more than 1,300 KBOs (Kuiper belt objects) have been identified and numbered. But there may be more than 100,000 of these icy objects, each with the potential of becoming a new comet in Earth's nighttime skies.

FUN FACT

The huge digital cameras used to take pictures of Kuiper belt objects have infrared light detectors that work only in extreme cold, so the cameras have to be kept at temperatures well below zero.

FACTS ABOUT THE KUIPER BELT

Distance from the sun	2.8–5.1 billion miles (4.5–8.2 billion km)
Objects over 62 miles (100 km) in diameter	More than 100,000
Largest members by diameter	
Pluto	1,476 miles (2,376 km)
Eris	1,445 miles (2,326 km)
2007 OR10	955 miles (1,535 km)
Makemake	918 miles (1,478 km)
Haumea	1,443 x 707 miles (2,322 x 1,138 km)

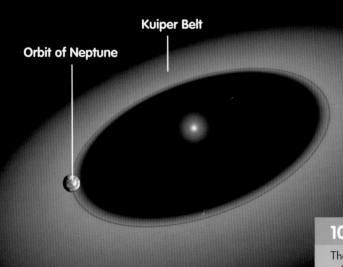

Orbit of Neptune

Kuiper Belt

100,000 OBJECTS

The vast Kuiper belt, which extends from Neptune's orbit to far beyond Pluto, may hold more than 100,000 comets, dwarf planets, and other unidentified objects.

ASTEROID ACTION

In the Kuiper belt, asteroids smash together, sometimes nudging each other into new orbits toward the sun. Here (art below), we see in the distance that they vaporize and grow large tails, becoming spectacular comets. Periodically returning comets, like Halley's comet, originate in the Kuiper belt.

PLUTO

For 76 years, Pluto reigned as the ninth planet in our solar system. In 2006, everything changed. Like a popular sports star who gets demoted to second string, Pluto was reclassified as a dwarf planet.

Originally, astronomers thought Pluto might be about the size of Earth. Its true size was difficult to tell because it was so far away. No matter what telescope was used to look at it, no details could be seen. It simply appeared as a speck of light. The best the Hubble Space Telescope could do was capture an image of a small ball with patches of dark and light. We now know Pluto is smaller than our own moon.

Pluto is located in the Kuiper belt, where comets that return again and again originate. In 2015, the New Horizons space probe became the first craft to fly past the distant world. Surrounding Pluto's rocky core is a thick layer of ice, with huge flat plains and spiky ice mountains. The dwarf planet has a thin, blue atmosphere that freezes and falls to the surface when Pluto is at the far parts of its orbit.

Pluto also has a large moon named Charon (SHAR-on). Because of their sizes, Pluto and Charon together are considered a dwarf double-planet by many astronomers. Four other moons, much smaller, also orbit the dwarf planet: Nix, Hydra, Kerberos, and Styx.

FACTS ABOUT PLUTO

Average distance from the sun	3,670,092,055 miles (5,906,440,628 km)
Position from the sun in orbit	Tenth
Equatorial diameter	1,476 miles (2,376 km)
Mass (Earth = 1)	0.002
Density (water = 1)	2.05
Length of day	6.39 Earth days
Length of year	248 Earth years
Average surface temperature	–378°F (–228°C)
Known moons	5

Earth

Pluto

SKY-WATCHER
NEW HORIZONS

Launched in 2006, the New Horizons probe is making one of the longest journeys ever undertaken by a spacecraft. After it was rocketed into space, the probe swung past Jupiter and used the giant planet's gravity as a boost to speed toward Pluto. Wrapped in gold-covered insulation to hold in its heat, the spacecraft is carrying seven science instruments. They include cameras and tools to map surfaces, study the dwarf planet's atmosphere, and measure the solar wind and space dust.

On July 14, 2015, New Horizons made its closest pass to Pluto's surface. What it saw was amazing. Pluto and its moon Charon were much more complex than scientists had thought. Pluto had ranges of sharp, icy mountains and a vast heart-shaped plain of ice. Charon had a strange, reddish north pole and a deep canyon.

New Horizons did not go into orbit around Pluto. Instead, it continued its journey deeper into the Kuiper belt, heading for a Kuiper belt object called 2014 MU69. By studying this little world, scientists hope to learn more about the Kuiper belt and how the solar system formed in its earliest years.

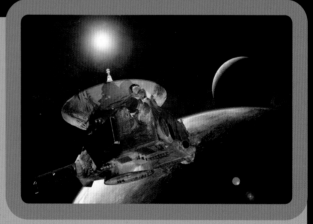

Nix

Kerberos

Pluto

Charon

PLUTO'S MOONS

The Milky Way galaxy stretches behind the dwarf planet Pluto and its largest moon, Charon (art above). In the distance, Pluto's four smaller moons, Nix, Hydra, Kerberos, and Styx, can be seen silhouetted against the starlit sky.

ICY MOUNTAINS

Pluto and Charon's very peculiar orbit around the sun is egg-shaped instead of circular. They orbit so far out on the edge of the solar system that from the surface of Pluto, the sun would look like just another bright star in the sky.

In 2015, when the New Horizons spacecraft reached the dwarf planet, Pluto was fairly close to the sun in its orbital journey. Scientists were surprised by its varied landscape. Near its heart-shaped plain, now named Tombaugh Regio after the discoverer of Pluto (see below), are high, jagged mountains that have been named after Edmund Hillary and Tenzing Norgay, the first climbers to safely reach the top of Earth's Mount Everest. A large crater is now known as Burney, after 11-year-old Venetia Burney, the girl who came up with the name "Pluto" for the planet.

FUN FACT

In 1930, Venetia Burney, an English school girl, suggested naming Clyde Tombaugh's new discovery after Pluto, the Roman god of the underworld—and Tombaugh liked it. Many think the Disney dog Pluto was then named after the planet.

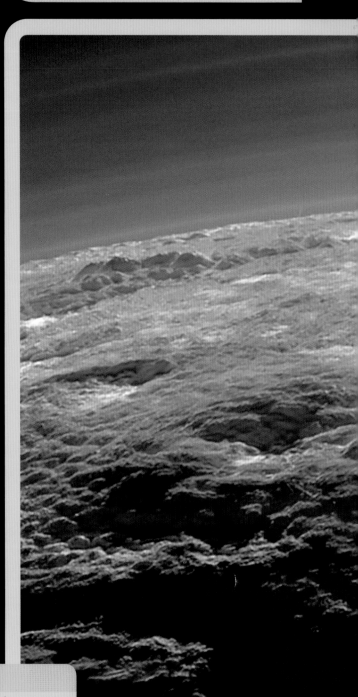

SUPER STARS

Pluto's story begins with Neptune. Astronomers thought that something was disturbing Neptune's orbit. Was there another undiscovered planet out there? Today, we know that Pluto is too small to have had any influence on Neptune, but while looking for the mysterious Planet X, a night assistant at Arizona, U.S.A.'s Lowell Observatory named Clyde Tombaugh (1906-1997) found Pluto.

Tombaugh was an Illinois farm boy with a knack for building telescopes. At 22 years old, he built his own six-inch (15-cm) reflector and sent drawings of Mars and Jupiter to the Lowell Observatory. Scientists there offered him a job, and he began taking pictures of the same area of the sky a week apart. If an object changed position on one of the photographic plates, it might be Planet X. On February 18, 1930, something showed up on one of Tombaugh's plates. Everyone was amazed. This object became the ninth planet in the solar system.

The right to name it belonged to the Lowell Observatory. The observatory scientists asked for name submissions, and an 11-year-old English girl came up with Pluto. All planets have an astronomical symbol, used by astronomers instead of spelling out the planet's name. Pluto's astronomical symbol is PL. It stands for the first two letters in its name and also honors the initials of Percival Lowell, the founder of the Lowell Observatory.

DEEP FREEZE

Pluto is one of the coldest objects in the solar system. In 2015 NASA's New Horizons spacecraft captured its rugged, icy mountains. When it's at its farthest from the sun, its atmosphere freezes, like an ice frosting on the ground.

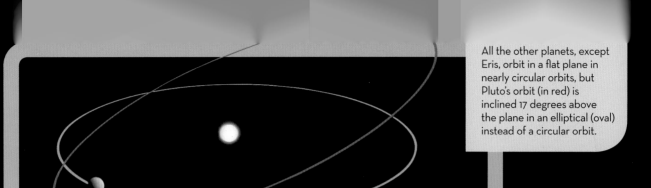

All the other planets, except Eris, orbit in a flat plane in nearly circular orbits, but Pluto's orbit (in red) is inclined 17 degrees above the plane in an elliptical (oval) instead of a circular orbit.

SEPARATE PICTURES OF TWO FRIGID WORLDS—
Pluto in the foreground and its moon Charon in the background—are joined here in one image from NASA's New Horizons spacecraft. Pluto's surface has smooth plains, sharp-edged craters, and tall icy mountains. Its huge, heart-shaped plain has been named Tombaugh Regio after Pluto's discoverer. The left lobe of the plain's "heart" is covered with carbon monoxide ice. Different chemicals frozen on the dwarf planet's surface give it a range of colors from dark red to light blue, which are enhanced in this image.

HAUMEA

Leaving Pluto behind, we travel even farther into the lonely reaches of the Kuiper belt in search of the next two dwarf planets. Before long, we spot one of the oddest members of the solar system.

Tumbling end over end is potato-shaped Haumea, circled by two tiny moons. Thin ice covers its rocky surface. The dwarf planet, about as long as Pluto is wide, spins so quickly that it has just a four-hour day. But its year is long—Haumea takes 285 Earth years to orbit the sun.

Haumea has one of the fastest rotations of any large body in the solar system. Astronomers think a collision early in its history sent it whirling, and that this motion gradually pulled it into its oblong shape. The impact may also have knocked off the chunks of rock that make up its moons, Namaka and Hi'iaka. Astronomer Mike Brown, one of the spinning world's discoverers, nicknamed it "Santa" because he spotted it just after Christmas in 2004. Its official name, Haumea, comes from the Hawaiian goddess of fertility and childbirth. The moons are named after two of the goddess's daughters.

SHIP LOG DAY 34: **Approaching Haumea, landing on one of its two tiny moons**

FACTS ABOUT HAUMEA

Average distance from the sun	4,017,165,000 miles (6,465,000,000 km)
Position from the sun in orbit	Eleventh
Equatorial diameter	1,443 x 707 miles (2,322 x 1,138 km)
Mass (Earth = 1)	0.00066
Density (water = 1)	1.8
Length of day	3.9 Earth hours
Length of year	285 Earth years
Average surface temperature	-396°F (-233°C)
Known moons	2

SKY-WATCHER
DOES HAUMEA HAVE RINGS?

Haumea is so far away that astronomers can't see it clearly. However, in 2017 they got a chance to see its shadow when the little world passed in front of a distant star. By measuring the way Haumea blocked the starlight, scientists were able to get a better sense of its size and elongated shape. They also saw something new: Just before and after the main body of Haumea passed in front of the star, the light dimmed. It seems as though Haumea may have rings, like the gas giant planets, that block the starlight.

The measurements suggest that the rings are about 43 miles (70 km) wide and circle the planet's narrow equator. Like other rings, they would probably be made of bits of ice and rock. If they do exist, they might support the idea that Haumea once banged into another large body in space. The blow would have knocked it spinning and created its rings and two little moons.

Earth

Haumea

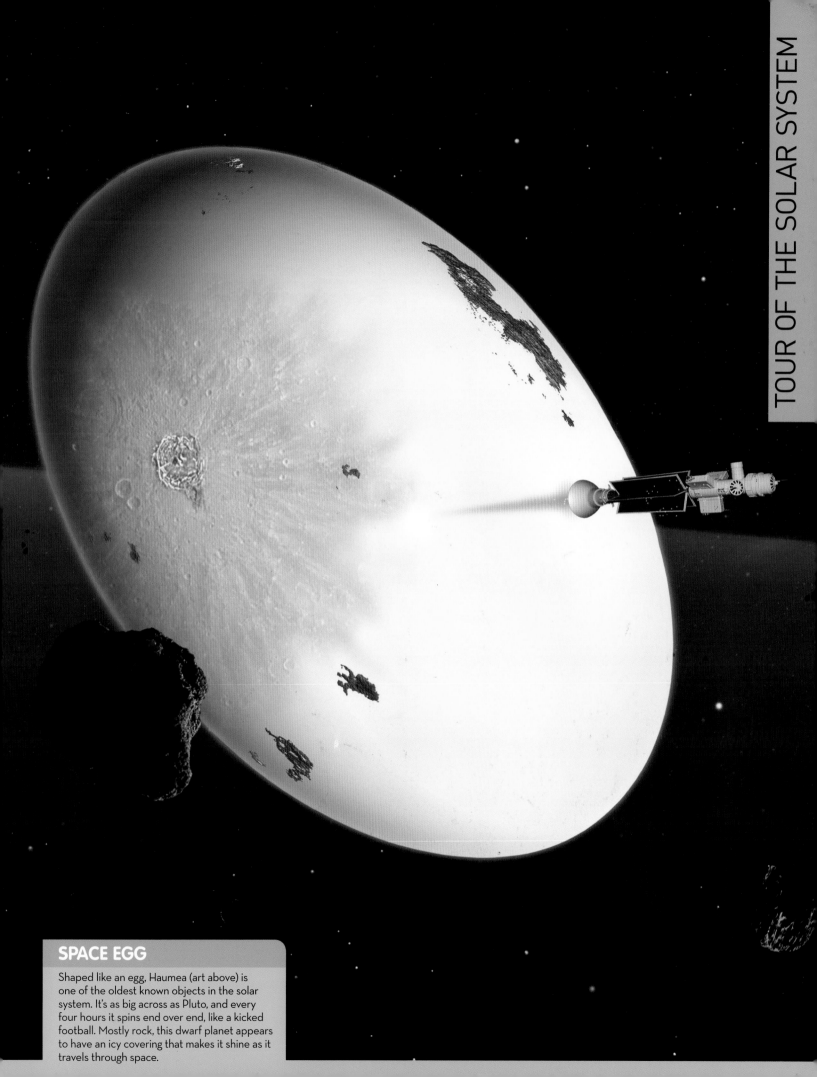

SPACE EGG

Shaped like an egg, Haumea (art above) is one of the oldest known objects in the solar system. It's as big across as Pluto, and every four hours it spins end over end, like a kicked football. Mostly rock, this dwarf planet appears to have an icy covering that makes it shine as it travels through space.

MAKEMAKE

Dwarf planet Makemake (pronounced MAH-kay-MAH-kay) is next on our tour of the solar system's chilly fringe. It shows up ahead of us, bright and surprisingly red. Unlike Haumea, Makemake has a normal round shape, though a bit flattened at the poles. It is somewhat smaller than Pluto. Just one orbit around the sun takes 310 years.

In 2015, the Hubble Space Telescope spotted a small moon, about 100 miles (160 km) wide, circling the dwarf planet. Nicknamed MK 2, the moon is as dark as charcoal. Scientists aren't sure why.

Makemake itself is thickly covered with ice—not water ice, but ice made of ethane, methane, and nitrogen. If sound could travel on its airless surface, you might hear the ice grains crunch under your feet. Radiation from the sun has turned the ice a reddish-brown color. It is cold cold cold down there—about minus 406°F (–240°C).

Makemake was originally nicknamed Easterbunny, because it was discovered just after Easter in 2005. Its official name comes from Easter Island, or Rapa Nui. Makemake is a chief god in the mythology of the Rapanui people.

SHIP LOG DAY 61: **Approaching Makemake, flyby of its flat north pole**

FACTS ABOUT MAKEMAKE

Average distance from the sun	4,260,898,000 miles (6,857,250,000 km)
Position from the sun in orbit	Twelfth
Equatorial diameter	918 miles (1,478 km)
Mass (Earth = 1)	0.0005
Density (water = 1)	1.70
Length of day	7.7 Earth hours
Length of year	310 Earth years
Average surface temperature	–406°F (–240°C)
Known moons	1

SKY-WATCHER
PALOMAR OBSERVATORY

Orbiting telescopes, such as the Hubble Space Telescope, have a big advantage over ground-based scopes: Earth's atmosphere and lights don't get in their way. Even so, big Earth-based observatories are still finding new astronomical objects. One of the most famous of these observatories is Palomar Observatory, which holds the telescope that astronomer Mike Brown used to discover Makemake.

Completed in 1939, the observatory was built on Palomar Mountain in Southern California. Eventually, the domed building held several telescopes, including one with a huge, 200-inch (5-m)-wide mirror that would be able to see distant stars and planets. The observatory describes it as "a giant pupil that collects light from the Universe." Mike Brown, however, used a smaller telescope there, the 48-inch (1.2-m) Samuel Oschin photographic telescope, to find Makemake. The scope is good for imaging large areas of the sky to spot distant, moving objects—like dwarf planets. The Samuel Oschin and other telescopes at Palomar Observatory are continuing to make important discoveries about everything from exoplanets to supernovae.

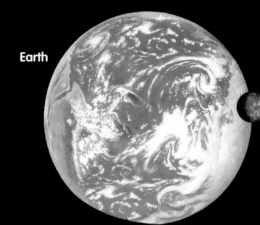

Earth

Makemake

RED REFLECTOR

The odd, red-colored dwarf planet Makemake reflects just enough dim sunlight to be seen in large telescopes back on Earth. To the right, a stunning open star cluster, the Pleiades, shines like sapphires.

ERIS

The coldest object ever found in our solar system is now looming before us. Eris was discovered in 2005. It has an orbit that goes through the Kuiper belt but also extends beyond it—nine billion miles (14 billion km) from the sun. Eris orbits the sun about every 558 Earth years! It's about the same size as Pluto and has a moon named Dysnomia.

Eris's discoverer, Mike Brown, was amazed to find something so far out in the solar system. When it became classified as a new planet, some astronomers weren't too happy. If Pluto remained a planet, and Ceres and Eris were added to the list too, the solar system might keep expanding until we had more planets than anyone could name. Instead, at the 2006 meeting of the International Astronomical Union, scientists came up with the new classification of dwarf planet, which included Pluto.

Pluto, Ceres, Haumea, Makemake, and Eris are different from the other eight planets. They're actually smaller than some of the moons of Jupiter, they're a combination of rock and ice, and their orbits are different from the others.

Right now, our solar system has 13 planets. But there are probably more out in space we haven't discovered yet.

SHIP LOG DAY 84: **Approaching Eris, initiate return journey to Earth!**

FACTS ABOUT ERIS

Average distance from the sun	6,325,635,000 miles (10,180,123,000 km)
Position from the sun in orbit	Thirteenth
Equatorial diameter	1,445 miles (2,326 km)
Mass (Earth = 1)	0.0028
Density (water = 1)	2.1
Length of day	1.1 Earth days
Length of year	558 Earth years
Average surface temperature	-382°F (-230°C)
Known moons	1

FUN FACT

Astronomer Mike Brown, who discovered Eris, knew that it would cause arguments over the definition of a planet. That's why he named it after a Greek goddess who stirs up fights.

LOL!

Q: How cold is Eris?

A: So cold that Jack Frost turned into Jack Froze!

END OF THE LINE

The new dwarf planet Eris and its moon, Dysnomia (art right), are as far as our expedition through the solar system takes us. This icy distant rock is the largest of the new dwarf planets and the most distant from the sun.

Earth

Eris

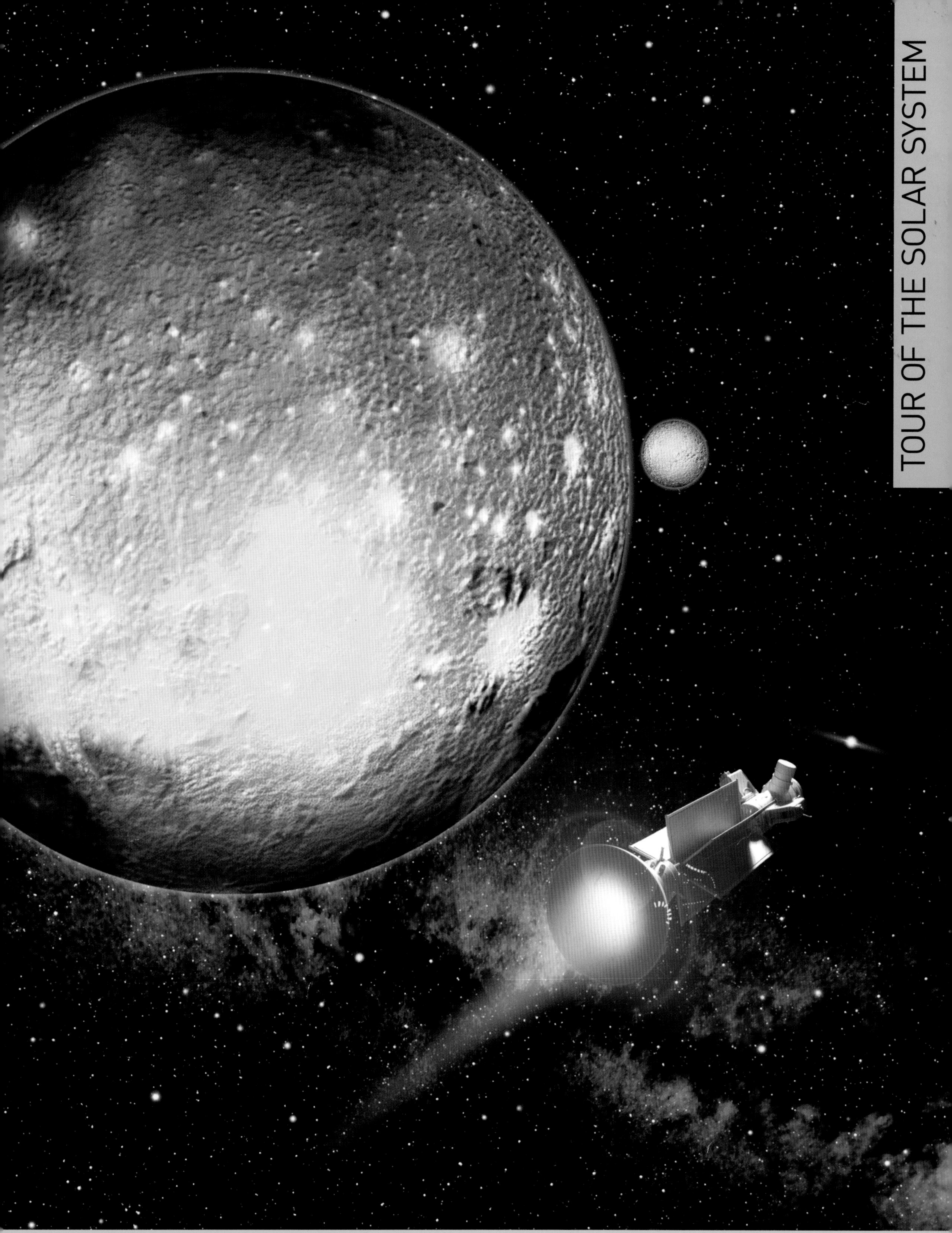

OORT CLOUD

f we could travel 465 trillion miles (748 trillion km) from the sun, out past the extreme edges of the solar system, astronomers think that we would encounter an enormous shell of icy rubble known as the Oort cloud. They also think this is the remains of the original nebula that coalesced to form our solar system nearly 4.6 billion years ago. The cloud marks the outer boundaries of the sun's gravitational field.

In 1950, Dutch astronomer Jan Oort set out to determine the origin of comets. He proposed that a vast and remote reservoir existed one to two light-years from the sun, far beyond Pluto's orbit. Although no one has actually observed the Oort cloud, astronomers believe it's the base camp for most comets. These icy fragments probably orbit the sun here until a passing star's gravity nudges one of them, sending it on a new journey in toward the sun. Since comets zoom in from all directions, astronomers think the Oort cloud wraps around the solar system.

Other stars may also have Oort-like clouds around them. The icy comets in these clouds could help future space travelers on their way. Water ice from the comets could provide hydrogen to power their ships, water to drink, and oxygen to breathe.

FACTS ABOUT THE OORT CLOUD

Distance	Between 5,000 and 100,000 AU (1 AU = 92,955,807 miles/149,597,870 km)
Number of objects	About 2 trillion
Materials	Ammonia, methane, and water ice
Mass (Earth = 1)	4–100

SUPER STARS

Jan Oort (1900-1992) was one of a group of very few astronomers who saw Halley's comet twice. The first time was in 1910, when he was 10 years old. The next was 1986, when he was 86 and a famous scientist.

Oort was Dutch, the son of a doctor, and he became interested in outer space in part because he read science fiction novels. He spent most of his career in the Netherlands and made many major contributions to modern astronomy. Among other things, he showed that the Milky Way spun like a wheel and that the sun was not at its center but located toward the outer edges.

Oort is best remembered today for suggesting that the solar system must be surrounded by a bubble of icy debris that gives rise to many comets. (This theory was also suggested by Estonian astronomer Ernst Öpik in 1932.) Before it turned into a short-period comet (see page 86), Halley's comet itself may have originally started out in that icy shell, now known as the Oort cloud.

OTHER OORT CLOUDS?

Though the Oort cloud (art at right) has not yet been detected by astronomical instruments, scientists believe that not only our solar system but other star systems as well may have Oort clouds. The art below shows a cloud around our solar system (middle), Alpha Centauri (lower right), and other, more distant stars.

COMETS

O f all the objects in the night sky, comets are the most spectacular. Most of these unexpected visitors originate far out in the Oort cloud, where they take hundreds, even millions, of years to complete one orbit around the sun. A second major group comes from the Kuiper belt. They're called short-period comets because their orbital periods are less than 200 years. Halley's comet, one of the most famous short-period comets of all time, comes from this area.

The word "comet" comes from the Greek word *kometes*, which means "long-haired." Today, we know that these objects are leftovers from the formation of the solar system 4.6 billion years ago. Made of sand, water ice, and carbon dioxide, comets have been called big, dirty snowballs.

As they pass by Jupiter on their way toward the sun, comets begin to defrost. Solar heating vaporizes ice, which forms a halo of gas and dust, or coma, around the comet's nucleus. As they near the orbit of Mars, comets may start to form long spectacular tails, sometimes hundreds of millions of miles long. Blown by the solar wind, the tails of comets always point away from the sun.

Parts of a Comet

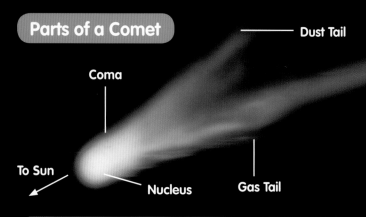

Dust Tail

Coma

To Sun

Nucleus

Gas Tail

COMET'S PATH

As a comet shoots toward the sun, its ice heats up and vaporizes into a coma, a halo of gas and dust around its nucleus. The dust tail streams behind the comet (above), while the gas tail is blown away by the solar wind and always points away from the sun (below).

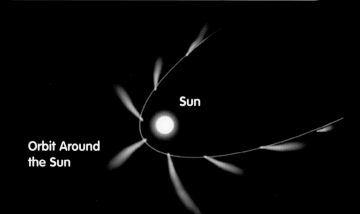

Sun

Orbit Around
the Sun

FAMOUS COMETS

Name	Last Seen	Next Visit
Halley's	1986	2061
Swift-Tuttle	1992	2126
Shoemaker-Levy 9	1994	Destroyed in collision with Jupiter
Hale-Bopp	1995	4385
Hyakutake	1996	71196
McNaught	2007	94607

LONG-PERIOD COMET

Low in the west, just after sunset, the tail of a brilliant comet lights up the evening sky (art below). Short-period comets, such as Halley's comet, return every 200 years or less in their journeys around the sun. The comet pictured here is a long-period comet that will not return again for thousands of years.

COMET-WATCHING

You don't have to be a professional astronomer to observe comets. Every year or two a comet shows up in Earth's skies that is bright enough to be seen through binoculars. About every five to 10 years, a bright comet visible to the naked eye visits. The grand prize, a brilliant "great comet" that out-shines the stars, may pass near Earth every 10 or 20 years. The easiest way to find out when a bright comet will visit Earth is to go online with an adult and search for "bright comets" and the year. Good astronomy sites will tell you when the next bright comet will be closest and where to look for it. With a pair of binoculars, on a clear night, find a dark place away from street or house lights. (Make sure you have a trusted grown-up with you.) It helps to have a star map that shows you constellations and major stars, which will help you find the comet based on online directions. Of course, if you're very lucky and a truly great comet comes by, you can see it and its beautiful tail even in the daytime sky.

EARTH

Our tour of the solar system is coming to an end, and we're heading home. Now that we've visited other planets, we can appreciate more than ever what a Garden of Eden our Earth is.

From space, Earth appears deep blue because of the nitrogen in the atmosphere and the oceans that cover 71 percent of its surface. Since Earth spins on its axis more than 1,000 miles an hour (1,600 km/h) and travels around the sun at 66,700 miles an hour (107,300 km/h), all of us who live on Earth are actually traveling through space all the time!

Located at just the right distance from the sun, Earth is warm enough for water to exist as a liquid, which is an essential element for most life. Its atmosphere is oxygen-rich and swirled by white clouds. And Earth has the most diverse terrain of any planet. The polar caps are covered with sheets of ice. Along the Equator, vast deserts border grasslands that give way to lush tropical jungles. In temperate zones, green forests surround mountains thrust up by volcanoes or the movements of tectonic plates.

So far, our planet is the only place in the universe we know of that has life on it.

SHIP LOG DAY 199: **Back to Earth. It's a long, strange trip back home.**

FACTS ABOUT EARTH

Average distance from the sun	92,956,050 miles (149,598,262 km)
Position from the sun in orbit	Third
Equatorial diameter	7,900 miles (12,750 km)
Mass (Earth = 1)	1
Density (water = 1)	5.51
Length of day	24 hours
Length of year	365.25 days
Surface temperatures	-126°F (-88°C) to 136°F (58°C)
Known moons	1

Earth

Moon

FUN FACT

Earth isn't perfectly round. It bulges a bit at the Equator and is slightly lumpy.

LOL!

Q: How do Earth, Neptune, and Saturn organize a party?

A: They planet!

CROWN JEWEL

Earth is the crown jewel of our solar system, at least from a human perspective. Returning to this blue world, we can see in this art that it is daytime in India (center), the Middle East (slightly to the left), and Africa (far left). On the opposite side of the world, it's nighttime.

THE STORY OF EARTH IN A YEAR

f you were to compare the age of the solar system, which is 4.6 billion years, to the length of time in a year, you could look below to see how long it—and its life-sustaining planet Earth—would take to form and develop. Now take a look at the right page. You'll see that the amount of time we humans have been on Earth relative to the age of the superancient solar system is so brief that instead of looking at a one-year calendar, you are now using a one-minute stopwatch!

January 1
On New Year's Day, the solar system begins condensing out of a swirling cloud of stardust.

January 7
The nuclear fires of our sun ignite.

January 28
A truly memorable day—Earth forms.

February
Through the month of February, Earth continues to shrink and cool.

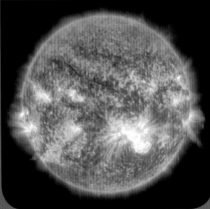

March 10
Escaped water vapor returns to Earth as rain, and oceans form.

April 15
Somewhere within Earth's warm blue-green waters life begins.

May 22
Oxygen starts to form in the atmosphere.

July to August
Life continues to develop.

September 14
Somewhere in the oceanic depths, single-cell plants begin reproduction.

October
Multicell creatures and plants burst onto the scene.

December 2
Some animals and plants begin to live on land.

December 13
Dinosaurs appear.

December 25
Dinosaurs disappear.

December 31

At 5:00 in the evening, "Lucy," the oldest recognizable ancestor of the human tree, is born in Africa.

52 seconds before midnight

On the last day of the year, Cro-Magnon humans, anatomically like modern humans, appear in Europe. Their cave paintings indicate they have an appreciation of culture.

40 seconds before midnight

The pyramids are built in Egypt.

23 seconds before midnight

The golden age of Greece is celebrated.

33 seconds before midnight

A succession of tribal peoples in what is now Britain assembles Stonehenge.

8 seconds before midnight

The Middle Ages begin.

5 seconds before midnight

The Middle Ages end.

3 seconds before midnight

The Pilgrims land in the New World.

1.5 seconds before midnight

The industrial age begins.

1 second before midnight

The U.S. Civil War begins.

1/2 second before midnight

WWI breaks out.

3/8 second before midnight

WWII begins, ushering in the atomic age.

1/8 second before midnight

Neil Armstrong walks on the moon.

1/16 second before midnight

The computer age begins.

1/64 second before midnight

Humans begin to realize that their use of Earth, its creatures, and its resources, begun less than one second ago on the cosmic timetable, have dramatically altered the natural balance of the planet. At no time in Earth's history has a species had such an impact. What could that mean for the future of Earth?

1/32 second before midnight

The age of artificial intelligence and virtual reality follow.

EARTH'S ORIGINS

Earth formed about 4.6 billion years ago from the spinning cloud of gas and dust that gave birth to the sun and the rest of the solar system. As rocky debris rained down on the planet's young molten surface, an unexpected cosmic collision suddenly changed everything. Around 4.5 billion years ago, an object about the size of Mars slammed into Earth, tilting it 23.5 degrees on its axis. This collision also knocked off a big chunk of the planet. The chunk broke into pieces and formed a gigantic ring around Earth. The pieces, still hot and molten, quickly came back together and formed the moon. This may explain why the moon's composition is nearly identical to that of Earth's crust.

Once formed, the moon's gravitational pull on Earth helped stabilize Earth's rotation on its journey around the sun. That's one of the lucky events that made it possible for life to survive here. If Earth were spinning upright on its axis, the sun would heat up the Equator much more than it does today. We would have no change of seasons, and the weather on our planet would be much more severe.

A Wet World

As Earth and the moon began the long process of cooling down, changes took place on the planet. Erupting volcanoes released water vapor that formed into clouds. The clouds quickly returned water to the surface as rain. Comets still raining down on the surface also brought in staggering amounts of water that slowly filled basins. Gradually, Earth's surface was completely covered with one global salty ocean averaging two miles (3.2 km) deep. Biologists believe life first began in these warm, salty oceans.

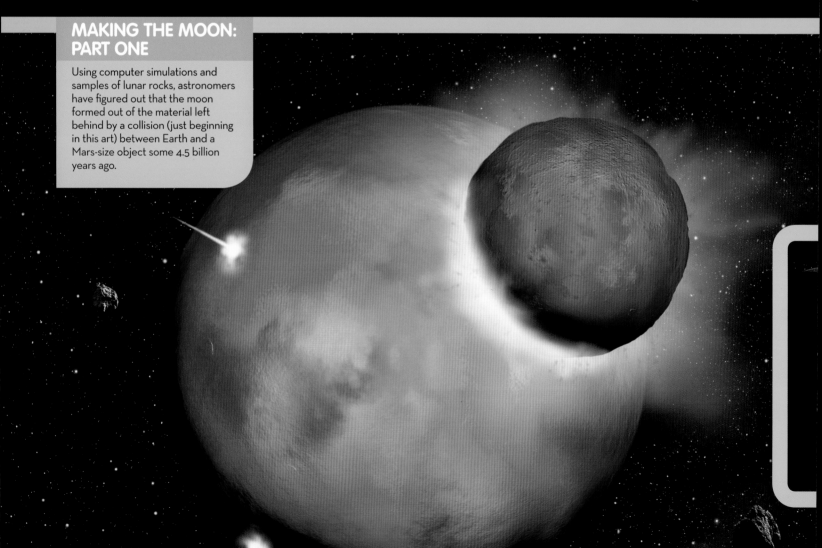

MAKING THE MOON: PART ONE

Using computer simulations and samples of lunar rocks, astronomers have figured out that the moon formed out of the material left behind by a collision (just beginning in this art) between Earth and a Mars-size object some 4.5 billion years ago.

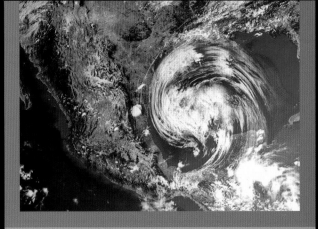

PROGRESS OF LIFE ON EARTH

ABOUT 3.5 BILLION YEARS AGO

Earth was covered by one gigantic reddish ocean, whose color came from hydrocarbons. The first life on Earth were simple bacteria that could live without oxygen. These bacteria released large amounts of methane gas into an atmosphere that would have been poisonous to us.

SKY-WATCHER
EYES ON THE EARTH

In 1900, a Category 4 hurricane struck Galveston, Texas, U.S.A., with deadly force. The city was completely unprepared for the storm and between 6,000 and 12,000 people were killed by wind and water. Today, hurricanes are still dangerous, but we can see them coming many days in advance and warn the people in their path—thanks to orbiting spacecraft, known as artificial satellites.

Today, hundreds of these spacecraft observe Earth from orbit, viewing the planet in a range of visible wavelengths and with radar. Some of the satellites track changes in the environment. They can see where trees are being cut down in the Amazon Basin, or where deserts are spreading in Africa. Others watch the atmosphere and Earth's ever changing weather. From orbits 22,300 miles (35,880 km) above Earth's surface, weather satellites have a wide view of clouds, snow, pollution, and even volcanic eruptions. When Category 4 Hurricane Harvey approached the coast of Texas in 2017, this time Texans had plenty of warning: NASA's GOES 16 satellite had been tracking the storm since it was far out to sea.

ABOUT THREE BILLION YEARS AGO

Something new appeared in the global ocean. Erupting volcanoes linked together to form larger landmasses. A new form of life also appeared— blue-green algae, the first living things that used energy from the sun.

TWO BILLION YEARS AGO

These algae filled the air with oxygen, killing off the methane-producing bacteria. Colored pools of greenish-brown plant life floated on the ocean waters. The oxygen revolution that would someday make human life possible was now under way.

ABOUT 530 MILLION YEARS AGO

The Cambrian explosion occurred. It's called an explosion because it's the time when most major animal groups first appeared in our fossil records. Back then, Earth was a place of swamps, seas, a few active volcanoes, and oceans teeming with strange life.

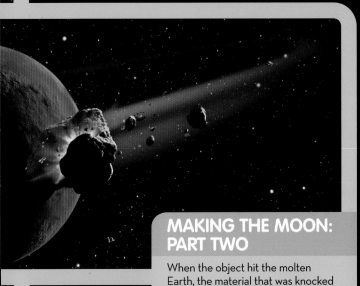

MAKING THE MOON: PART TWO

When the object hit the molten Earth, the material that was knocked off the planet first stabilized into a ring of molten rock, then fused back together, and eventually re-formed into the moon we see today in this art. In the early solar system, collisions like this happened all the time.

MORE THAN 450 MILLION YEARS AGO

Life began moving from the oceans onto dry land. About 200 million years later, along came the dinosaurs. For more than 150 million years, they would dominate life on Earth.

EARTH'S LAYERS

Over time, landmasses thrust up by volcanic activity began to rise out of Earth's oceans. These landmasses began to drift and collide, growing larger and larger until they formed a giant supercontinent called Rodinia about 425 million years ago. Rodinia eventually broke apart into smaller continents. About 225 million years ago the smaller continents pushed together again to form Pangaea. Slowly, after another 94 million years, that supercontinent separated into the continents we see today.

Even today, the continents are drifting. Scientists predict that 250 million years from now North America will collide with Africa, and South America will wrap around the southern tip of Africa. By then, the Pacific Ocean will cover half of Earth.

The idea that the solid ground we are standing on may be slowly moving is difficult to believe. Even more amazing is that the interior structure of Earth is still pretty much a big mystery to us. Scientists believe the structure of Earth consists of four separate layers. Covering the outer surface, the part where we build houses and plant trees, is the rocky crust. It averages five miles (8 km) thick under the oceans and up to 45 miles (72 km) thick under the continents. If Earth were the size of an apple, the crust would be about the thickness of the apple peel.

In 1970, Soviet scientists began trying to drill through the crust. They only succeeded in digging a hole about a third of the way through it before they gave up. It took them 20 years to drill down 7.6 miles (12 km). Even though they did not make it beyond the crust, what they found surprised them. First, the temperatures down there were hot enough to cook a turkey or bake a pie! And second, the rock at that depth was saturated with water—something nobody believed was possible.

Below the crust is the mantle, a layer of dense, semisolid rock. It flows out through cracks onto the surface as lava when volcanoes erupt. Beneath the mantle is a liquid outer core that spins like a motor, generating a magnetic field around Earth that repels damaging solar radiation. At the center of our planet is a solid core, where the temperatures may reach 9000°F (5000°C)—about as hot as the surface of the sun.

THE AIR ABOVE US

Our layered atmosphere (art below) is composed mostly of nitrogen and oxygen, with small amounts of carbon dioxide and other gases mixed with water vapor. All weather occurs in the lowest level, the troposphere.

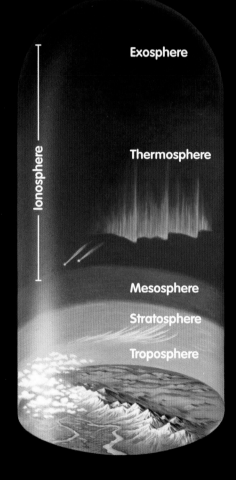

Exosphere

Thermosphere

Ionosphere

Mesosphere

Stratosphere

Troposphere

EARTH'S UNIQUE ATMOSPHERE

Unlike any other place that we know of in our solar system, the oxygen in our atmosphere is provided and replenished by living organisms. Plant life on Earth "exhales" oxygen that animals need. Without plants, there would be no animal life. In turn, animals exhale carbon dioxide that plants use in the process of photosynthesis.

Today, Earth's atmosphere is nearly 80 percent nitrogen and 21 percent oxygen, with traces of carbon dioxide, water, and argon. The small amount of carbon dioxide in the atmosphere helps moderate the temperatures of our planet. If there were too little carbon dioxide, Earth would become too cold, but too much and it would grow unbearably hot.

Earth's atmosphere has no definite boundary. It just becomes thinner as it fades into outer space. The atmosphere is divided into layers. The layer closest to the ground is called the troposphere. It extends about eight miles (13 km) into the sky. This is the layer where all weather occurs and where most planes fly. Above the troposphere is the stratosphere, which continues out to about 30 miles (50 km) above the surface. In the lower stratosphere is the very important ozone layer. A special form of oxygen, ozone blocks deadly ultraviolet radiation from the sun. Without it, plants and animals wouldn't survive.

500 million years ago

ON THE MOVE

The surface of Earth is always changing. The crust is made up of plates that move slowly, carrying the oceans and continents with them.

200 million years ago

100 million years ago

LOL!

Q: What does Earth say to tease the other planets?

A: You guys have no life!

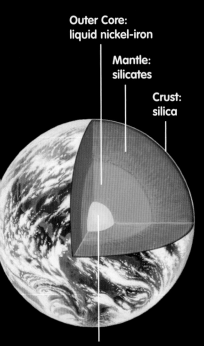

50 million years ago

Today

FUN FACT

Earth's magnetic field reverses direction about every 200,000 to 300,000 years. If that happened today, the north-pointing needle in your compass would spin around and point south.

Outer Core: liquid nickel-iron

Mantle: silicates

Crust: silica

Inner Core: solid nickel-iron

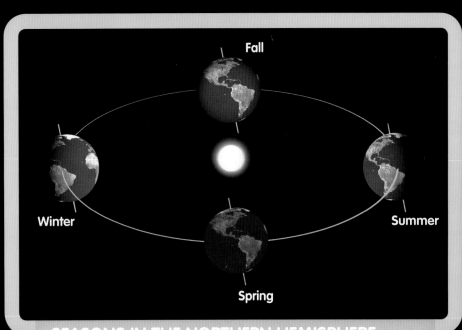

Fall · Winter · Summer · Spring

EARTH OUTSIDE-IN

A thin layer of cooled rock, Earth's crust supports the oceans and the continental plates. Just beneath the crust lies the molten rock of the mantle, which becomes lava when it is spewed out onto Earth's surface during an eruption. Beneath the mantle are two layers of core.

SEASONS IN THE NORTHERN HEMISPHERE

The reason we have seasons can be confusing. Some people think summer occurs in the hemisphere closest to the sun, and that the hemisphere farthest away experiences winter. This sounds like a great explanation, but, unfortunately, it's wrong. Seasons occur because Earth tilts 23.5 degrees on its axis. That tilt affects the intensity of the sunlight hitting the surface, and that in turn causes the seasons. When North America, Europe, and northern Asia are having summer (above), it's because they're tilted toward the sun and receiving the most concentrated sunlight. During the same time, in the Southern Hemisphere, South America, Africa, and Australia are tilted away from the sun, so sunlight is less concentrated and there's less heat. Six months later, when Earth has circled around to the other side of the sun, everything reverses. The Northern Hemisphere has winter and the Southern Hemisphere has summer. In January, when people in Vermont are out skiing down snowy slopes, Australians down under are waxing their surfboards and sunbathing on the beach.

LIFE ON EARTH

Living things are found everywhere on Earth, from the tropical Equator to the frozen poles, from the bottom of the oceans to the tops of mountains, inside other organisms (including us) and inside scalding volcanic sulfur pools. The diversity and distribution of life on Earth are staggering. From amoebas to elephants, electric eels to butterflies, scientists have yet to catalog all the species of life existing on our planet.

Taxonomists, the scientists who try to group life-forms into similar categories, have identified about 1.2 million distinct animal and plant species, mostly mammals and birds. But it's estimated that the number of undiscovered species—mostly fish, fungi, insects, and land animals—is more than seven million. (This total does not include simple organisms such as bacteria.) Scientists say that if you want to discover a new animal, all you have to do is spend a day in a tropical rainforest in South America, looking under a log or a rock.

Scientists are not quite sure how life began on Earth, but they're fairly certain where it began—in the sea. Most living creatures, including human beings, carry the fossil record of this past inside them. Since 71 percent of Earth is covered by water, and our bodies are about 60 percent water, in a way we are walking containers of ocean.

The earliest life on Earth probably looked like the bacteria we find everywhere on the planet today. Over the past 3.7 billion years, organisms on Earth have diversified and adapted to almost every environment imaginable. Now we wonder: Has this same process occurred elsewhere in our solar system or on other planets circling distant stars? Within the next 25 years, we may well have an answer to this question.

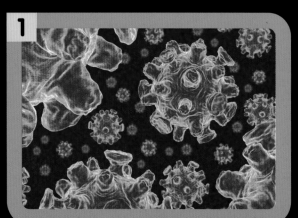

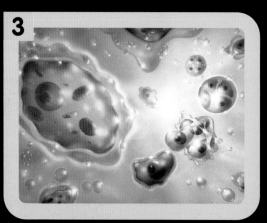

CLASSIFYING LIFE ON EARTH

Kingdom	Cell Type	Examples
Eubacteria	Single cell	Bacteria such as staphylococcus
Archaea	Single cell	Microbes in undersea vents
Protista	Mostly single cell	Amoebas
Fungi	Mostly multicell	Mushrooms
Plantae	Multicell	Flowering plants
Animalia	Multicell	Insects, mammals, birds

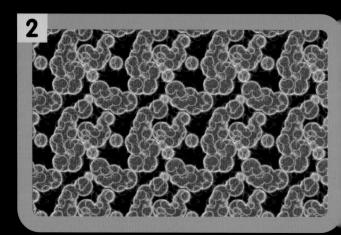

6

10

7

11

DIVERSE LIFE

Life on Earth is as beautiful as it is diverse. These photographs are just a sampling. (The first four are tiny organisms seen under a microscope.)

1 an influenza virus

2 bacteria cells

3 amoebas

4 phytoplankton

5 a field of daisies

6 desert cacti

7 garter snakes

8 a flock of geese

9 honeybees inside their hive

10 a school of pilot fish

11 a herd of sheep

12 different kinds of coral

13 people gathered for a football game

12

8

9

13

THE MOON

The moon is our closest companion in space. Only three days away by spacecraft, it's a dramatic reminder of how violent and chaotic the early solar system was. With just a pair of binoculars, we can see how the moon's terrain was smoothed by the lava flows of ancient volcanoes or scarred with impact craters a hundred miles (160 km) in diameter.

Earth's atmosphere causes most space objects to burn up before impact, but the moon has no atmosphere. Everything heading for it hits its surface. None of these impact scars is erased over time by the actions of weather. The footprints left by the Apollo astronauts in 1969 will remain on the moon's surface for at least another 10 million years.

There are two types of terrain on the moon: the deeply cratered highlands and the relatively smooth lowlands called "maria," from *mare*, the Latin word for "sea." Maria are found mostly on the near side that faces Earth. They formed four billion years ago, when asteroids smashed into the moon, causing lava to flow out and resurface vast areas. The far side of the moon has almost no maria because the crust there is thicker, which kept lava from reaching the surface.

FACTS ABOUT THE MOON

Average distance from Earth	238,855 miles (384,400 km)
Equatorial diameter	2,159 miles (3,475 km)
Mass (Earth = 1)	0.012
Density (water = 1)	3.34
Length of day	27.3 days
Length of one orbit around Earth	27.3 days
Average surface temperature	–387°F (–233°C) to 253°F (123°C)

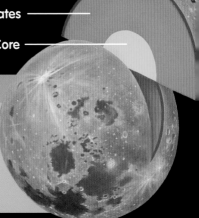

Crust: silicate rock

Mantle: silicates

Iron Core

LIGHTWEIGHT

The moon contains less rock and iron, a heavy metal, than Earth. This combination gives the moon less mass, so it is not as compact, or dense, as Earth.

SOLAR AND LUNAR ECLIPSES

A solar eclipse occurs when the moon passes directly between Earth and the sun, blocking the sun from view. This can happen only during the new moon phase. A total solar eclipse can last up to 7.5 minutes. When the moon is at its farthest point from Earth, it doesn't completely cover the face of the sun but leaves a visible ring of sunlight. This type is called an annular eclipse. Up to five solar eclipses occur each year.

A lunar eclipse happens when the moon passes behind Earth as seen from the sun. This casts Earth's shadow on the moon. The moon passes into the shadow, or umbra, and becomes dim until it emerges from Earth's shadow. Lunar eclipses may be partial or total, and they can happen only at full moon. Total lunar eclipses may last for up to a hundred minutes.

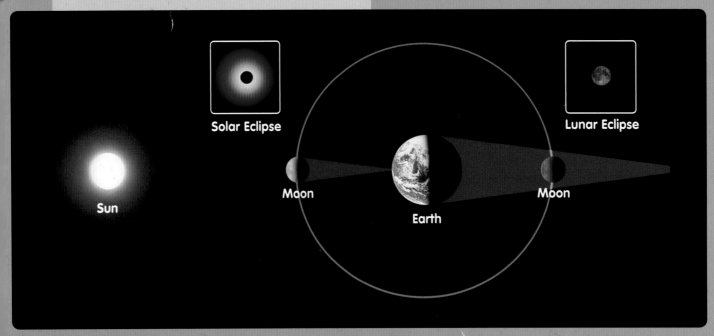

Solar Eclipse

Lunar Eclipse

Sun

Moon

Earth

Moon

EERIE GLOW

If you were standing on the moon like the astronauts in this art, and Earth moved in front of the sun, you would observe a solar eclipse almost 20 minutes in length. Sunlight, passing through the edge of Earth's atmosphere, would cast an eerie red glow over the lunar landscape.

ON THE MOON

Like Earth, the moon has mountain ranges. Many are found along the edges of large craters, where the impacts of asteroids suddenly thrust them up. One of the biggest surprises for the Apollo astronauts was that the mountains of the moon are not sharp and jagged but soft and rounded. Since the moon doesn't have an atmosphere, there are only dark black shadows on its surface, not the soft gray ones we have on Earth. Because of this, and because there are no familiar objects like telephone poles, it is impossible for astronauts standing on the moon to tell whether a mountain is large and distant or small and close by.

The gravitational forces of Earth and the moon pull on each other. This causes some interesting results, including the tides along our shorelines. When the moon formed more than four billion years ago, it was six times closer to us than it is today. Over time, it has edged away in its orbit. Now it takes the same amount of time—almost 28 days—for the moon to rotate once on its axis and to revolve around Earth. This is called tidal lock, and it's the reason we see only one side of the moon. Most of the larger moons in the solar system are in tidal lock with their planets, too.

The moon is still moving away from Earth, adding 1.5 inches (3.8 cm) a year to its orbit around the planet. It won't ever leave Earth and float away, though—the solar system will end before that could happen.

Humans on the Moon

NASA plans to return humans to the moon—or at least to an orbit around the moon—within the next 20 years. Since the moon's gravitational force is only a sixth of Earth's, visiting astronauts weigh less there. A 100-pound (45-kg) person would weigh only 16.6 pounds (7.5 kg), and a solidly hit baseball could travel for half a mile (0.8 km).

Astronaut Buzz Aldrin described the moon as a world of "magnificent desolation." It offers no oxygen to breathe and no global magnetic field to protect it from deadly solar radiation.

Maria (Seas) · Sea of Tranquility · Highlands · Tycho Crater · Rays

WATCHING THE MOON THROUGH BINOCULARS

The moon's bright light can interfere with seeing planets or stars. But the moon itself is a great object for beginning sky-watchers to observe. With just a pair of binoculars, you can see wonderful craters, mountains, and plains in detail.

Though a full moon is spectacular in its own way, you may want to start off by looking at the moon when it is a waxing crescent—that is, when its crescent shape is growing from night to night. Look along the line between light and dark, where the mountains and crater edges cast sharp shadows. You'll see flat gray maria (*maria* is Latin for "seas") and white highlands. When the moon is closer to full, you can see bright streaks called rays stretching out from craters. These show the path of debris that was blasted across the moon's surface when the crater was formed. You won't be able to see discarded spacecraft, but on the eastern half, near the equator, you can spot the dark plains of the Sea of Tranquility, where astronauts first walked in 1969.

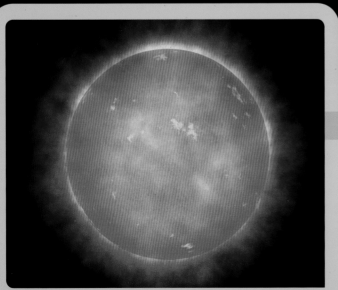

THE MOON'S FUTURE

The moon was created out of an ancient collision, and scientists believe it is headed for further catastrophe. In about five billion years, the sun will enter its red giant phase and begin to expand in diameter. As it reaches the orbit of Earth, it will bring the moon's orbital path back in toward Earth. Eventually, this will tear the moon apart. At first, the lunar pieces will create a rather lumpy ring system around our planet, then they will crash onto Earth's surface.

FUN FACT

In western cultures, moon-watchers see a "man in the moon" in its dark and light patches. Eastern cultures see a rabbit or a pair of hands.

LUNAR RAIN

About five billion years from now, Earth will gain a system of rings as the moon breaks apart. Earth and its moon will be reunited when lunar debris rains down from the burning heavens, as shown in this art.

TO THE STARS AND BEYOND

The first stars are just beginning to form in the young universe.

THE MILKY WAY
SEEN FROM EARTH

I f you're on a dark countryside hill some night, look up at the heavens. Arcing overhead, you may see a faint band of light that looks like milk spilled across the sky. The ancient Romans called that band the *via lactea*, which means the "milky road" or "milky way." The name has stuck for 2,000 years.

A lot of people around the world use the term Milky Way, but some cultures have different names for the band of light. In China, it's called the silver river, and people of the Kalahari Desert in southern Africa call it the backbone of the night.

In 1610, Galileo and his telescope finally revealed that this band was actually made up of stars. We now know that there are hundreds of billions of them in our galaxy. Even on a clear night, though, the average person can see only about 2,000 with the naked eye. The Milky Way also has dark patches sprinkled through it. Those patches aren't areas without stars. They're clouds of interstellar dust that block the light from the stars behind them.

SKY-WATCHER
HOW TO SEE THE MILKY WAY

Before electric lights were invented, most people on Earth could see the beautiful Milky Way in the night sky. Now, light pollution from cities, houses, and roads makes that difficult. To see this beautiful river of stars, you'll need to find a sky-watching spot in the countryside or in a big park, far from local lights. Be sure to go with a trusted adult. Pick a clear night with no moonshine. In the Northern Hemisphere, the best viewing time is late summer, when the Milky Way stretches from the southwest to the northeast sky. It won't look as colorful as it does in photographs: You'll see it as a soft, white, cloudlike band of light. That band is the core of our galaxy, where the stars are thickest. Dust clouds in the galaxy will show up as darker spots.

FUN FACT

If our solar system was located close to the center of the Milky Way, instead of farther out along one of its arms, our night skies would be lit up by such a brilliant mass of stars that it would never get truly dark.

RIVER OF LIGHT

Meteors slash across the pristine night sky on Easter Island in the southern Pacific Ocean, far from distracting city lights. Here, our Milky Way galaxy shines brightly overhead with visible dark dust clouds obscuring parts of the galactic center, while other areas glow by reflected starlight radiating from billions of distant suns.

CONSTELLATIONS:
SKY DREAMS

Long ago, people looking at the sky noticed that some stars made shapes and patterns. By playing connect-the-dots, they imagined people and animals in the sky. Their legendary heroes and monsters were pictured in the stars.

Today, we call these star patterns constellations. There are 88 constellations in all. Some are visible only when you're north of the Equator, and others, only south of it.

The ones visible in the Southern Hemisphere, such as the Southern Cross, have names given them by European ocean voyagers. In the 16th-century age of exploration, their ships began visiting southern lands. Astronomers used the star observations of these navigators to fill in the blank spots on their celestial maps.

Constellations aren't fixed in the sky. The star arrangement that makes up each one would look different from another location in the universe. Constellations also change over time, because every star we see is moving through space. Over thousands of years, the stars in the Big Dipper, which is part of the larger constellation Ursa Major (Great Bear), will move so far apart that the dipper pattern will disappear.

A WHEEL OF STARS

Centered on Polaris, the North Star, the time-lapse photograph above shows how stars seem to spin around the sky as Earth spins on its axis. Our ancestors imagined people and animals in star patterns, as in the constellation wheel (top).

KEYS TO SPOTTING CONSTELLATIONS

The first thing to know about seeing constellations is that they move from east to west in the night sky as Earth rotates on its axis. A constellation will rise in the east and set in the west, just like the sun. The second thing to know is that constellations change during the year, as Earth moves around the sun and faces different parts of the galaxy. So constellation maps, found in books or online, are your best bet for finding which star pattern is over your head at a particular time and date. To start learning the constellations, pick one or two that are easy to spot. In the winter, for instance, Orion the Hunter (left) is easy to locate by his three-star belt. In summer, look for Scorpius, the scorpion that stung Orion, on the southern horizon. It has a curving tail and a bright star, Antares, near its head. Once you're familiar with a few easily seen constellations, you can find others around them. The two dogs Canis Major and Canis Minor, for instance, trail along behind Orion.

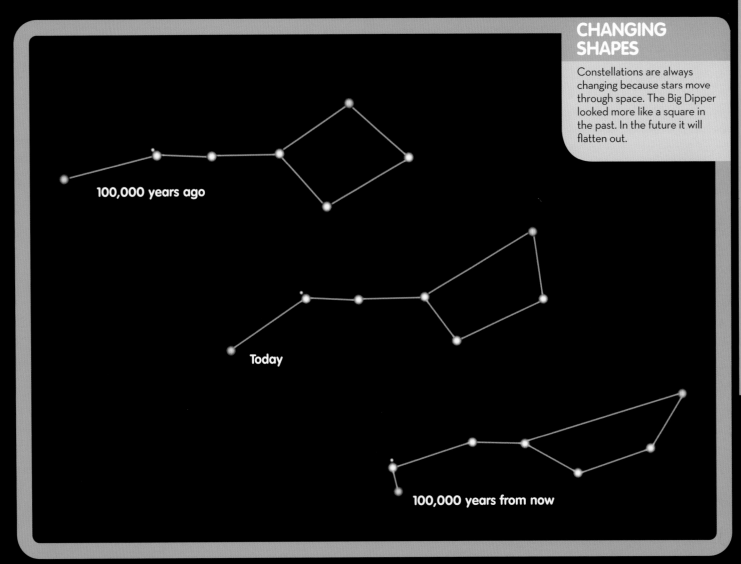

CHANGING SHAPES

Constellations are always changing because stars move through space. The Big Dipper looked more like a square in the past. In the future it will flatten out.

100,000 years ago

Today

100,000 years from now

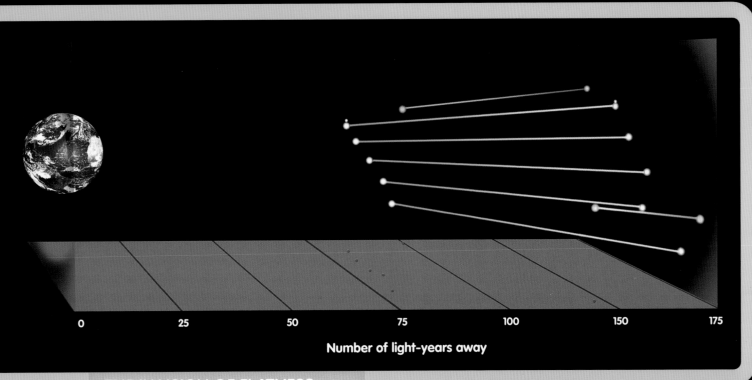

Number of light-years away

THE ILLUSION OF FLATNESS

When we look up at the sky, the stars that seem to form patterns along a flat plane and to be close together may actually be in very different locations in space. Some stars in the Big Dipper are twice as far away from us as others (above).

EVERYTHING WE SEE IS HISTORY

A telescope is a time machine, but a time machine that only takes you into the past. That's because a telescope shows things in the sky not as they are now but as they were.

To understand this, remember that a telescope collects light from the heavens. It takes time for that light to reach us, even moving at 186,000 miles a second (300,000 km/s)—the speed of light. Light from the sun reaches Earth in about eight minutes, so we see the sun as it looked about eight minutes ago. Light from Pluto takes about four hours to reach us because it has to cross three billion miles (5 billion km) of space.

Big Distances

Beyond the solar system, the distances get unbelievably big. In one Earth year, light travels six trillion miles (9.6 trillion km). The closest star to the sun, Alpha Centauri, is 24 trillion miles (41 trillion km) away. The center of the Milky Way is 125 thousand trillion miles away (201 thousand trillion km). The numbers get so big that astronomers have created a word to describe cosmic distances: the light-year. One light-year is the distance light travels in an Earth year, so a light-year equals six trillion miles. Since light from Alpha Centauri takes four years to reach us, we say that Alpha Centauri lies four light-years away.

DISTANCES FROM EARTH TO PLANETS, STARS, AND GALAXIES

Our sun	8.3 light-minutes
Mars	12.5 light-minutes
Neptune	4 light-hours
Sirius (star)	8.6 light-years
Deneb (star)	2,600 light-years
Large Magellanic Cloud (galaxy)	14,000 light-years
GN-z11 (galaxy)	13.4 billion light-years

FLASH FROM THE PAST

A telescope is like a time machine because it allows us to see things as they were in the past. Light from the sun takes approximately 8 minutes 20 seconds to arrive at Earth, so we see the sun as it was 8.3 minutes ago.

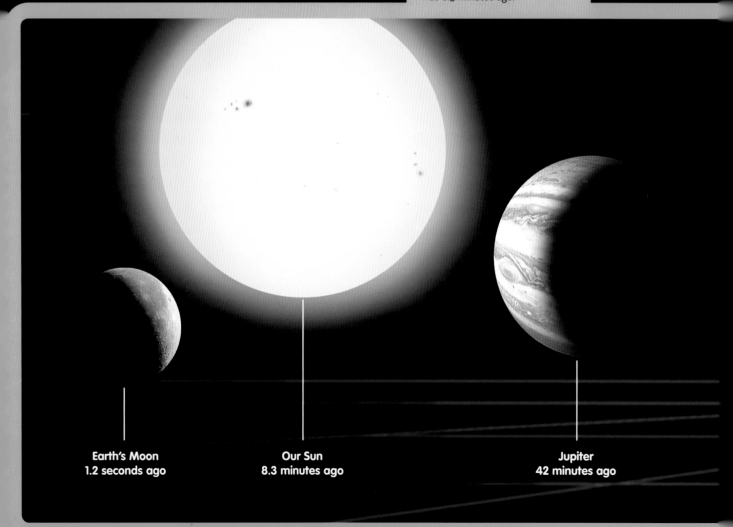

Earth's Moon
1.2 seconds ago

Our Sun
8.3 minutes ago

Jupiter
42 minutes ago

LOOK-BACK TIME

Look-back time is how far back in time we are seeing something in the sky. The look-back time for Alpha Centauri is four years. The red star Aldebaran (shown here) in the constellation Taurus is about 65 light-years away, so it has a look-back time of 65 years. Looking at Aldebaran, we see that star as it was 65 years ago. It's like looking at pictures of your grandparents when they were just children.

The travel time of light gets even longer when you look outside the Milky Way galaxy. For example, the closest large galaxy to us is the Andromeda spiral galaxy (bottom of page), 2.5 million light-years away. The light we see from Andromeda left there when the earliest ancestors of humans first appeared on Earth 2.5 million years ago.

LIGHT SPEED

If you could shine a flashlight around Earth, its light beam would circle the planet more than seven times in one second because that is the speed that light travels. The much slower space shuttle circled Earth once every hour and a half.

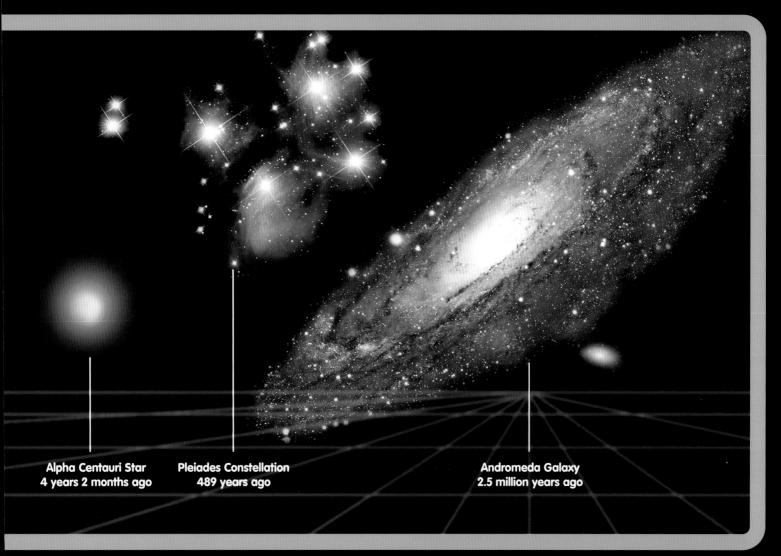

Alpha Centauri Star
4 years 2 months ago

Pleiades Constellation
489 years ago

Andromeda Galaxy
2.5 million years ago

WHAT IS THE MILKY WAY?

Our galaxy, the Milky Way, appears to be a band of stars in the sky, but it's actually a disk. Hundreds of billions of stars are clumped into lines called spiral arms because they spiral outward. When we look up at the night sky, we're seeing the edge of the disk, like the side of a Frisbee.

Earth is located about halfway between the center of the Milky Way and its outer edge, in one of the spiral arms. Light from the galaxy's center takes 25,000 light-years to reach us.

Our solar system orbits the galactic center about once every 230 million years. The last time we were on this side of the Milky Way, the earliest dinosaurs were just starting to emerge.

At the galaxy's center, frequent star explosions fry huge sections of space. Those explosions would wipe out any life on nearby planets. We're lucky that Earth is located where it is, far away from the center.

SUPER STARS

"My job is amazing," says astronomer Munazza Alam. "I get to explore the universe, and think about stars, planets, and black holes." The young astronomer, a graduate student at Harvard, is one of a new generation of scientists who are studying some of the most fascinating objects in our galaxy: exoplanets (planets in other solar systems). After graduating first in her high school class, Alam began researching brown dwarfs while an undergraduate in college. Brown dwarfs begin like stars but cool off and turn into giant gas worlds. Alam now hopes to apply what she's learned to understanding the atmospheres of alien planets. "It is my goal to find an Earth-twin exoplanet," she says—a world that might support life like that on Earth.

Alam's work has taken her to some of the world's biggest observatories, including Hawaii's Mauna Kea and the Las Campanas Observatory in Chile. In 2015, she was named a National Geographic Young Explorer. In her spare time, she also helps out younger students who might want to follow in her footsteps. "If you're interested in becoming an astronomer," she notes, "I'd suggest being curious. Ask questions. Ask why. And look up at the night sky."

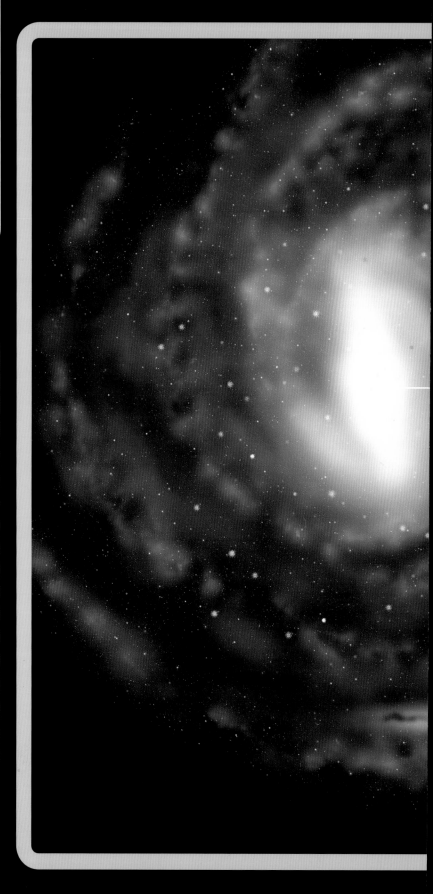

FACTS ABOUT THE MILKY WAY

Shape	Barred spiral
Diameter	100,000 to 160,000 light-years
Thickness of disk	1,000 light-years
Number of stars	100 to 400 billion
Oldest star	13.7 billion years old
Mass of central black hole	4.3 million solar masses

THE GRAND SPIRAL

Our Milky Way galaxy (art below) has a bulge in its middle that surrounds the galactic center, or nucleus. In the nucleus is a giant black hole. The central bulge is surrounded by a flat disk. Within the disk, spiral arms of stars and gas wrap around the center. Outside the disk, globular star clusters orbit like swarms of bees. Companion galaxies called the Magellanic Clouds also pass by the Milky Way.

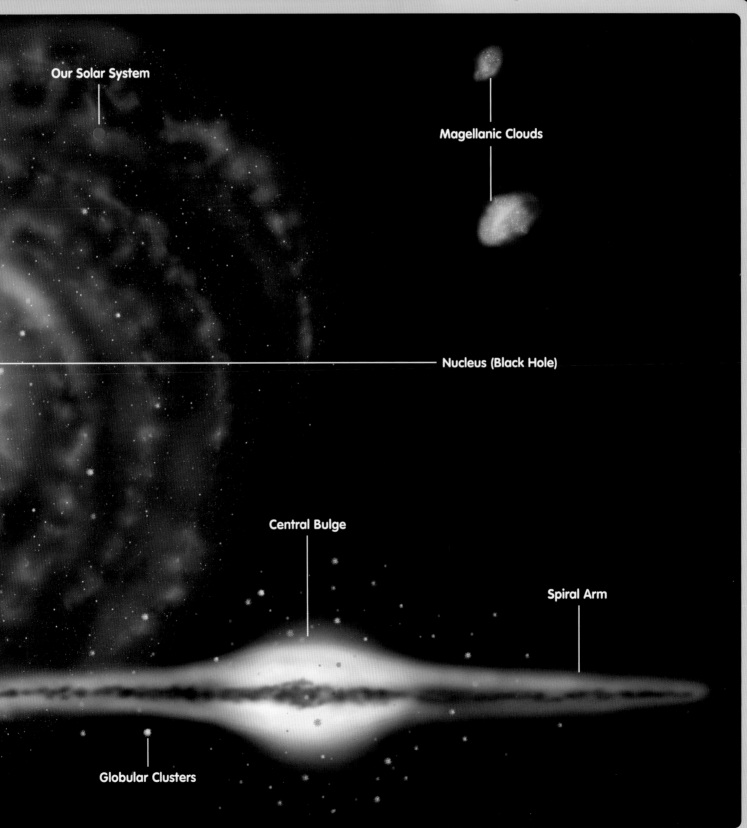

Our Solar System

Magellanic Clouds

Nucleus (Black Hole)

Central Bulge

Spiral Arm

Globular Clusters

A CHANGING UNIVERSE

The Milky Way may look like a peaceful, static arrangement of sparkling lights in our night sky, but it's really like a bustling restaurant kitchen, always cooking up something new. And stars are its main dish.

New stars form continually. In our galaxy, most of the action takes place in the spiral arms, which contain plenty of hydrogen gas to make stars. On average a few stars are born every year in the Milky Way. Our galaxy is getting older, though, and the rate of star birth is slowing down.

The births and deaths of stars are linked. When stars die, their remains mix with the remains of other stars over time to create new stars—or new solar systems.

Stars aren't the only things that are changing. Galaxies are moving through space, sometimes bumping into each other and re-forming. Scientists even think new universes might be forming and re-forming.

SUPER STARS

Danish astronomer Tycho Brahe (1546-1601) is famous for his highly accurate observations of the stars and planets. He is also famous for his nose. As a young nobleman studying medicine at the University of Rostock, he got into a duel with another student over who was the best mathematician. His opponent sliced off most of Brahe's nose with his sword. For the rest of his life, Brahe wore a brass nose.

The nose incident did not keep him from becoming a great astronomer. In 1572, Brahe observed a "new star" in the sky, a sight that we now know was a supernova, an exploding star. His description of this event proved that the old ideas about the heavens being fixed and unchangeable were wrong. Brahe also built the world's best observatory on the island of Hven, in those years part of Denmark. There, he made excellent notes of the orbits of the moon and planets using just his own eyes and instruments such as sextants, which measure distances. These studies allowed his assistant, Johannes Kepler, later to work out for the first time the true orbits of the planets. Brahe died suddenly in 1601 after attending a banquet. Craters on the moon and Mars are named after Brahe, as is the supernova he discovered.

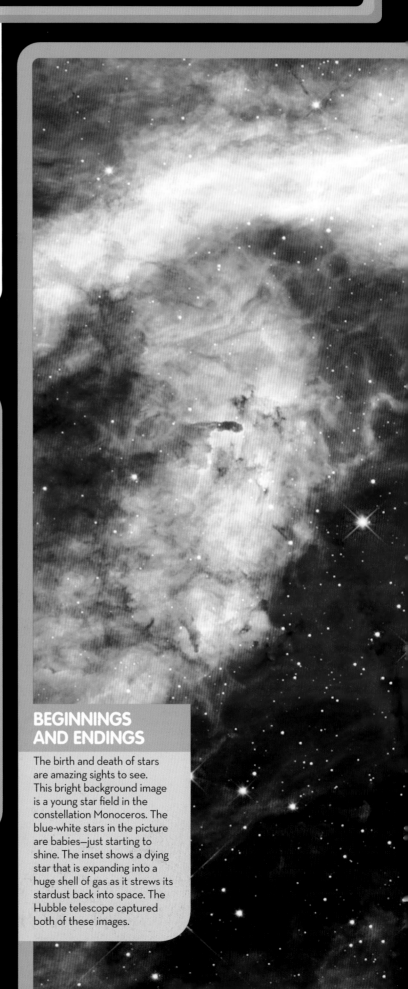

BEGINNINGS AND ENDINGS

The birth and death of stars are amazing sights to see. This bright background image is a young star field in the constellation Monoceros. The blue-white stars in the picture are babies—just starting to shine. The inset shows a dying star that is expanding into a huge shell of gas as it strews its stardust back into space. The Hubble telescope captured both of these images.

FUN FACT

In the Milky Way, the hottest stars glow blue, medium-hot stars yellow or white, and cooler stars red. Young stars are typically hot and energetic, so they will shine blue among cooler, redder gases. When we look at these stars through regular telescopes, the colors are dimmer than they are in images such as the one below. That's because the cameras on space telescopes, such as Hubble, capture a much wider range of light than our eyes do, and computers turn the data from those cameras into colorful images.

LIFE CYCLE OF A STAR

Poets might say that the stars are forever, but scientists know that's not true. All stars eventually die when they run out of fuel.

You might think a more massive star would live longer because it has more fuel to burn. But the heavier a star is, the faster it burns through its fuel, and the shorter its lifetime is. The most massive stars will live for only a few million years, whereas the least massive stars can live for trillions of years.

All stars spend most of their lives fusing hydrogen and turning it into helium in their cores. This nuclear fusion creates the energy we see as starlight. Eventually, the star's core runs out of hydrogen. This is the end for low-mass stars like our sun.

When higher-mass stars run out of hydrogen, they can start fusing the helium in their cores, creating carbon and oxygen. The most massive stars can keep fusing heavier and heavier elements until their core is full of hot, dense iron. That's the end of the road, because no energy comes from fusing iron. When a massive star reaches this point, it undergoes a titanic explosion and blows off part of itself. If it is very massive, the remainder of the star collapses into a black hole—a place in space with such strong gravity that not even light escapes. If the star is a bit less massive, it becomes a superdense neutron star—the collapsed center of the star.

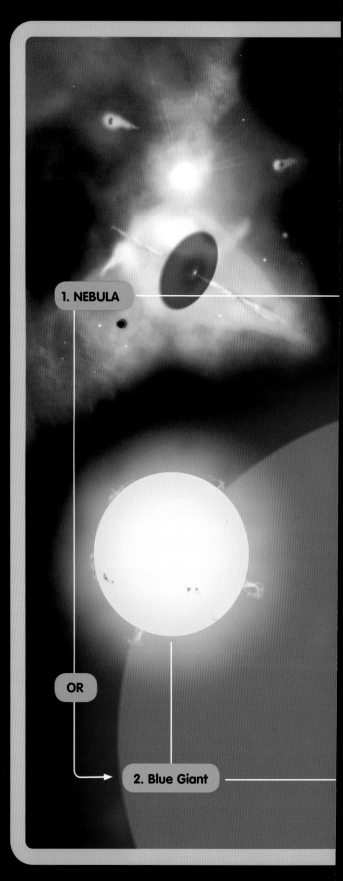

1. NEBULA

OR

2. Blue Giant

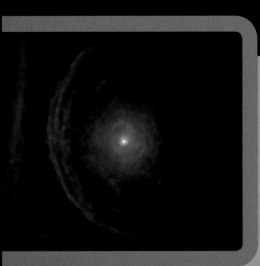

SKY-WATCHER
FINDING GIANT STARS

The biggest stars in the night sky— giant and supergiant stars—aren't always the brightest. How brilliant they appear depends both on their natural brightness and on how close they are to our solar system. However, you can spot some truly massive stars, such as the ones below, with the naked eye. As always, pick a clear dark night away from lights and use a star chart that matches the time of year to find these giants.

Mu Cephei: A red supergiant sometimes called the "Garnet Star," Mu Cephei is one of the biggest stars in the Milky Way, about 1,200 times as big as our sun. Look for it in the constellation Cepheus, near the Little Dipper.

Betelgeuse: Located in Orion, on the hunter's arm, Betelgeuse (above left) is a red supergiant about 1,000 times as wide as our sun. Look for it in winter.

Antares: Sometimes called the heart of the scorpion, Antares is a red supergiant in the constellation Scorpius, best seen in the summer. It's about 700 times as large as our sun.

Rigel: A blue-white supergiant, it's about 100 times as wide as our sun. Look for it at the base of the Orion constellation in the winter.

Aldebaran: Big and bright, Aldebaran is an orange giant 44 times as wide as our sun. You can see it in the constellation Taurus, near Orion, in the winter.

STAR FATES

All stars come from nebulae (top left in art below), but then their lives take different courses to their final end. Smaller stars (top row) end as tiny, dead white dwarfs. The more massive stars (bottom row) explode as supernovae and leave behind crushing black holes or neutron stars.

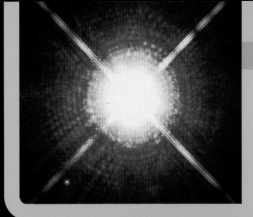

SIRIUS B

Some day, billions of years in the future, our sun will turn into a small, hot white dwarf star. Such a star is only about as big as Earth but is extremely dense. Astronomers would like to take a closer look at white dwarfs, and there's one nearby. The brilliant star Sirius is actually a double star with a white dwarf companion, known as Sirius B (left). Recently, the Hubble Space Telescope has been able to single out the little star, which had been hidden in its bright partner's light. What we learn about it will help us understand the fate of our own solar system.

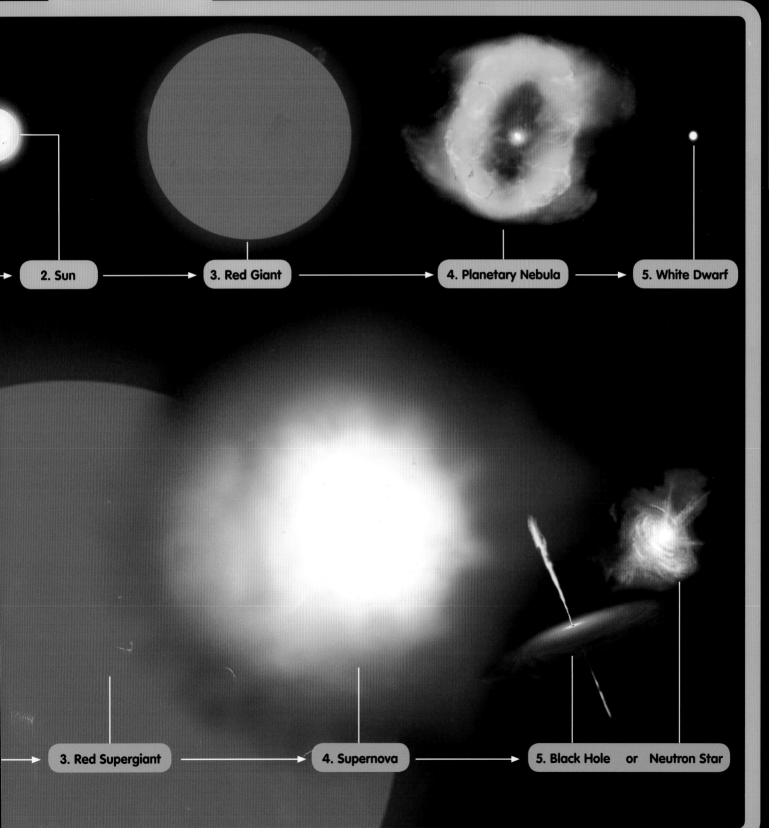

2. Sun → **3. Red Giant** → **4. Planetary Nebula** → **5. White Dwarf**

3. Red Supergiant → **4. Supernova** → **5. Black Hole or Neutron Star**

NEBULAE: STAR NURSERIES

A star is born inside an enormous cloud of hydrogen and other gases. This gas cloud is called a nebula. As clumps in a nebula attract more gas, they grow larger and hotter until they ignite and become stars.

Newborn stars light up the surrounding nebula the way car headlights light up the fog. A long-exposure photograph reveals a nebula's true colors, but in a telescope, it glows an eerie grayish green. Many backyard astronomers look for nebulae, using a list compiled by French astronomer Charles Messier.

MESSIER NEBULAE

Backyard astronomers often look for the so-called Messier objects—the list of stars, nebulae, and more first published by Charles Messier in 1771. Some even challenge themselves to a "Messier marathon" and try to observe all 110 in a single night.

The photographs on these pages show three nebulae in the Messier catalog. In each photo, the nebula is the glowing reddish formation near the center.

ORION NEBULA

M42 (far right), the Orion Nebula, is the most well known and easy-to-find nebula on Messier's list. It's visible to the unaided eye as the middle point of light in the sword of the constellation Orion, hanging below Orion's belt, where the red X is in the circled diagram (near right). The nebula contains hundreds of young stars, including a famous grouping of four bright stars called the Trapezium.

Orion

SUPER STARS

Many nebulae that are easy to find with telescopes have several names. For example, the Orion Nebula is also called Messier 42, abbreviated M42. It was the 42nd object on a list compiled by legendary French astronomer Charles Messier.

Messier (1730-1817) became hooked on astronomy at the age of 14 when an amazing, six-tailed comet appeared in the sky. When he was in his early 20s, he got his first job as an astronomer. The only telescopes available to Messier were fairly small, and lots of different objects looked similar in them. It was easy to confuse a comet with a nebula or a galaxy. They all looked like faint fuzz balls in the telescope eyepiece.

To help clear up the confusion, Messier began keeping track of objects that looked like comets but didn't move across the sky the way comets do. He worked from his observatory in Paris, France, and published his first catalog of 45 objects in 1771. Messier continued to add to the list throughout his lifetime until it had 103 objects. In the 20th century, the catalog was revised to include 110 objects.

Sagittarius

SWAN NEBULA

M17 (right), called the Swan or Omega Nebula, is located 5,000 light-years from Earth in the constellation Sagittarius. The nebula contains enough hydrogen to make hundreds of stars like our sun.

Sagittarius

X

TRIFID NEBULA

M20 (left), or the Trifid Nebula, also in the constellation Sagittarius, gets its name from its three-part appearance. Filaments of dark dust seem to divide it into sections. The red color comes from hot hydrogen gas heated by young stars, while the blue is the usual color of massive young stars.

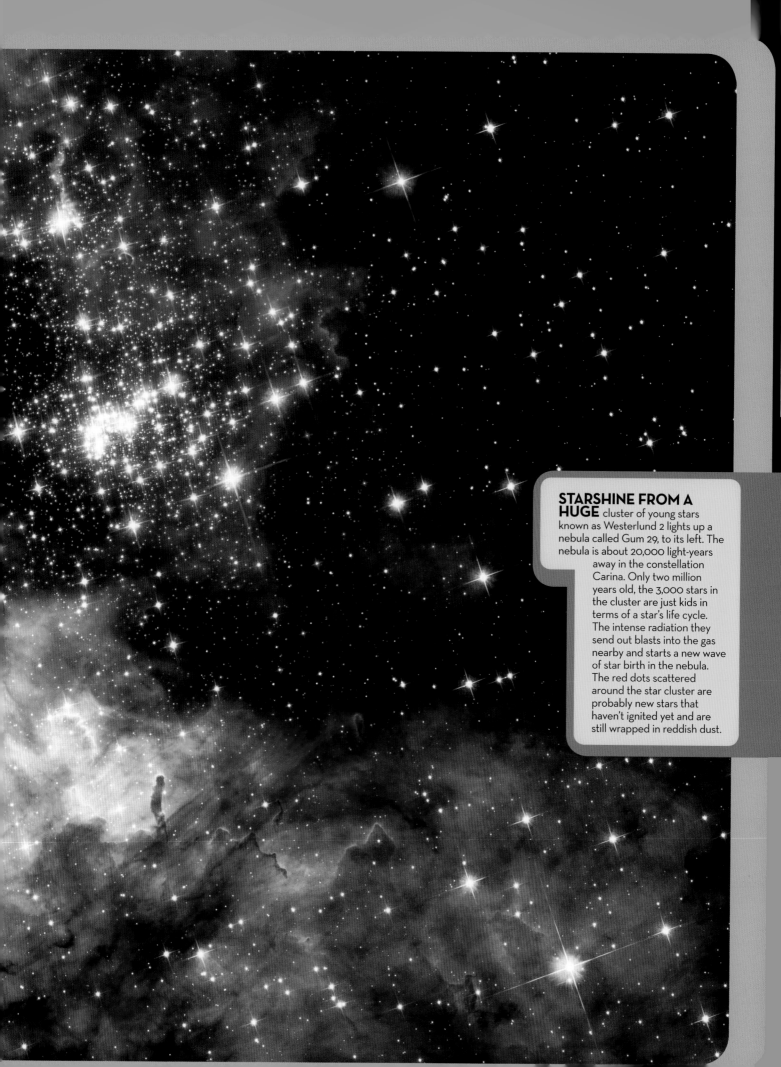

STARSHINE FROM A HUGE cluster of young stars known as Westerlund 2 lights up a nebula called Gum 29, to its left. The nebula is about 20,000 light-years away in the constellation Carina. Only two million years old, the 3,000 stars in the cluster are just kids in terms of a star's life cycle. The intense radiation they send out blasts into the gas nearby and starts a new wave of star birth in the nebula. The red dots scattered around the star cluster are probably new stars that haven't ignited yet and are still wrapped in reddish dust.

TYPES OF STARS

Astronomers classify stars based on their size, temperature, color, and luminosity. When astronomers talk about the size of a star, they usually mean the star's mass, or how much "stuff" it contains. This classification system is for young and middle-age stars. The rule changes when stars get old.

A Star's Prime of Life

Scientists say that when a star is in the prime of its life, it is on the "main sequence." That means it's producing energy by converting hydrogen to helium (sidebar opposite).

The mass of a star determines everything else about it: how hot it is, what color it is, and how long it will live. Massive stars are hot and blue; small stars are cool and red.

To identify main sequence stars more easily, astronomers assign letters to the different star types. For historical reasons, some of the letters are skipped, so the labels are not in alphabetical order. Instead, they are O, B, A, F, G, K, and M. The hottest stars are type O, while the coolest are type M.

The smallest stars are about one-tenth the mass of our sun. They're cool, dim, and red. They can live for trillions of years, burning slowly and steadily. The largest stars are about a hundred times the mass of our sun or more. They're hot, bright, and blue. They live fast and die young, burning out in only a few million years.

Old Stars

A star's size changes as it stops fusing hydrogen and leaves the main sequence. It begins burning hydrogen in a thin shell-like area surrounding its core. Fusion energy from this shell heats the star and makes it swell up, expanding to many times its previous size. Small and medium-size stars, like our sun, expand to be much, much bigger than an O star, but with far less mass. At this stage, they're called red giants. In the end, they fade into white dwarfs.

Large stars become red supergiants. One famous supergiant is the star Betelgeuse in the constellation Orion (see pages 114-115).

(see pages 114-115).

THE MAIN SEQUENCE

Stars come in a variety of sizes and masses. When they're on the main sequence, they range from hefty, hot O stars to lightweight, cool M stars (art at right). As smaller stars like our sun age, they swell in physical size to become red giants, then fade away into dying embers called white dwarfs.

FUN FACT

Red supergiant star UY Scuti may be the biggest star in our galaxy. If it were in the place of our sun, it would swallow up all the planets through Jupiter. You can't see it with the naked eye, though, because it is far away and hidden by the gases of the Milky Way.

O Star
(blue)

B Star
(blue-white)

1. Two protons (P) speed toward each other.

2. The force of their collision jars energy from one of the protons, turning it into a neutron (N) and releasing a neutrino (ν).

3. The resulting release of energy is starlight.

HOW A STAR BURNS

A star gets its energy from nuclear fusion. In other words, a star combines (fuses) two hydrogen atoms to make a helium atom. At a star's center, the temperature and pressure are so high atoms get squeezed and slammed together. Some of them hit so hard that positively charged subatomic particles called protons in the atoms' nuclei get changed into neutrons, subatomic particles with no electric charge. At that point, the atoms become helium atoms. That fusion process releases a little bit of energy. The sun fuses more than 650 million tons of hydrogen each second. Even at that rate, it will live for another five billion years before it runs out of usable fuel.

Red Giant Star

A Star (white)

F Star (yellow-white)

G Star—Our Sun (yellow)

K Star (orange)

M Star (red)

White Dwarf

DEATH OF STARS LIKE OUR SUN

The end of a star like our sun is both beautiful and peaceful. For a short time, it creates a brilliantly glowing, gaseous nebula.

When this kind of star runs out of hydrogen in its core, it begins fusing hydrogen in a shell-like layer that surrounds the core, the way an eggshell surrounds a yolk. Energy from the hydrogen-burning shell heats the star's outer layers, puffing them up. The star becomes a red giant.

These outer layers swell more and more until they blow off completely, leaving behind the star's hot, dead core. That core is called a white dwarf. It lights up the surrounding gas, creating a glowing planetary nebula.

Over the course of about 10,000 years, the gas slowly spreads out until there is not enough left for us to see. The white dwarf gradually cools and fades away as well. All that remains is a cold black dwarf.

THE LIFE STORY OF OUR SUN

4.57 billion years ago	4.52 billion years ago	4.52 billion years ago–present	Present–5 billion years in future	5 billion years in future	5.2 billion years in future
Spinning gas and dust cloud collapses into cool young star and surrounding disk.	Hydrogen fuses in center of condensing star. It stops condensing and enters main sequence.	Sun burns through half its hydrogen fuel, growing steadily brighter.	Sun burns steadily through remaining half of fuel, growing brighter.	Sun runs out of hydrogen fuel and becomes red giant.	Outer layers become planetary nebula. Sun collapses into white dwarf.

HALFWAY TO THE END

Our five-billion-year-old sun is a middle-aged star. In another five billion years, it will reach its end, puffing off its outer gas layers to form a shining nebula, like the three shown opposite.

FUN FACT

Billions of years from now, when the dying sun has expanded into a red giant, Earth will be too hot for life. The outermost planets and dwarf planets, such as Pluto, might be the best new homes for any humans who may still be living in the solar system.

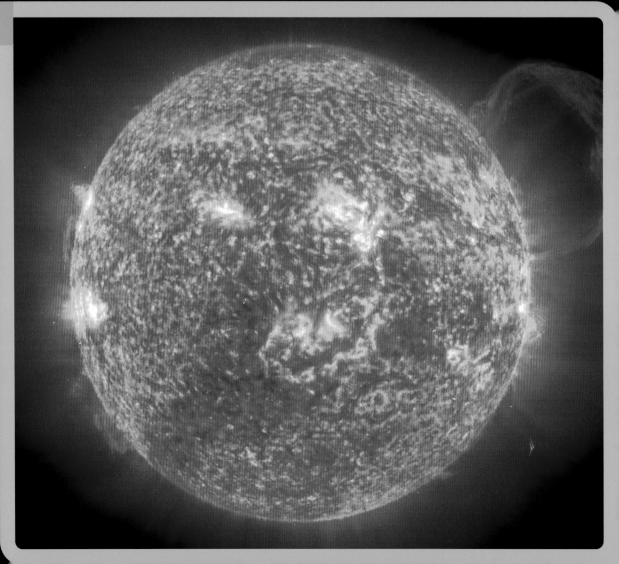

DUMBBELL NEBULA

The Dumbbell Nebula, or M27, was the first nebula from a dying, sunlike star ever discovered. It's one of the brightest such nebulae in the night sky. The star at the center ejected gas in two cones that we see from the side, giving the nebula its unique shape.

Cygnus

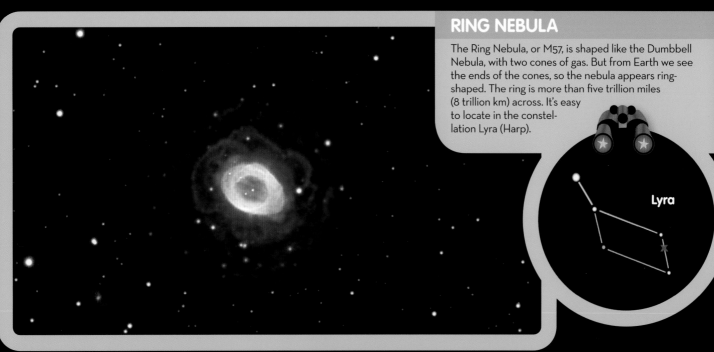

RING NEBULA

The Ring Nebula, or M57, is shaped like the Dumbbell Nebula, with two cones of gas. But from Earth we see the ends of the cones, so the nebula appears ring-shaped. The ring is more than five trillion miles (8 trillion km) across. It's easy to locate in the constellation Lyra (Harp).

Lyra

JUPITER'S GHOST

Found in the constellation Hydra, NGC 3242 is nicknamed Jupiter's Ghost because it looks similar to that planet when seen through small telescopes. But NGC 3242 is about 1,400 light-years from Earth, much farther away than Jupiter. The NGC in its name stands for New General Catalogue, a list of thousands of space objects first published in 1888. The most recent version of the NGC was published in 1988 and is now available online.

Hydra

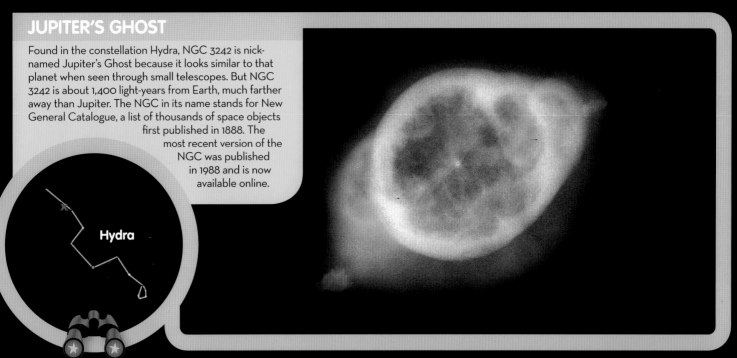

DEATH OF GIANT STARS

Compared to a medium-size star like our sun, the death of a giant star is dramatic and violent. It actually destroys itself.

Once a massive star runs out of hydrogen in its core, gravity pulls the core inward, making it dense enough and hot enough for its helium to fuse, making carbon and oxygen. That is when the star becomes a red supergiant. Then the carbon and oxygen fuse to make sodium, magnesium, silicon, and heavier elements. The final stage of fusion creates iron.

Fusing iron removes energy rather than releasing it. With no energy source left to push outward against the force of gravity pulling inward, the star's core suddenly collapses. The star's outer layers rush inward, collide, then blast outward again with immense energy. The star explodes into a supernova.

Many of the elements, from helium to iron, that were created in the star's interior are scattered into space, where they can be used by the next generation of stars and planets. The calcium in our bones and the iron in our blood come from ancient supernovae.

COUNTDOWN TO A SUPERNOVA

This is what happens in the core of a star that is 25 times as massive as our sun. At this size, the star's core is squeezed by the mass of the gas around it and burns through its elements until it collapses. The hot, massive core then blows up and flings the whole star out into space as a supernova.

Action	Time
Normal fusion (hydrogen to helium)	7 million years
Helium fuses to carbon	700,000 years
Carbon fuses to oxygen	600 years
Oxygen fuses to silicon	6 months
Silicon fuses to iron	1 day
Iron core collapses, star explodes	1/4 second

FUN FACT

Astronomers predict that when this binary star, Eta Carinae, explodes in a supernova, we'll see a massive light show from Earth.

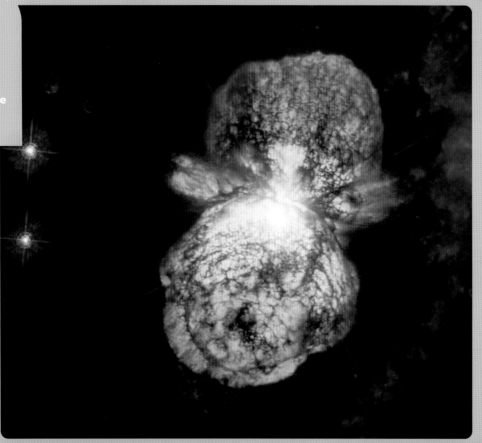

SUPER EXPLOSION

In this artwork, a massive star has just exploded as a supernova. The radiation given off from such an explosion would sterilize any planet orbiting the star, leaving behind a dead world.

SUPERNOVA REMNANTS

When a massive star explodes as a supernova, it scatters itself across space. Gas ejected by a supernova rushes out at a speed of millions of miles an hour. The supernova also creates a shock wave, which slams into surrounding gas ejected by the star before the explosion. That blast wave heats the gas to a temperature of millions of degrees—hot enough to glow. We call that glowing gas cloud a supernova remnant.

A supernova remnant is so hot that it emits high-energy x-ray radiation. Special telescopes are needed to detect and study those x-rays.

A supernova remnant may also emit visible light that we can see with our eyes, or radio waves that can be detected by radio telescopes.

Creators and Destroyers

The blast wave of a supernova can rip apart nebulae, but a supernova shock wave can also help new stars form. Interstellar gas compacted by the shock wave may clump together and gather more gas until it ignites as a star.

BETELGEUSE

No supernova has been observed in the Milky Way since the invention of the telescope. The next star to go might be Betelgeuse. In the art below, it's shown as a massive red glow consuming the moon (seen faintly toward the top of the art) of a nearby planet (the sphere in the foreground).

Orion

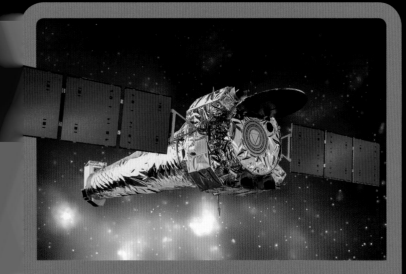

SKY-WATCHER
THE CHANDRA TELESCOPE

Very hot, energetic objects such as supernovae release high-energy radiation, including x-rays. In 1999, the National Aeronautics and Space Administration (NASA) launched into space a telescope that specializes in spotting x-ray light. Known as the Chandra X-ray Observatory, it orbits Earth once every 64 hours. Since Earth's atmosphere absorbs most x-rays, this space telescope orbits above our atmosphere where it is able to capture the x-ray light. The shiny, 64-foot (19.5-m)-long spacecraft has four very sensitive mirrors that reflect x-rays onto its detectors. In its years in space, Chandra has found all kinds of amazing objects: supernova shock waves, neutron stars, massive black holes, a halo of gas around our Milky Way, and more. We can't see x-rays with our own eyes, but information from Chandra has been translated into color images of some of the most spectacular sights in the universe.

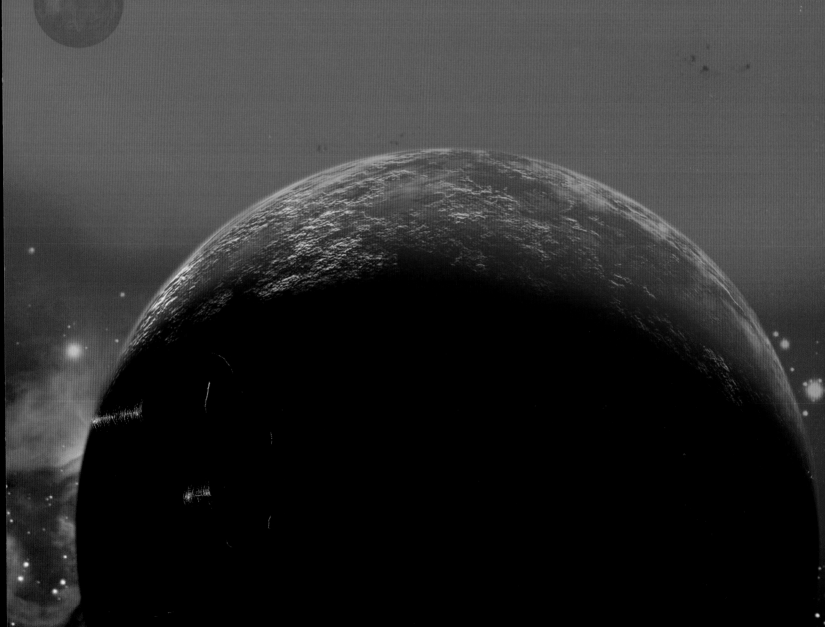

FUN FACT

In 2000, three U.S. high school students in North Carolina used information from the Chandra space telescope to discover a high-density neutron star.

Taurus

CRAB NEBULA

The Crab Nebula, or M1 (photo left), in the constellation Taurus is the only supernova remnant in Messier's catalog. A star that exploded in the year a.d. 1054 created M1. Sightings of the supernova were recorded in China and possibly in the Americas.

THE VEIL NEBULA

EIGHT THOUSAND YEARS AGO, a star near the constellation Cygnus (Swan) suddenly became very bright. This huge star, 20 times as massive as our sun, was exploding as a supernova. The blast wave from the explosion plowed into cooler gases around the star and started them glowing. Those long, bright strands of gas are now known as the Veil Nebula. This image shows just one small portion of the beautiful nebula, which is 110 light-years across. The red colors come from hydrogen gas, green from sulfur, and blue from oxygen. Parts of the nebula also give off x-rays and radio waves.

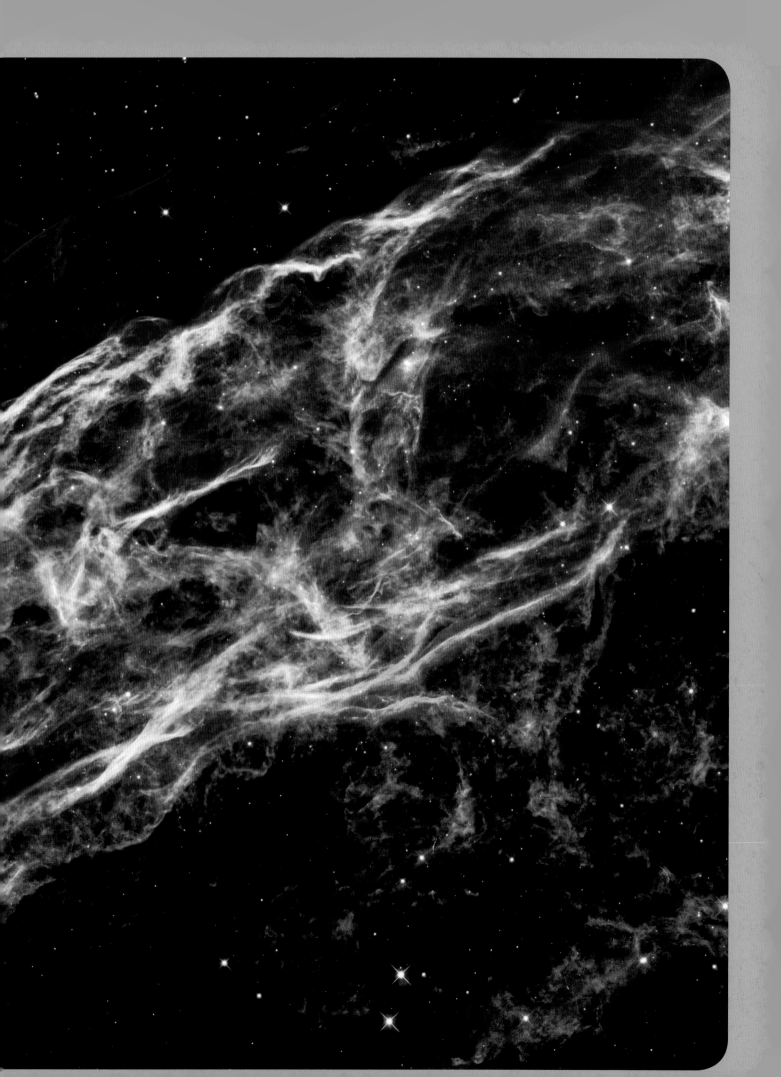

NEUTRON STARS AND PULSARS

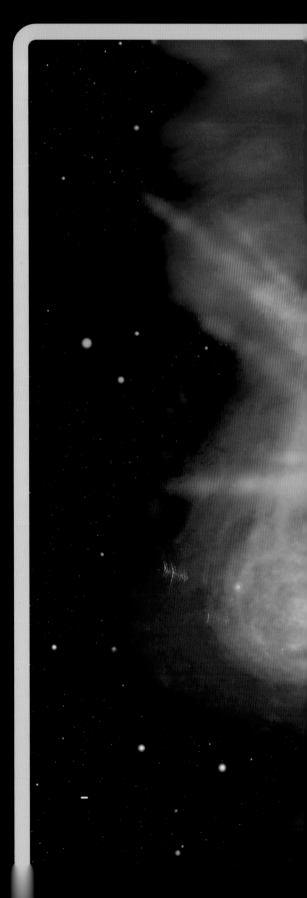

A supernova remnant can become either a black hole (see page 134) or a neutron star.

A neutron star isn't really a star. It's more like a giant atomic nucleus 5–10 miles (8–16 km) across, made entirely of neutrons. Normal atoms are made of three particles—protons, electrons, and neutrons. But the atoms in a supernova core have been squeezed together so tightly that protons and electrons have combined to form neutrons.

Since so much mass is stuffed into such a small sphere, a neutron star is very dense. A sugar cube–size lump would weigh about a billion tons, more than 10,000 aircraft carriers.

Pulsars

Some spinning neutron stars emit beams of radio energy that sweep across space like the beam of a lighthouse or searchlight. If the beam happens to pass over Earth, we detect a pulsing radio signal every time the beam hits. The neutron stars that create these signals are called pulsars.

SUPER STARS

Astronomer Jocelyn Bell Burnell (b. 1943) was born in Northern Ireland to a family that encouraged her interest in reading and science. Although her school did not allow girls to study science until her parents protested, Bell persisted and eventually earned a degree in physics from the University of Glasgow. She went on to Cambridge University in England to study astronomy. She helped to build a radio telescope and began studying the radio signals it detected, reading through hundreds of feet of paper charts every few days.

One day in 1967, on one inch (2.5 cm) of the recording paper, she discovered a strange radio signal that blinked on and off about once every second. She labeled it LGM-1 for "little green men," a joke about possible alien life.

No one really thought that the signal was from aliens, but astronomers weren't sure what was causing it. Not long after the discovery, a scientist calculated that a spinning neutron star could make radio pulses. The strong magnetic field of a pulsar traps electrons that escaped when the star's core collapsed. Those electrons generate radio waves that are funneled outward by the star's magnetic field into beams of radiation. As the pulsar spins, the beam of radiation sweeps across the sky. Jocelyn Bell Burnell's little green men were the first signals ever discovered from a pulsar.

Since the discovery of the first pulsar, about 2,000 others have been found. Some spin so fast that they flicker on and off hundreds of times every second.

"The surprises keep rolling in," says Burnell, "and that's I think what surprises me most: the uncertainty about astronomy."

FACTS ABOUT NEUTRON STARS

Number of neutron stars in Milky Way	About 100 million
Average diameter	12.4 miles (20 km)
Average mass (Earth = 1)	1.4–3
Surface gravity (Earth = 1)	2 billion
Average surface temperature	1,080,000°F (600,000°C)
Fastest spinning pulsar	716 times a second

PULSAR HEART

As shown in this artwork, the center of the Crab Nebula is a region of powerful energy. Hot gas swirls around a compact pulsar. That pulsar is all that remains of a once mighty star.

GAMMA-RAY BURSTS

The most powerful supernovae do more than announce the death of a star. They create huge blasts of high-energy radiation called gamma rays. Gamma-ray bursts are the brightest explosions in the universe. They would destroy any life that existed on nearby planets.

A gamma-ray burst has been called the birth cry of a black hole. When a massive star's core collapses, it can form a black hole (see pages 134-135). If the star was rotating very quickly, a fast-spinning disk of gas will surround the new black hole, and some material from the disk will shoot out in cone-shaped jets. Those jets, coming from deep in the interior of the dying star, will punch through it and rip the rest of the star apart.

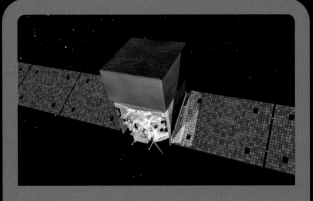

SKY-WATCHER
FERMI GAMMA-RAY SPACE TELESCOPE

Earth's atmosphere blocks gamma rays from reaching the surface. That's a good thing: These super-high-energy particles are dangerous to humans. To see where they're coming from, scientists at NASA and European space agencies launched the Fermi Gamma-ray Space Telescope in 2008. This boxy-looking spacecraft orbits about 330 miles (531 km) above Earth and can scan the entire sky every three hours. It has a big telescope that scans for gamma rays and a detector that looks specifically for very quick gamma-ray bursts. In 2013, it spotted one of the highest-energy bursts ever detected, coming from the region of the constellation Leo. The radiation had 35 billion times the energy of visible light. It released more energy in a few seconds than our sun will give off in its entire lifetime.

GAMMA-RAY BURSTS

A gamma-ray burst (art above) is the most powerful explosion in the universe. The orbiting Fermi Gamma-ray Space Telescope (above left) records these cosmic events, which are often the result of merging neutron stars and the formation of massive black holes. We don't know the cause of other gamma-ray bursts.

FUN FACT

There's a lot still to learn about gamma-ray bursts like this one in April 2013. Scientists don't know what causes more than half of them.

BLACK HOLES

A black hole really seems like a hole in space. Most black holes form when the core of a massive star collapses, crushing itself into oblivion.

A black hole has a stronger gravitational pull than anything else in the universe. It's like a bottomless pit, swallowing whatever gets near enough to it to be pulled in.

Black holes come in different sizes. The smallest has a mass about three times that of our sun. The biggest one scientists have found so far has a mass about 800 billion times the sun's. Really big black holes at the centers of galaxies probably form by swallowing enormous amounts of gas over time.

One of NASA's spacecraft has found thousands of possible black holes in the Milky Way, but there are probably many more. The nearest one to Earth is about 2,800 light-years away.

A BLACK HOLE'S NEIGHBORHOOD

After hydrogen gas from a yellow star (at right in the art) fell into a black hole, it formed a disk around the hole (the small, black circle). The multicolored disk of gas is held in place by the black hole's gravitational pull. The two bright white cones are some of the star's hydrogen gas that got close to the hole but escaped, thanks to a push from the hole's magnetic field.

SKY-WATCHER
GRAVITATIONAL WAVES

Many star systems in the universe are twins: two stars held close together by gravity. What happens when both of these stars turn into black holes? You get a pair of black holes that orbit each other. And what happens if these black holes get so close that they crash into each other? That collision is so immense that it shakes the very fabric of space and time, sending out waves of gravity that can make our own planet vibrate.

Scientists were finally able to "see" this happening using an unusual kind of detector called the Laser Interferometer Gravitational-Wave Observatory (LIGO). LIGO (below) consists of two pairs of L-shaped steel tubes, each arm of which is 2.5 miles (4 km) long and just over 3 feet (1.2 m) in diameter. One pair is in Louisiana, U.S.A., and the other some 2,500 miles (4,023 km) away in rural areas of Washington State, U.S.A. Laser beams bounce back and forth between mirrors inside the tubes. If a gravity wave passes through the tubes, the wave pushes and pulls the mirrors a tiny bit. The very sensitive lasers measure this tiny wiggle. In September 2015, the detectors wobbled by a tiny amount, seven milliseconds apart, meaning they were measuring gravitational waves from the distant collision of two black holes. It was the first time these waves had been detected. In August 2017, there was another first: Gravitational waves helped scientists detect light from a distant elliptical galaxy.

FALLING INTO A BLACK HOLE

Imagine falling into a black hole. As you move closer to it, the black hole's forces pull at your body, stretching it. As the pull grows stronger, the atoms in your body are pulled apart. Those atoms are stretched and torn into smaller and smaller bits until nothing recognizable is left. You have just been "spaghetti-fied" by the might of a black hole.

White Cone

Disk of Hydrogen

Black Hole

Gas From Star

Yellow Star

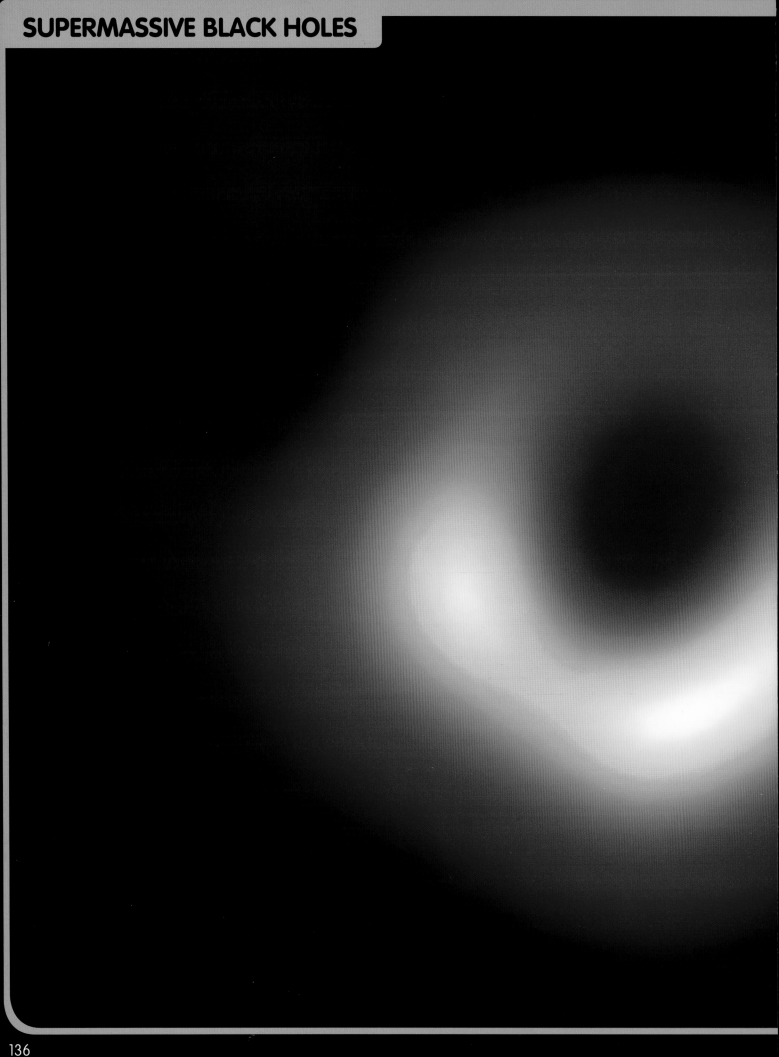

A SUPERMASSIVE BLACK HOLE at the heart of the Messier 87 (M87) galaxy drags in gases, heating them into a brilliant red ring. This image, produced by radio telescopes around the world working together, is the first photograph ever taken of a black hole—or at least of the dark shadow where it lurks within the bright ring—called its event horizon. Like a massive blockade, the event horizon keeps light and radiation from escaping the dark area inside its boundary. Located 55 million light-years from Earth, and with as much mass as 6.5 billion suns, the gigantic M87 black hole is almost as wide, from side to side, as our entire solar system.

FAILED STARS :
BROWN DWARFS

Not every clump in a star-forming nebula will become a star. Sometimes there's not enough gas nearby. Without that fuel, the object never gets dense enough and hot enough to maintain nuclear fusion. Instead, it fizzles.

Our sun contains about a thousand times as much mass as Jupiter. The least massive stars are about 75 times the mass of Jupiter. Anything less massive than that is a failed star.

Astronomers call them brown dwarfs, even though they're not really brown and they're not dwarf stars. They start out at their brightest, then become dimmer and redder than the dimmest star.

Brown Dwarf or Planet?

Astronomers are still debating what the difference is between planets and brown dwarfs. Most astronomers think that anything less massive than 13 Jupiters is a planet, whereas anything between 13 and 75 times the mass of Jupiter is a brown dwarf. The lower limit, 13 times the mass of Jupiter, is the mass at which a brown dwarf can briefly fuse a form of hydrogen called deuterium. Planets do not fuse hydrogen at all.

FACTS ABOUT BROWN DWARFS

Nearest to Earth	Luhman 16, 6.5 light-years
Most massive	J0104+1535, 90 times the mass of Jupiter
Least massive	OTS 44, 11.5 times the mass of Jupiter
Fastest spinning	J1122+25, turning once on its axis every 17 to 51 minutes
Coolest	WISE 0855-0714, -53°F to 9°F (-48°C to -13°C)

FUN FACT

Unlike planets, brown dwarfs give off their own light. However, these starlike objects can be as cool as your skin, and the light they send out may be very faint and red. In many other ways, brown dwarfs look like big gas planets. They can have atmospheres and storms. They may have auroras like our own northern lights. They might have planets orbiting them, although like the little planets in the illustration at right, they wouldn't get enough heat from their star to support any life.

FAILED STAR

Looking like a glowing red coal, a brown dwarf (art at right) is a stellar wannabe without enough mass to sustain nuclear fusion. It is destined to cool off slowly over billions of years, and without any heat, it will leave any planets orbiting it in a never-ending deep freeze.

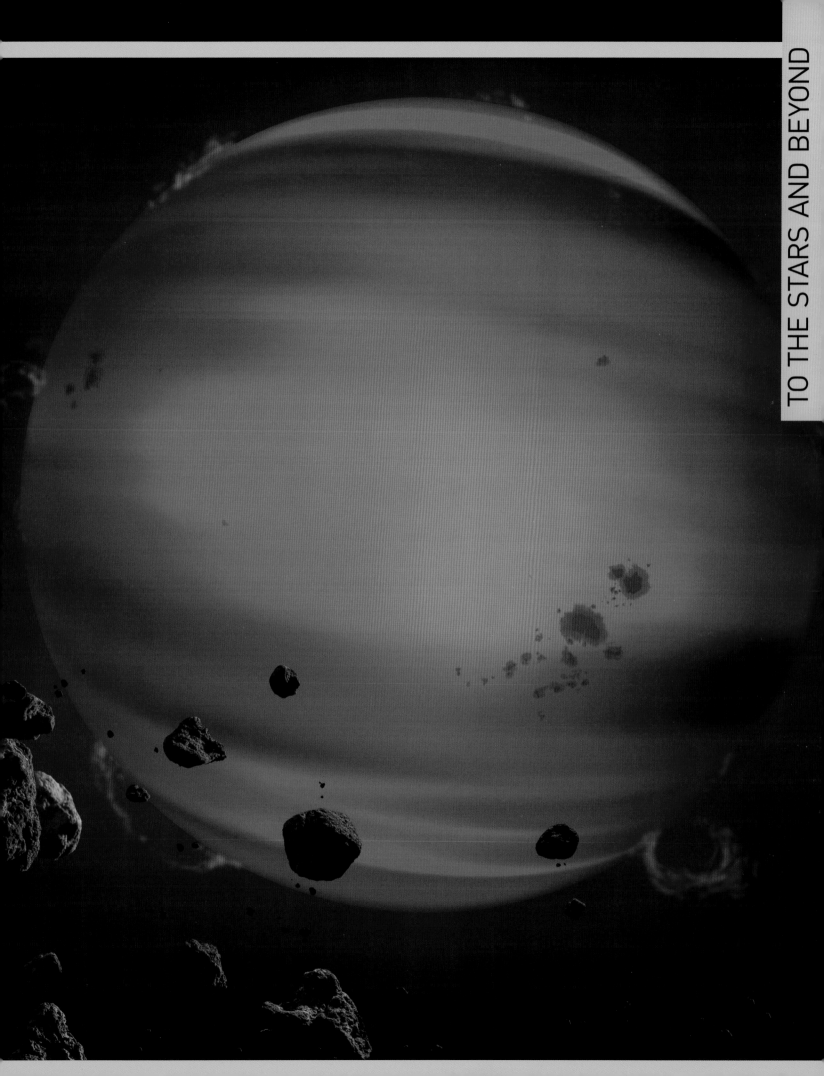

HOW PLANETS FORM

Planets arise as a natural result of the star-formation process. Stars are born from large clouds of gas and dust. That gas and dust spin in space, flattening into a disk the way pizza dough does when a baker tosses it. The center of the disk becomes a star, whereas the rest of the disk may form planets.

To form planets in the outer part of the disk, bits of dust begin to clump together. Those clumps eventually get bigger and become rocky objects called protoplanets. Protoplanets smack into each other and stick together—and planets are born.

The asteroids in our solar system are leftover planetesimals, or small planets from the early solar system. Jupiter's gravity stirred them up and prevented them from sticking together. Astronomers also have found evidence of asteroids in other star systems.

If a rocky planet grows large enough by pulling together enough rock and ice, it can collect and hold on to surrounding hydrogen gas. That's how the gas giants—Jupiter, Saturn, Uranus, and Neptune—of our outer solar system grew so big. Their rocky cores—bigger than the other planets—were large enough to grab and hold on to hydrogen gas.

LOL!

Q: What did one nervous protoplanet say to the other?

A: We'd better stick together!

PLANETS TAKE SHAPE

Follow the artwork below from top left to bottom right to see how a star and its planets form from a single disk of gas and dust. As the infant star gathers hydrogen gas, leftover rocky bits stick together like giant dust bunnies. The rocky bits continue to come together, and eventually, those cosmic clumps grow to become full-size planets. At last a full-fledged solar system forms. Here, a comet is streaking toward them.

Infant Star

Star Gathering Hydrogen Gas and Rock

Planets Forming Around the Star

SUPER STARS

The great German astronomer Johannes Kepler (1571-1630) was the first person to figure out how planets orbit our sun. He was a sickly child who developed bad vision as a result of smallpox, but he was brilliant at mathematics. When he was six years old, he saw the Great Comet of 1577, and when he was ten he observed a lunar eclipse, two events that confirmed his love for astronomy. By the time he was 23, Kepler was teaching math and astronomy and studying the motions of the planets. He realized that Copernicus was right that the planets orbit the sun, but he also saw that Copernicus's orbits were not mathematically correct. In 1609, after working for the great astronomer Tycho Brahe (see page 112), Kepler published a book, *Astronomia nova (New Astronomy)*, which included his first two laws of planetary motion: (1) all planets move around the sun in elliptical (oval-shaped) orbits, with the sun at the center, and (2) an imaginary line joining each planet to the sun sweeps out at equal distances in equal lengths of time. Kepler's findings revolutionized astronomy.

Kepler died in 1630. His work not only redrew the paths of the planets, but also helped Isaac Newton form the theory of universal gravitation in 1665-1667. That explains how objects in space, like the sun and the planets or the planets and their moons, have a strong gravitational pull on one another based on their mass and the distance between them.

Solar System Complete

OTHER WORLDS

stronomers didn't discover planets outside our solar system, called exoplanets, until 1992. Then, three Earth-size planets were detected about 900 light-years away. Instead of orbiting a normal star, they were orbiting a dead star known as a pulsar (see pages 130-131).

In 1995, Swiss astronomers found the first planet orbiting a normal star. Named 51 Pegasi b, it has about half the mass of Jupiter; unlike Jupiter, it orbits very close to its star and has a year that is only four days long.

Since the discovery of 51 Pegasi b, astronomers have confirmed more than 4,100 planets orbiting other stars. As well as "hot Jupiters," like 51 Pegasi b, they include such oddball characters as "puffy planets," as light as cork, and coal-black planets. Most discovered so far don't look like they would support Earthlike life. They are too hot or too cold, bathed in deadly radiation, or circle their suns in long loopy orbits. But a few are promising. Planet Kepler 44b, about 1,120 light-years away, is a "super-Earth" that seems to be in the life-friendly habitable zone of its small star.

Astronomers have even found a planet in our neighborhood. It circles Proxima Centauri, in the star system closest to Earth.

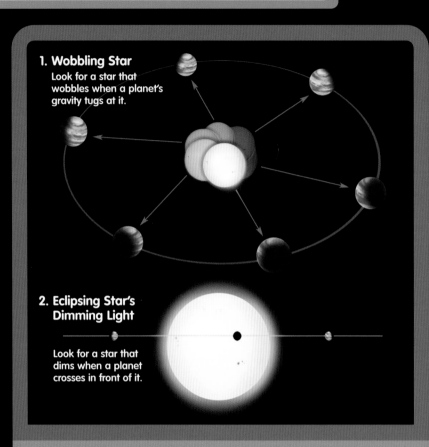

1. Wobbling Star
Look for a star that wobbles when a planet's gravity tugs at it.

2. Eclipsing Star's Dimming Light
Look for a star that dims when a planet crosses in front of it.

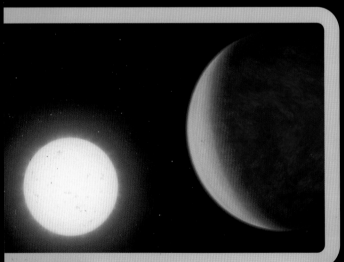

FUN FACT
In this art, exoplanet 55 Cancri e, about 40 light-years away, orbits close to its star with one side always facing that sun. Its hot bright side is almost 4400°F (2427°C), while its dark, cooler side is 2060°F (1127°C).

SKY-WATCHER
HOW WE FIND EXOPLANETS

It's hard to find planets around other stars. The stars are very far away, and planets are so small and dim that seeing one next to a star is like trying to see a firefly sitting next to a spotlight. Only in the past couple of decades have astronomers gained the tools they need to find alien worlds, such as the orbiting space telescopes Kepler, Spitzer, and CoRoT.

Since a star is much easier to see than a planet, astronomers usually hunt planets by looking for their effect on their host star. Many of the 4,100-plus known alien worlds were found by looking for wobbling stars. Just as the star's gravity tugs on the planet, the planet's gravity tugs on the star. In this gravitational dance, the star wobbles back and forth.

If it wobbles toward and away from us, we can use a spectrograph (an instrument similar to a prism that splits the light of the star into a spectrum of colors) to look for a slight shift in the star's movement. That is the way 51 Pegasi b was found. We can also look for stars that wobble left and right or up and down across the sky, but those searches are much harder because the wobble in the star's apparent position is so tiny.

Planet hunters have also had great success by looking for planets that eclipse their stars, making the star's light dim ever so slightly. (Since we are so far away, the planet appears to cover only a fraction of the star's disk.) Eclipse searches can find smaller planets than the search for "wobblers"— even planets as small as Earth.

Dozens of planets have been seen directly, using methods that block out or cancel out the glaring light of their suns. Astronomers are excited about this method, called direct imaging, because it may let them get a look at the planets' atmospheres. Still, exoplanets haven't been photographed, so all the art in this book is imagined.

TOO HOT
TO HANDLE

Many of the exoplanets discovered so far orbit very close
to their star (art below). Such
a heat-blasted world would be
covered with molten rock and
not welcoming to human life.

WEIRD WORLDS

E xoplanets are huge and tiny, hot and cold, bright and dark. Some are rocky, like Mercury. Others are gas giants, like Jupiter. So far, we've seen only a few of them directly in our telescopes. However, new telescopes will soon be able to see more of these distant worlds. We'll see if the reality is as weird as—or even weirder than—our imaginings.

CHILLED OUT

The gas giant planet Epsilon Eridani b, seen from one of its moons in this artwork, orbits a star a little cooler than our sun. Since the planet is more than 300 million miles (483 million km) from its star, the planet and its moons would be too cold to support life.

SKY-WATCHER
KEPLER SPACE TELESCOPE

When NASA launched the Kepler Space Telescope in 2009 (art above), thousands of new exoplanets came into view. Kepler orbits our sun, just as Earth does, and from its place in space it has a clear view of distant stars. Its powerful telescope and camera watch selected groups of stars to detect the tiny dimming of the light that happens when a planet crosses in front of its sun. These instruments are so sensitive that, from Kepler's orbit in space, it could detect a single porch light on Earth.

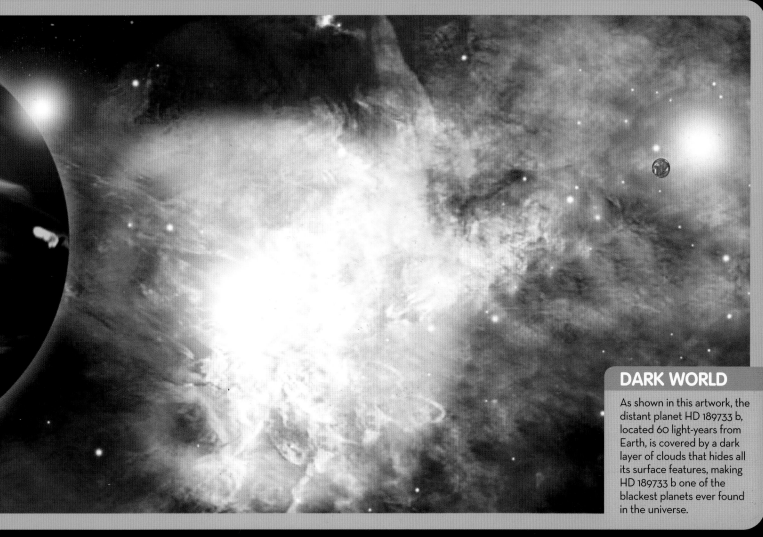

DARK WORLD

As shown in this artwork, the distant planet HD 189733 b, located 60 light-years from Earth, is covered by a dark layer of clouds that hides all its surface features, making HD 189733 b one of the blackest planets ever found in the universe.

GLOBULAR CLUSTERS

The Milky Way and other large galaxies are home to a special kind of star cluster: a globular cluster. These round balls hold up to a million stars. They are spread over a volume of several tens to about 200 light-years in diameter. If you think of the sun as living in a quiet suburb, then the stars in a globular cluster are living in a crowded city center.

If you were to visit a planet inside a globular cluster, the night sky would be spectacular! From Earth we see only a few thousand stars with the unaided eye. The sky of a globular-cluster planet would be filled with a hundred thousand stars or more.

These clusters contain the oldest stars in our galaxy—almost as old as the universe itself. Many aging red giants and dead white dwarfs live in globular clusters.

Globular clusters orbit the center of the Milky Way in all directions, some looping high above or below our galaxy. American astronomer Harlow Shapley mapped globular clusters as a way to figure out the size and shape of our galaxy. He argued that since we see more globular clusters in one direction than in the other, we must be off to the side of the Milky Way.

FUN FACT
Great big galaxies have lots of globular clusters. The supergiant galaxy M87, about 53 million light-years from Earth, has more than 10,000 of them.

FACTS ABOUT GLOBULAR CLUSTERS

First one discovered	M22, by Abraham Ihle in 1665
Largest	Omega Centauri, 150 light-years wide
Nearest	NGS 6397 and M4, 7,200 light-years away
Oldest	11 to 18 billion years old
Number in Milky Way	150 to 170

STARRY NIGHT

This art shows the night sky as seen from a cave opening on a rocky planet orbiting a star in a globular cluster. Thousands of nearby stars would make clear nights much lighter than they are on Earth.

ACROSS THE GALAXY

Since so many stars are packed so close together in globular clusters, they're very bright and visible across great distances of space. That makes them favorite targets for a lot of backyard astronomers. Through a large telescope, a globular cluster looks like a large ball of stars filling the eyepiece with a brilliant display.

In small telescopes, globular clusters look more like fuzzy cotton balls. In fact, they look a lot like comets, which is why Charles Messier's catalog of objects (see page 116) lists a lot of globular clusters.

Globular clusters are so crowded that sometimes two stars will collide to form a more massive star that burns hot and blue, appearing younger than it really is. Since those stars look like they've aged more slowly, lagging behind their neighbors, astronomers have named them blue stragglers.

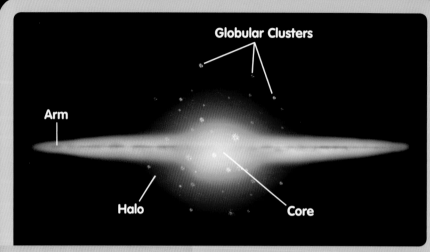

HALO OF CLUSTERS

All spiral galaxies are surrounded by a halo of globular clusters, as in this art. The stars in the globular clusters were the first to form as the galaxy structures grew.

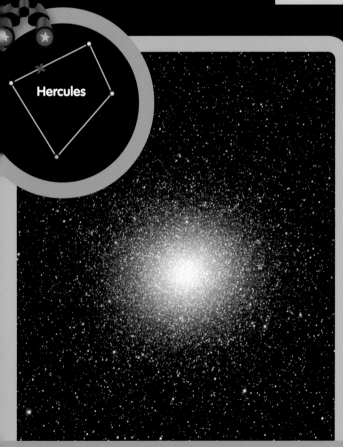

HERCULES CLUSTER

The Hercules globular cluster, or M13, is bright even though it is 25,000 light-years away. In 1974, astronomers used the Arecibo radio telescope in Puerto Rico to send a message toward it. If aliens live there, they won't get the message for 25,000 years.

M2 CLUSTER

The globular cluster M2 is compact, which makes it more easily visible in small backyard telescopes. It's located on the opposite side of the galactic center from Earth, more than 37,000 light-years away.

SKY-WATCHER
FINDING THE HERCULES CLUSTER

The Hercules globular cluster, M13, is a favorite target for sky-watchers in the Northern Hemisphere. Look for it on a clear, dark, moonless summer night. Using a star chart, face south and find the Hercules constellation between the bright stars Arcturus and Vega. M13 is located on a line between the two western stars of the constellation's four central stars. In binoculars, it will look like a fuzzy round glow. In a good telescope, it will be a gorgeous collection of stars.

FUN FACT
Globular clusters are held together in a spherical, or egg, shape by gravity. In 1764, Charles Messier described the Hercules cluster as "a nebula which I am sure contains no star." He was wrong—astronomers estimate it has about 300,000!

OMEGA CENTAURI
Omega Centauri is the largest and brightest globular cluster in the Milky Way. It contains millions of stars in a sphere 150 light-years across. Omega Centauri is best viewed from locations near Earth's Equator.

Billions, maybe trillions, of galaxies with hundreds of billions of stars populate our universe. Galaxies come in many varieties. Our home, the Milky Way, is a spiral galaxy. All spiral galaxies have a disk of stars. The stars gather into curlicues called spiral arms that extend from the galaxy's center to its edges. Some galaxies have tightly wound spiral arms; others have loosely wound spiral arms.

Some spiral galaxies are just a disk and are as flat as a pancake. Others, including the Milky Way, have a big, central ball of stars called a bulge. The bulge often contains older stars, whereas the flat disk holds younger stars.

A barred spiral galaxy has a central bar, or rectangular clump, of stars that lies across the middle of the galaxy. The spiral arms extend from the ends of the bar instead of from the center of the galaxy. Astronomers think that a galactic bar might form when a galaxy is disturbed by the gravity of another galaxy that passes nearby, or even collides with it.

The Milky Way is a barred spiral galaxy, but from Earth we're looking almost directly at one end of the bar, so it's hard to see from our location.

Another common type of galaxy is the elliptical galaxy. Elliptical galaxies are all bulge and no disk. They can be round, football-shaped, or anything in between. They tend to be made up of only old stars.

Some galaxies have no definite shape. Because of that, they're called irregular galaxies. The nearby Magellanic Clouds are irregular galaxies, and in the beginning of the universe, the first galaxies that formed were irregulars.

ELLIPTICAL GALAXY

The galactic zoo is shown in this art. An elliptical galaxy has a distinctly orange-yellow color because it contains mostly old, redder stars. Unlike spiral galaxies, ellipticals like this one typically hold little or no dust.

FACTS ABOUT GALAXIES

Number in universe	200 million to 2 trillion
Biggest known	HFLS3 starburst galaxy, 35 billion stars
Oldest known	GN-z11, 13.4 billion years old

SPIRAL GALAXY

A spiral galaxy has older stars in its central bulge and young, blue stars in its disk and spiral arms. Dark patches show where large clumps of interstellar dust block starlight.

LENTICULAR GALAXY

This unusual galaxy is in between a spiral and an elliptical in form, sharing characteristics of both. It has the flattened shape of a spiral, but its yellowish color and lack of dust are more like an elliptical.

SUPER STARS

The 20th-century physicist Edwin Hubble (1889-1953) tried out different jobs before finally becoming an astronomer. A bright student, he earned an undergraduate degree in mathematics and astronomy, but because he had promised his father he would become a lawyer, he studied law at Oxford University in England. Back in the United States, he worked as a high school teacher and basketball coach. Eventually, though, his passion for astronomy led him to earn a Ph.D. in astronomy and, after another detour serving in the army in World War I, he started working at the Mount Wilson Observatory in California in 1919. At that time, people thought that our galaxy, the Milky Way, was the entire universe. They believed that the blurry spots seen in the night sky, known as nebulae, were just clouds of gas and dust. However, Hubble used a way of measuring distances to certain kinds of stars in nebulae and realized that they were millions of light-years away. The nebulae weren't gas clouds after all, but separate galaxies. With the discovery, Hubble transformed our picture of the universe from a single galaxy into a huge expanse full of galaxies of all shapes and sizes.

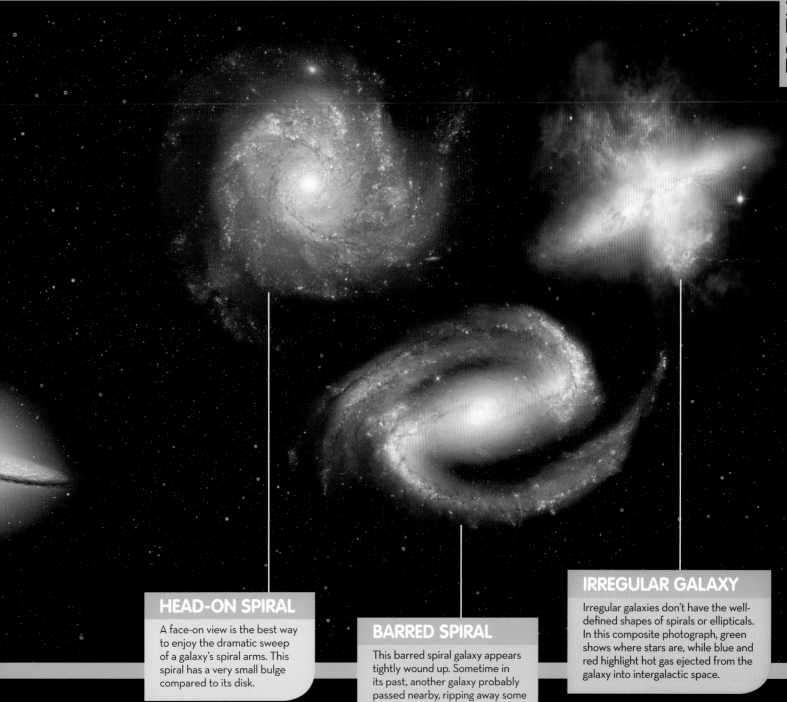

HEAD-ON SPIRAL

A face-on view is the best way to enjoy the dramatic sweep of a galaxy's spiral arms. This spiral has a very small bulge compared to its disk.

BARRED SPIRAL

This barred spiral galaxy appears tightly wound up. Sometime in its past, another galaxy probably passed nearby, ripping away some of its stars and gases and spinning

IRREGULAR GALAXY

Irregular galaxies don't have the well-defined shapes of spirals or ellipticals. In this composite photograph, green shows where stars are, while blue and red highlight hot gas ejected from the galaxy into intergalactic space.

OUR NEXT-DOOR NEIGHBORS

The Milky Way has dozens of galaxies in its neighborhood, clustered together by gravitational attraction. Together, they are known as the Local Group. The closest large galaxy to the Milky Way is Andromeda, also called M31. Andromeda is like the Milky Way's big sister, since it's more than twice as large as our galaxy. The Milky Way is 100,000 light-years across and holds about 400 billion stars. By comparison, Andromeda is about 220,000 light-years across and holds a trillion stars.

Another close neighbor of the Milky Way is the Triangulum galaxy, or M33. M33 is a runt compared to Andromeda. It is only 60,000 light-years across, with about 100 billion stars. Unlike many galaxies, M33 has no giant black hole at its center.

Until the 1920s, astronomers thought M31 and M33 were nearby gaseous nebulae and part of the Milky Way. Then Edwin Hubble (see page 151) discovered that M31 and M33 are separate galaxies. Sometime in the future, the Milky Way and Andromeda will collide, temporarily forming one big galaxy some astronomers call Milkomeda. Then, to complicate matters, M33 may collide with this large galaxy, creating an even larger one. We'll leave it up to future astronomers to name this new galaxy!

FACTS ABOUT THE LOCAL GROUP

Largest galaxy	Andromeda, 220,000 light-years wide
Second largest galaxy	Milky Way, 100,000 light-years wide
Third largest galaxy	Triangulum, 60,000 light-years wide
Number of spiral galaxies	3
Number of elliptical galaxies	1
Number of irregular galaxies	13
Number of dwarf elliptical galaxies	5
Number of dwarf spheroidal galaxies	40

ANDROMEDA

Andromeda is a beautiful spiral galaxy. This long-exposure photograph taken with a small telescope shows its full glory.

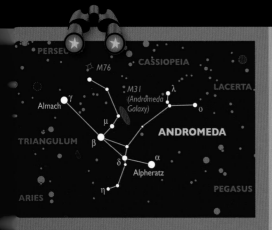

SKY-WATCHER

WHERE TO FIND THE ANDROMEDA GALAXY

The Andromeda galaxy is the only galaxy that you can see with the naked eye in Northern Hemisphere skies—but binoculars or a small telescope are even better for viewing it. It's best seen on clear, moonless nights in October or November. As always, it's handy to have a star chart. Face south and look high overhead. You'll see a big square made of four stars, which forms the body of the constellation Pegasus. The Andromeda constellation is a V of stars that starts at the upper-left corner of this square. Follow the right-hand line of this V and look for an oval glow to the right of it, about halfway up. That's the Andromeda galaxy. Don't be disappointed if it looks just like a fuzzy blob to the unaided eye. Remember, you're seeing something that's 2.5 million light-years away!

FUN FACT

The Triangulum galaxy is sometimes called the Pinwheel galaxy, also M33, and you can see why. Its loose spiral arms twirl around its center like a child's toy. Triangulum is the third largest member of the Local Group of galaxies. Inside its hydrogen gas clouds, many hot young stars are being born. Radiation from these stars makes the galaxy shine bright in ultraviolet light, which NASA's Swift satellite captured in this image.

COLLIDING GALAXIES

Stars don't collide too often because they're very far apart, relative to their size. Galaxies are much closer to each other relative to their size, so they collide frequently. Galactic collisions were even more common in the past, when the universe was smaller and galaxies were closer together.

When galaxies collide, strange things can happen. Sometimes a small galaxy with only a hundred million to several billion stars, called a dwarf galaxy, punches through the center of a larger galaxy with up to 400 billion stars. The dwarf galaxy leaves a hole and a surrounding ring of stars and creates a ring galaxy. Sometimes a large galaxy consumes a small one, destroying all signs that the smaller one ever existed. If the giant black holes at the centers of two galaxies collide, the impact can send one of them flying through space like a monstrous billiard ball at millions of miles an hour.

Right now, the Milky Way is swallowing at least one dwarf galaxy. On the far side of the galactic center from Earth, the Sagittarius dwarf elliptical galaxy is plunging through the disk of the Milky Way. The Milky Way's stronger gravity is ripping apart the dwarf galaxy. Eventually its stars will become part of the Milky Way.

More than 200 million years ago, M32, a dwarf galaxy, punched through the disk of Andromeda. Ripples of interstellar dust spread out through Andromeda like water ripples in a pond. M32 survived the encounter, but one day it will be devoured by Andromeda.

When two galaxies close to the same size interact, the results are even more dramatic. Gravity can fling off streams of stars as the galaxies whip around each other. Gas clouds in the two galaxies may merge, fueling bursts of star formation.

In some colliding galaxies, stars form a hundred times faster than in calm galaxies like the Milky Way. Those stars live fast and die quickly. A star explodes as a supernova every couple of years there, compared to an average of once every hundred years in the Milky Way. Astronomers call colliding starburst galaxies "supernova factories" since they produce supernovae so quickly.

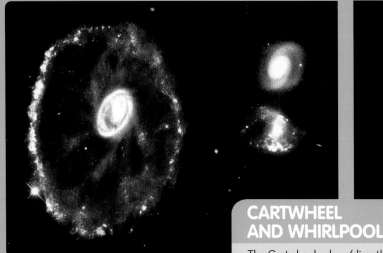

CARTWHEEL AND WHIRLPOOL

The Cartwheel galaxy (directly above), 500 million light-years from Earth, suffered a head-on collision with another galaxy. Gravitational forces from the collision formed the two stunning rings of gas and newborn stars. The Whirlpool galaxy (top) has a small companion known as NGC 5195. As the two galaxies brush past each other, gravity from NGC 5195 may be molding the dramatic spiral structure seen in the Whirlpool galaxy.

MOUSE COLLISION

The Hubble Space Telescope captured this view of two galaxies playing a game of cat and mouse or, in this case, mouse and mouse. These colliding galaxies were nicknamed "the mice" because of the long tails of stars and gas thrown off them during the collision. They're located 300 million light-years from Earth.

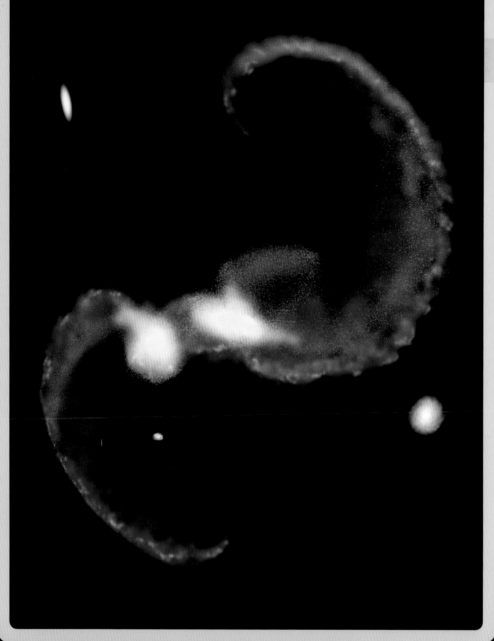

MILKY WAY AND ANDROMEDA COLLIDE

The Milky Way and Andromeda are on a collision course, approaching each other at a speed of about 300,000 miles an hour (483,000 km/h). In a few billion years, these two galaxies will ram together to become a football-shaped, elliptical galaxy.

Since the Milky Way and Andromeda are both large, their collision will be particularly dramatic. The "damage" will be greater, just as the collision of two dump trucks would bend a lot more metal than if a small vehicle were to smack into a truck.

As the two galaxies interact gravitationally, some stars will be tossed outward, escaping into intergalactic space. Others will be flung from a galaxy's outskirts into the core (art at left). Stars that once orbited in an orderly disk may be sent into new orbits that zoom outward before plunging back down, looping around and out again.

By the time the Milky Way and Andromeda collide, our star, the sun, will be no more than a white dwarf.

Both the Milky Way and Andromeda hold plenty of gas that could form new stars. Most likely, a burst of star formation will take place when the collision happens. Thousands of new stars and planetary systems will be born. Older stars will be lost, ejected from both galaxies. Many new stars will quickly die off and explode as supernovae. The new galaxy will be an energetic place for millions of years after the collision.

FUN FACT

In the long history of the universe, probably every galaxy has interacted with another galaxy at least once, such as these two—NGC 2201, at left, and IC 2163, right—in a NASA photograph from January 2014.

LONELY PLANETS

When galaxies collide, chaotic collisions and disruptions occur. One of the consequences is that planets can be ejected into space, as in this art. Without a star to warm them, these orphaned planets now travel through space alone.

CLOUDS OF MAGELLAN

The twin Magellanic Clouds, or Clouds of Magellan, are not really clouds at all. They're galaxies visible deep in the southern half of the sky. North of the Equator you can't see them. Because of this, they remained unknown to most of the Western world until the voyage of Ferdinand Magellan.

In 1519, he sailed from Spain with a crew of about 270 men, hoping to travel around the world. Magellan died along the way, but 18 members of his crew returned safely in 1522. With them, they brought their observations of the southern sky. When European astronomers used the mariners' records to make sky charts, they named two objects after Magellan, calling those objects the Large and Small Magellanic Clouds.

FACTS ABOUT THE MAGELLANIC CLOUDS

LARGE MAGELLANIC CLOUD

Where to find it	Constellations Dorado and Mensa
Distance	163,000 light-years
Diameter	14,000 light-years
Mass	10 billion solar masses
Number of stars	30 billion

SMALL MAGELLANIC CLOUD

Where to find it	Constellations Tucana and Hydrus
Distance	200,000 light-years
Diameter	7,000 light-years
Mass	7 billion solar masses
Number of stars	3 billion

ABOUT THE CLOUDS

Although they may look like glowing clouds fixed to the sky, the Magellanic Clouds are both irregular galaxies that have been twisted and warped by the Milky Way's gravity.

Astronomers used to think that the Magellanic Clouds were permanent companions of the Milky Way, orbiting around our galaxy. Now scientists generally think these travelers may be "just passing through."

The Large Magellanic Cloud is located about 160,000 light-years from Earth. It's about one-fourteenth as large as our galaxy in diameter and holds about one-tenth as many stars. The Small Magellanic Cloud is located about 200,000 light-years from Earth. It's less massive than its companion and a hundred times smaller than the Milky Way.

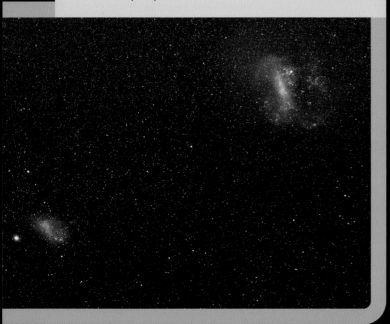

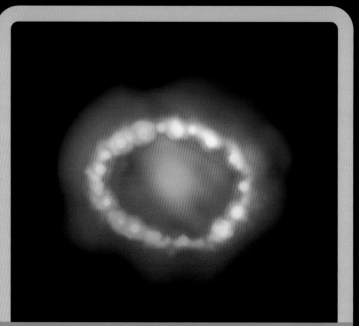

SUPERNOVA 1987A

In February 1987, astronomers spotted an exploding star in the Large Magellanic Cloud. Since it was the first supernova observed that year, it was named Supernova 1987A. This was the closest supernova to Earth seen since the invention of the telescope.

At its brightest, Supernova 1987A shone with the energy of a billion suns and could be seen with the unaided eye despite how far away it was. It slowly faded over time and now is visible only with a telescope.

Debris from Supernova 1987A formed a supernova remnant. Astronomers have searched the remnant looking for a neutron star that might have been created by the explosion, but they haven't found it. The explosion may have created a black hole instead.

SAILING BY THE STARS

When Magellan sailed into the Southern Hemisphere, his crew spotted two objects (top right in art) that no European had seen before. He used them as markers to navigate, not realizing they were actually companions to the Milky Way (middle, reflected on the sea).

SUPER STARS

How far are other galaxies? We never really knew until Henrietta Swan Leavitt (1868-1921) figured it out. Born in Cambridge, Massachusetts, U.S.A., the serious, hardworking young woman graduated from Radcliffe College and went to work at the Harvard College Observatory, earning 30 cents an hour. Her job was to study photographs of thousands of stars in the Magellanic Clouds and measure their brightness. She and her fellow workers were called "computers."

At the time, no one could be sure if another galaxy's stars were bright because they were close, or because they were naturally very bright.

Leavitt realized that she could link one type of star, called a Cepheid variable, to its natural brightness. Knowing that, astronomers could measure any Cepheid's dimness as seen from Earth, compare that to the star's natural brightness, and figure out how far it was. When other galaxies were discovered, scientists looked for Cepheid variables among their stars. Measuring the distances to those stars told scientists how far away their galaxies were. Leavitt's work told us for the first time how big the universe is.

157

CLUSTERS AND WALLS

Astronomers used to think that galaxies were scattered randomly throughout the universe. But when they began mapping galaxies carefully, they were in for a surprise.

In 1989, astronomers Margaret Geller and John Huchra announced that, rather than being random, galaxies are clustered into gigantic structures. Dozens of galaxies they measured were lined up at about the same distance, forming a "great wall." Scientists have found many more walls of galaxies since then.

The universe started out very smooth, with matter spread out almost evenly through space. Over the past 13.8 billion years, gravity has pulled that matter together. Now, the part of the universe close to us is very clumpy.

Galaxy walls, like the one that Geller and Huchra discovered, are huge formations. Along with superclusters—groupings of galaxies—they make up the largest structures in the universe.

THE LARGEST STRUCTURES IN THE UNIVERSE

Hercules-Corona Borealis Great Wall	Diameter: 10 billion light-years
Giant GRB* Ring	Diameter: 5.6 billion light-years
Huge LQG*	Diameter: 4 billion light-years
U1.11 LQG*	Diameter: 2.5 billion light-years
Clowes-Campusano LQG*	Diameter: 2 billion light-years
Sloan Great Wall	Diameter: 1.37 billion light-years

* GRB = gamma-ray burst; LQG = large quasar group, a group of massive, starlike objects at the center of galaxies

FUN FACT
When astronomers map the distant universe, it looks like a bubble bath, with foamy-looking strings and sheets of galaxies separated by huge empty spaces.

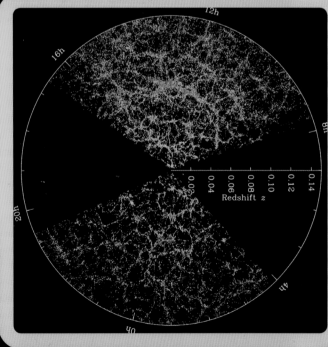

COSMIC WEB

Illuminated in the background by glowing strings of the earliest galaxies, called primordial galaxies, most modern galaxies cluster into huge cosmic walls (art below) pulled together by their mutual gravity. More-distant galaxies are red in color because of dust in the space between us and them. Scientists have discovered that the redder they become, the more they are moving away from us.

FUN FACT

It would take our fastest current spacecraft more than five trillion years to travel from one side of the Sloan Great Wall to the other.

HUBBLE ULTRA DEEP FIELD

In 2004, astronomers unveiled the longest time-length photograph of the sky ever made (shown at right). The Hubble Ultra Deep Field shows an area (a field) of the sky one-fiftieth the size of the full moon, or smaller than a grain of sand held at arm's length. It required a total exposure time of a million seconds, or 11.3 days, and it reveals objects 10 billion times fainter than those that can be seen with the human eye.

"Deep" refers to areas of space outside our solar system. Some galaxies in this photograph are very faint because they're almost 13 billion light-years away. That means we're seeing them as they were 13 billion years ago, when the universe was young.

The Hubble Ultra Deep Field shows approximately 10,000 galaxies. Some are spirals and ellipticals similar to nearby galaxies, but many others are oddballs—galactic toddlers still growing and developing.

The Ultra Deep Field will remain our best view of the early universe until Hubble's successor, the James Webb Space Telescope, is launched in 2021.

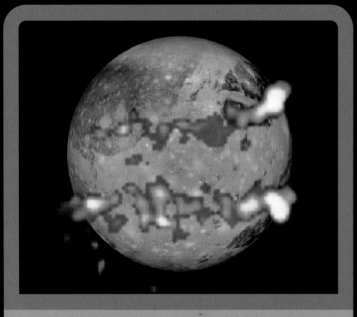

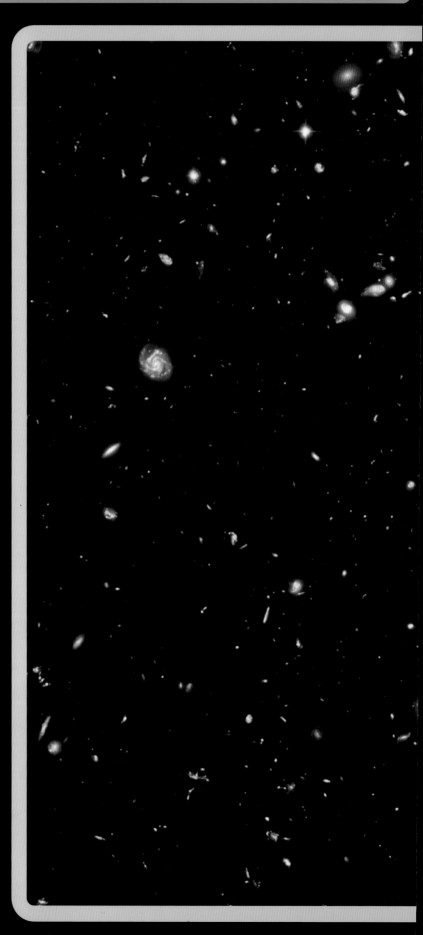

SKY-WATCHER
THE ULTRAVIOLET SKY

Many hot, energetic astronomical objects shine with ultraviolet (UV) light. We can't see this light with our eyes, but specially designed telescopes can capture it. Because our atmosphere blocks UV light, these telescopes need to be in space. Probably the most famous UV observatory is the Hubble Space Telescope. Hubble can see a range of wavelengths of light, including UV light, and has produced some spectacular images. Aurorae on Jupiter's moon Ganymede (above), hot stars in distant galaxies, exoplanet atmospheres, and galaxies billions of light-years away show up brightly in UV light. These are just a few of the objects Hubble has been able to capture.

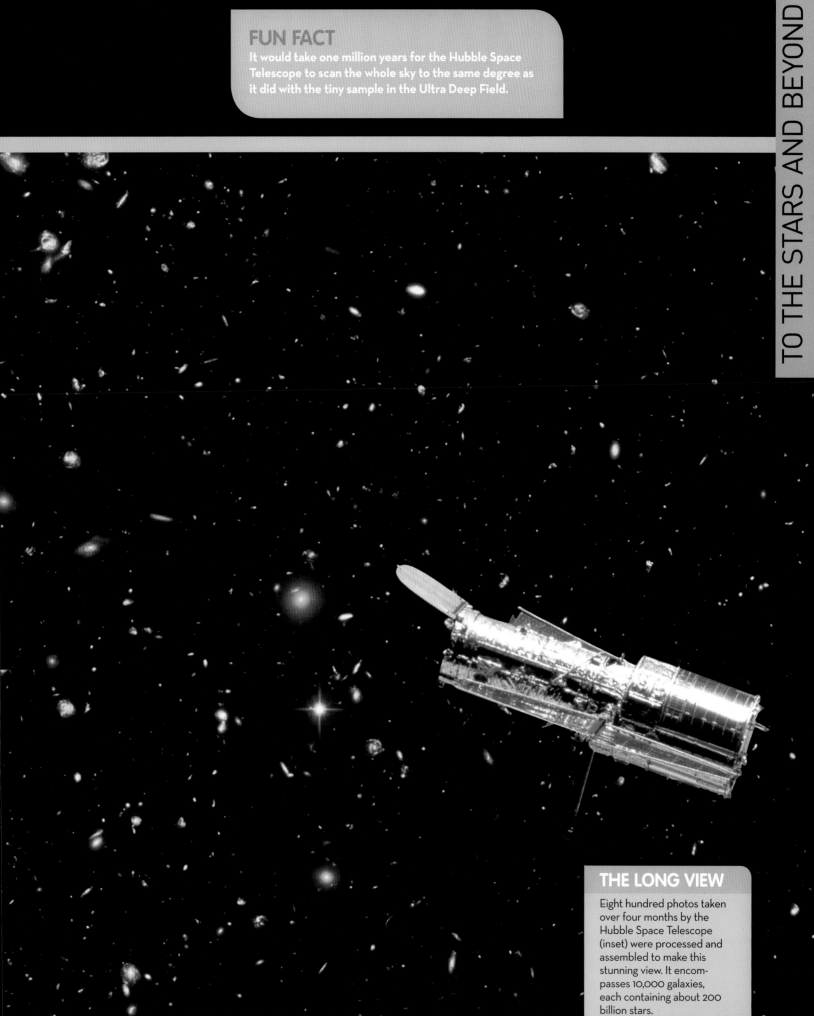

FUN FACT

It would take one million years for the Hubble Space Telescope to scan the whole sky to the same degree as it did with the tiny sample in the Ultra Deep Field.

THE LONG VIEW

Eight hundred photos taken over four months by the Hubble Space Telescope (inset) were processed and assembled to make this stunning view. It encompasses 10,000 galaxies, each containing about 200 billion stars.

DARK MATTER

Seeing the light of very distant galaxies is a great achievement for astronomers. But they face an even more difficult problem: seeing the dark.

Scientists have known since the 1930s that the universe has unseen matter whose gravity pulls on visible matter. No one knows, however, what this dark matter really is. Trying to solve this puzzle is one of the most important problems in modern astronomy.

Some scientists think this mysterious stuff might be made of heavy, dark chunks of matter, such as lightless brown dwarf stars. These kinds of objects are called MACHOs (MAssive Compact Halo Objects). But most scientists think that dark matter probably consists of huge numbers of tiny subatomic particles, known as WIMPs (Weakly Interacting Massive Particles).

They are hunting for these particles using large, sophisticated detectors. For now, though, the true nature of dark matter is a mystery.

Astronomers did find hints of dark matter when they studied rotating spiral galaxies, including the Milky Way. Rotating galaxies are like merry-go-rounds. Their speed depends on how much weight is on them and where it is located, whether in the middle or on the edges.

All the galaxies the astronomers examined were rotating faster than expected—so fast that they should fly apart, scattering stars like riders who aren't holding on to the handles. Strong gravity had to be holding the galaxies together. That gravity came from unseen dark matter.

There are many other clues that dark matter exists. For one, galaxy clusters hold hot intergalactic gas. The gas is so hot that it should escape like steam from a teapot. The gravity of dark matter holds on to it.

In 2006, scientists got more evidence that dark matter is real. They studied a pair of colliding galaxies and found that gas and stars were clustered in one spot, whereas the strongest gravity was concentrated in a different spot. The collision had dragged visible matter and dark matter in opposite directions.

Even the clumpiness of the universe shows that dark matter exists. Without the extra gravity of dark matter, visible matter wouldn't have had time to pull itself together to form galaxies and galaxy clusters. In that sense, we owe our very existence to something we've never seen.

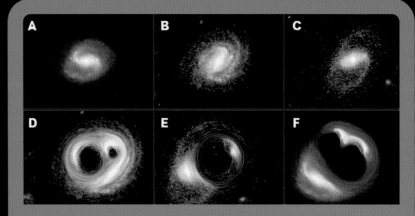

SKY-WATCHER
GRAVITATIONAL LENSES

You know what a lens looks like in eyeglasses or a camera. But what's a gravitational lens?

You won't find it in your household. A gravitational lens is a very massive object in space—a dense collection of galaxies, for instance—that bends the light traveling around it, just as a glass lens bends the light that travels through it. When a gravitational lens is located between a bright, distant object and Earth, the light from that object will be warped or magnified when we see it.

Gravitational lenses help us find dark matter. By studying the distorted light from distant galaxies as it curves around a gravitational lens, as shown in steps A-F above, astronomers can measure how massive the galaxies are. Then they can compare the mass that they can actually "see" with the total mass of the galaxies to figure out how much dark matter the object holds.

FUN FACT
A few scientists believe that dark matter doesn't exist—even though this 2017 Hubble photograph may show it in the dark ring at the center. They think that we just don't understand how gravity works yet.

UNLOCKING A MYSTERY

We thought we knew what the universe was, but we don't. About 95 percent of all matter is unseen and unknown. Astronomers hope to find the door (symbolized in this art) that opens onto the answer to the mystery of dark matter.

THE ACCELERATING UNIVERSE

To understand the accelerating universe, you first have to understand the birth of the universe—the big bang. This was not an explosion that tossed a bunch of atoms and energy into empty space. The big bang was an explosion of space itself. It created space where none existed before. And space is still being created right now.

When we say the universe is expanding, we mean that space itself is expanding. Galaxies rush away from each other not because they are speeding through space, but because the space between them is growing. A galaxy is like a person standing on a moving walkway. The person moves because the walkway moves.

Surprise!

Astronomers thought that the expansion of the universe had been slowing ever since the big bang. The pull of gravity from all the matter in the universe, both normal matter and dark matter, should see to that. The only debate was whether the universe would slow to a stop and reverse, collapsing into a "Big Crunch," or whether the universe would just keep slowing down without ever really stopping.

In 1998, astronomers got a big surprise. Two teams studying distant supernovae found that those star explosions were dimmer than expected. Since light grows dimmer the farther away the light source is, the supernovae were more distant than expected. So the universe must be expanding faster than scientists had expected.

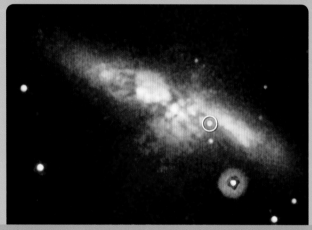

DARK ENERGY

Measurements of how fast supernovae are moving through space have shown us that the universe wasn't just growing faster than we thought; it was actually speeding up. Something must be providing a cosmic push. Astronomers named that mysterious something dark energy. The reverse of gravity, dark energy is pushing things away from each other. This 2014 NASA photograph shows the remnant of a supernova (circled in yellow) that exploded in the Cigar galaxy, M82, in 2014. Its superheated plasma shell blasted out into space at tens of millions of miles an hour.

No one knows what dark energy is, but many scientists are trying to answer that question. So far, it seems that dark energy is a property of space itself. The more space grows due to cosmic expansion, the more dark energy grows, and the more "push" there is to speed up the universe.

Whatever dark energy may be, its influence will decide the fate of our universe.

SKY-WATCHER
SUPERNOVA YARDSTICKS

It can be hard to measure distances in space, especially when it comes to distant stars and galaxies. No one has a yardstick that long! But astronomers have learned that a particular kind of supernova, called a Type Ia, can help them out.

A Type Ia supernova starts with two stars orbiting each other. If one star is a white dwarf, it can pull gas off its partner as they orbit. Eventually, when the white dwarf steals enough gas, it becomes massive enough to explode as a supernova.

These kinds of supernovae have a predictable brightness, so astronomers can compare their brightness as seen on Earth to their true brightness to measure their distances. Astronomers call this kind of measurement a "standard candle." By studying Type Ia supernovae in 1998, astronomers saw that the galaxies that held them were moving away from each other much faster than predicted—a finding that led to the discovery of dark energy.

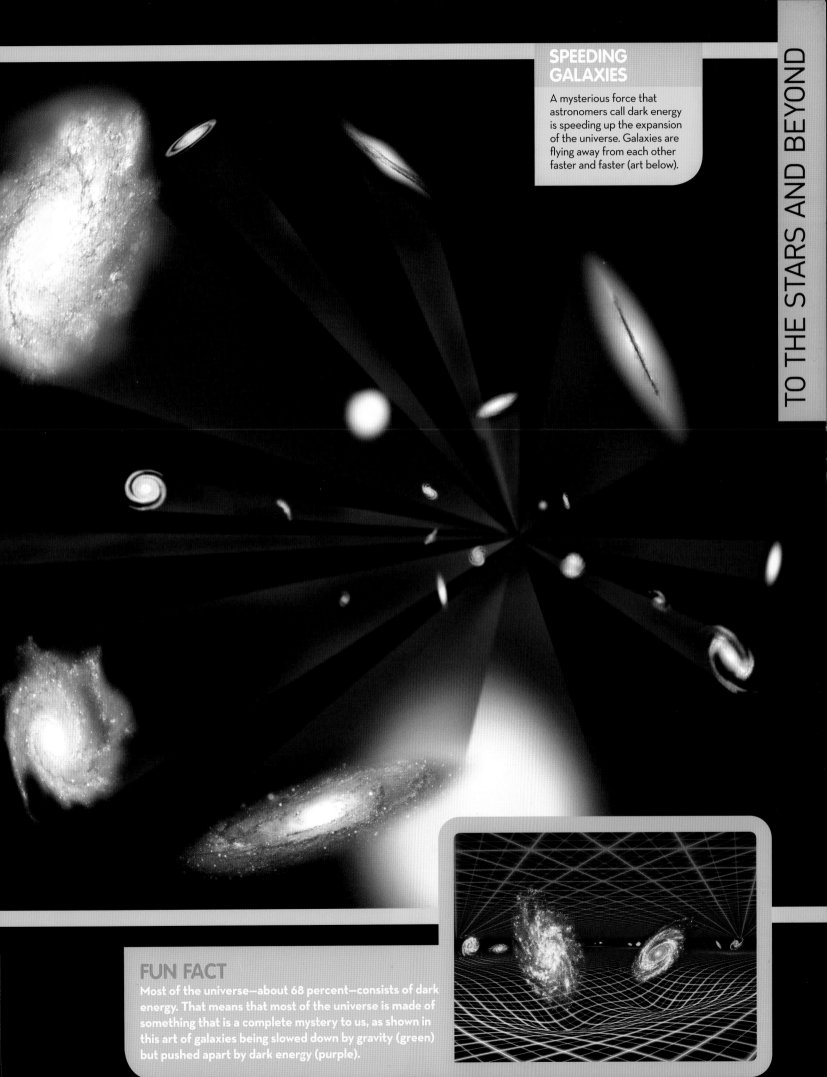

SPEEDING GALAXIES

A mysterious force that astronomers call dark energy is speeding up the expansion of the universe. Galaxies are flying away from each other faster and faster (art below).

FUN FACT

Most of the universe—about 68 percent—consists of dark energy. That means that most of the universe is made of something that is a complete mystery to us, as shown in this art of galaxies being slowed down by gravity (green) but pushed apart by dark energy (purple).

HOW THE UNIVERSE WILL END

We are on a one-way trip. Since the universe is expanding, everything is getting farther and farther apart. At some point, even our closest neighbors will have moved on. Before that happens, however, the Milky Way and Andromeda will collide. In a few billion years, they'll form a new combined galaxy that will pull in all the smaller galaxies in our neighborhood and swallow them up. More-distant galaxies will escape and move beyond our sight, leaving only one visible galaxy: our own.

Astronomers think our galaxy, and our universe, may end in one of two ways. In the "Big Chill" version, the universe will suffer a slow and steady decline. Stars and gases will drift apart and cool down. No new stars will be born. Stars that already exist will live their lives and burn out. Many trillions of years from now, all that will be left is a galaxy of black holes, neutron stars, and cold, black dwarfs that gradually fade away.

In the "Big Rip" version, the universe will expand faster and faster over time. Planets, stars, and galaxies will be violently torn apart, right down to their atoms.

Which version turns out to be correct depends on what we learn about dark energy. When we find out what it is, and whether it will always be in effect, we will know whether the universe will end with a sigh or a bang.

FUN FACT

A third possibility for the end of the universe is called the "Big Crunch" (art below). If dark energy were to slow down for some reason, as represented by the fading orange and yellow track, the universe might collapse back in on itself in a reverse of the big bang. Right now, most astronomers think this is unlikely.

TIMELINE OF A COOLING UNIVERSE

Today	4–8 billion years from now	100 billion–1 trillion years	2 trillion years	100 trillion years and onward
Stars are being created. Our solar system is 4.6 billion years old.	Milky Way and Andromeda galaxies merge.	Local Group galaxies merge.	All distant galaxies vanish from view.	Stars burn out. Eventually, black holes dominate the universe.

BIG CHILL

Tens of billions of years in the future, stars like our sun will have died. In this "Big Chill" scenario, only faint red stars that live for a long time will remain. Those fading embers will shed little warmth on worlds grown cold and quiet (art above).

167

OTHER UNIVERSES

When astronomers speak of the universe, they mean the observable universe—everything that we can see or detect with instruments. But what if there is more out there that we can't observe?

Using mathematics, scientists not only can imagine but also can describe in detail other possible universes, with different laws of physics. This is more than idle speculation. Other universes may actually exist.

To understand this mind-bending idea, consider what the word "dimension" means. In our everyday experience, a dimension is a direction in space. We live in a three-dimensional world—we can move forward and backward, left and right, up and down.

Physicist Albert Einstein showed that time also is a dimension, linked permanently to the other three. Past-future is the fourth dimension. So physicists have described the fabric of the cosmos as being four-dimensional space-time.

A Fifth Dimension?

Recently, physicists have begun to think there may be more than the four familiar dimensions. The true nature of everything may involve many dimensions, but we can't perceive other dimensions with our senses.

We're like ants crawling on the surface of a giant hot-air balloon. The ants perceive only the flat, two-dimensional fabric stretching off in all directions as far as they can see. We perceive four-dimensional space-time stretching in all directions, when actually other dimensions may exist.

Scientists speculate that the visible universe may be a four-dimensional membrane, or brane for short, moving through unseen dimensions. Other branes, or parallel universes, may also exist. We would never be able to communicate with these other universes, much less travel among them.

SUPER STARS

Some scientists study the really big picture: How did the universe begin? Why does it look the way it does? How will it end—or will it end at all? This kind of science is called cosmology. The most famous cosmologist in recent history was probably Stephen Hawking.

Hawking (1942-2018) was born in Oxford, England. He was a brilliant boy who wanted to study math in college. However, University College, Oxford, where he went to school, did not have a math major, so he studied physics instead. Physics came easily to him and he wanted to be challenged, so Hawking went on to Cambridge University, in England. There, he began to study how the universe began and how it might end.

While at Cambridge, the young physicist began to have trouble with his speech and movement. He had developed amyotrophic lateral sclerosis (ALS), a disease that gradually shut down his ability to move or speak. He wasn't expected to live more than a few years. He beat all the medical odds and lived to be 76 years old, getting around with a motorized wheelchair and speaking with computerized help. He was known for his sense of humor and interest in space travel.

Hawking made major contributions to our understanding of the big bang, black holes, and the nature of the universe. "Science predicts that many kinds of universe will be spontaneously created out of nothing," he once said. "It is a matter of chance which we are in."

FUN FACT

Beings living in a flat, two-dimensional world would never be able to see a three-dimensional object, such as a ball. They would only see a circle where the ball met their two-dimensional land.

COLLIDING BRANES

New research suggests that the event we call the big bang actually occurred when our brane collided with a neighboring brane. The collision generated the heat energy and push of expansion that we call the big bang. This art shows two branes colliding then separating, releasing energy that creates stars and galaxies.

BRANE MEETS BRANE

The most recent theory for the birth of our universe suggests that colliding branes (art at right) may be the power source behind the big bang. If such collisions happen over and over, then universes may have been formed and re-formed many times in the past.

THE BIG POP

Astronomers have several ideas about how our universe formed. Some believe that a universe can pop into existence from a black hole (art at left). If that's true, there could be thousands of other universes that we can't detect.

LOL!

Q: How do astronomers start off their bedtime stories?

A: "Once upon a space-time ..."

ARE WE ALONE?

In this imagined, alien world, creatures don't see the colors that we do. Instead, they detect infrared heat like an infrared camera does.

A PERFECT WORLD

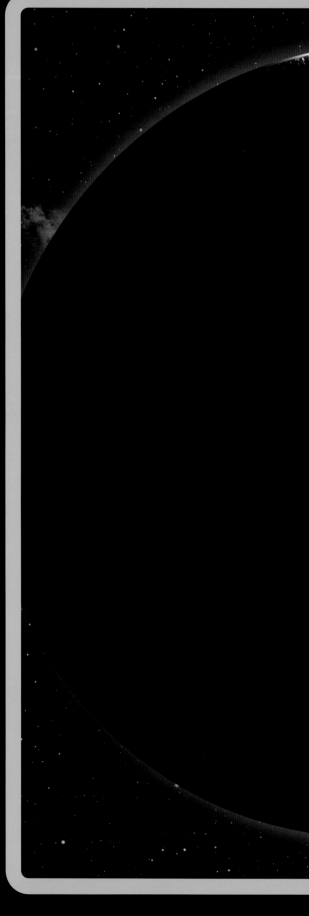

Earth is the perfect world for life. But what makes it so special? Actually, there are a number of things.

To begin with, Earth is in the right orbit circling the sun. Not too hot and not too cold, it has just the right temperature range to support life and keep the water in our oceans from freezing or boiling. Astronomers call this kind of orbit the "habitable zone."

Next, we orbit the right kind of star. Some stars have much shorter lifetimes than ours, leaving little time for life to evolve on the planets orbiting them. Some stars send out lethal amounts of radiation, which fry the surrounding planets and their moons. Our sun is a long-lived, stable star—perfect for supporting life.

Earth is also the right size. It's large enough to generate the gravity needed to hold an atmosphere and not let it float away. We have a stabilizing moon as well, and a tilted axis that moderates weather cycles.

Finally, Earth is located out in an arm of the Milky Way where there aren't devastating explosions. All of these things put together mean we live on a perfect world.

BODIES IN OUR SOLAR SYSTEM'S HABITABLE ZONE

Range	0.38 to 10 AU (1 AU = 1 astronomical unit, 92,955,807 miles/149,597,870 km)
Venus	0.72 AU: too hot due to greenhouse effect
Earth	1 AU: just right to support life
Mars	1.5 AU: cold, slight atmosphere, but life could be possible
Ceres	2.8 AU: too small to hold water; no atmosphere, life cannot survive

FUN FACT
Salt water can hold a lot more heat than air can. Earth's oceans act like big radiators, storing heat and releasing it slowly. They help keep the planet's temperature stable.

JUST RIGHT FOR LIFE

Light from the sun (peeking over the edge of Earth in the art) gives Earth just the right temperatures for life. The moon helps stabilize its rotation. Jupiter protects us from asteroids; its gravity pulls them in before they reach us.

WHAT IS LIFE?

This seems like such an easy question to answer. Everybody knows singing birds are alive and rocks are not. When we start studying plants, bacteria, and other odd microscopic creatures, though, things get more complicated. So what exactly is life?

Most scientists agree that if something moves on its own, reproduces to make more copies of itself, grows in size to become more complex in structure over time, takes in nutrients to survive, gives off waste products, and responds to external stimuli such as increased sunlight and changes in temperature, it's alive!

Biologists classify living organisms by how they get their energy. Algae, green plants, and some bacteria use sunlight as an energy source. Human beings, fungi, and some archaea use chemicals to provide energy. When we eat food, chemicals in our digestive system turn the food into fuel.

Living things inhabit land, sea, and air. Life also thrives deep beneath the oceans and embedded in rocks miles below Earth's crust, in ice, and in other extreme environments. The life-forms that thrive in these environments are called extremophiles. Some of these draw directly upon the chemicals surrounding them for energy. Since these are very different forms of life than what we're used to, we may not think of them as alive, but they are. If there is life on Mars, Titan, or somewhere else in the solar system, it could be like these extremophiles, and if we find it, we want to be sure to recognize it as life.

Bacteria

To understand how a living organism works, it helps to look at one example of its simplest form—the single-cell bacteria called streptococcus. There are many kinds of these tiny organisms, and some are responsible for human illnesses. What makes us sick or uncomfortable are the waste products the bacteria give off in our bodies.

A single streptococcus bacterium is so small that at least 500 of them could fit on the dot above this letter *i*. Under a microscope, magnified to a thousand times their true size, they look like little round water balloons joined in long strings. Like a water balloon, they have an outside covering. Sort of like the skin on our bodies, this cell membrane separates the outside world from the inside, working parts of the bacterium. Inside the membrane, thousands of molecules in different shapes and structures float in a gel.

These bacteria are among the simplest forms of life we know. They have no moving parts, no lungs, no brain, no heart, no liver, no leaves or fruit. And yet, this life-form reproduces and makes more of itself, grows in size by producing long chain structures, takes in nutrients, and gives off toxins. That's why your body runs a temperature when it detects a strep infection. It's defending itself from a living invader!

How did a random collection of nonliving molecules come together, get organized, and become alive? We're not sure, but these are questions scientists are trying to answer.

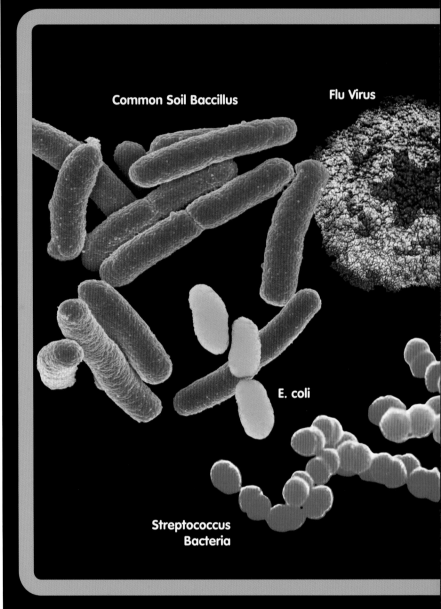

Common Soil Baccillus

Flu Virus

E. coli

Streptococcus Bacteria

EXAMPLES OF EXTREMOPHILES

Acidophil	Lives in acidic environments, such as hot springs
Anaerobe	Lives in places without oxygen, such as the deep ocean
Cryophile	Lives in places with temperatures far below freezing, such as Antarctica
Halophile	Lives in very salty environments, such as the Dead Sea
Hyperthermophile	Lives in places with temperatures close to, or above, the boiling point, such as deep-sea vents
Radioresistant	Lives in environments with high radiation, such as uranium mines
Xerophile	Lives in extremely dry environments, such as deserts

THE SMALLEST LIFE

Scientists think life began on Earth some 4.1 to 3.9 billion years ago, but no fossils exist from that time. The earliest fossils ever found are from the primitive life that existed 3.6 billion years ago. Other life-forms soon followed, and some of these are shown in the images below. Scientists continue to study how life evolved on Earth and whether it is possible that life exists on other planets.

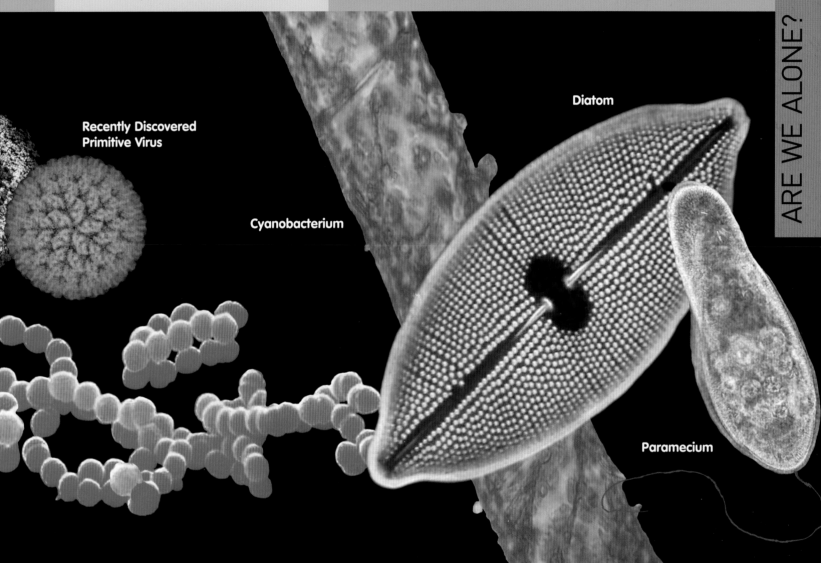

Recently Discovered Primitive Virus

Cyanobacterium

Diatom

Paramecium

SUPER STARS

The invention of the lens was important not only for astronomy but also for biology. Without microscopes, early scientists couldn't see all the teeming microbes that make up so much of life. One of the first people to truly explore this formerly invisible world was the Dutch inventor Antoni van Leeuwenhoek (1632-1723). Born in Delft, in what was then the Dutch Republic, Leeuwenhoek was not educated as a scientist. He was a draper—a cloth merchant. He began making his own glass lenses and microscopes as a hobby. Purely out of his own interest, he began looking at everyday objects with these microscopes: worms, seeds, insects, and more. In letters to Britain's scientific Royal Society, he was the first to describe seeing microscopic single-cell organisms, which he called "animalcules," in water. "[The] motion of most of these animalcules in the water was so swift, and so various upwards, downwards and round about that 'twas wonderful to see: and I judged that some of these little creatures were above a thousand times smaller than the smallest ones I have ever yet seen." The scientists were so skeptical about this that they sent some observers to visit Leeuwenhoek and make sure what he was saying was true. The visitors discovered Leeuwenhoek's findings were correct. The Dutch amateur's discoveries made him famous as the father of microbiology.

IT'S NOT AN ALIEN—
but it could be! The tardigrade, shown here in a greatly magnified electron microscope image, is an animal from right here on Earth.
These eight-legged creatures are only the size of a grain of sand, but they are extremely tough. They live in every environment from deserts to volcanoes to Antarctic waters. Experiments show they can even survive in the vacuum of outer space.

OTHER LIFE IN THE SOLAR SYSTEM

n 1976, when a Viking lander set down on the surface of Mars, no Martians were there to greet it. In one moment, the hope of finding intelligent life on Mars vanished. Now, more than 40 years later, no traces of life, not even microbes, have been discovered on Mars. The planet appears to be a vast desert wasteland. The surface water it used to have is locked up in the frozen polar ice caps or underground. Life-supporting liquid water doesn't exist on the surface anymore. However, the Curiosity rover is investigating an area of the planet to find out if conditions were once suitable for microbial life.

On Venus, life might have existed billions of years ago, but today the planet's extreme atmospheric pressure and heat would crush or cook life.

A few scientists still hold out hope that alien forms of life may be found bobbing along like cosmic jellyfish in the upper cloud layers of Venus or Jupiter, but this is very unlikely. So where else do we search for life in our solar system? The answer is three distant moons—one circling Jupiter and two orbiting Saturn.

Jupiter's moon Europa has dark, salty oceans under a thick shell of ice. A lake on the moon has also been discovered. Studies have hinted that other moons could also carry liquid water, and maybe even life. There are three conditions on Europa, though, that may bump it off the list for harboring life. First, its oceans are not just dark—they're pitch black. No sunlight penetrates through the ice. Life could form without sunlight, but it would be much more difficult for that to happen. Second, the water is too acidic to support life. Third, Europa is bathed in lethal radiation emitted by Jupiter. Anything on or near the surface of Europa's icy world would be killed. If there is life on this moon, it will surely be small and very hardy. And if there are warm, hydrothermal vents on the ocean floor, it will probably be living in the thick ooze next to them.

Saturn's moon Titan may be another place to look for life in our solar system. There's a good chance Titan's methane-rich atmosphere may be the result of primitive living organisms. Underneath its frozen methane lakes, there may be layers of liquid ammonia. Even though it's poisonous to life on our planet today, ammonia wasn't harmful to the first life-forms on Earth. So if there is life on Titan, it could be similar to early life on Earth, but not like any kind of life here now.

Life of some sort may also be found on Saturn's moon Enceladus (see sidebar opposite).

WHERE MIGHT WE FIND LIFE?

Venus	Probably too hot, but could support life in its atmosphere
Mars	Very cold and dry, but may have life under the surface
Europa	Life possible near the floor of its subsurface ocean
Titan	Very cold, but has the chemicals that could support life
Enceladus	Very cold on surface, but has a subsurface ocean and chemicals that could support life

DISTANT LAKES

On Saturn's moon Titan there are whole lakes of liquid methane, which would usually appear greenish blue. In this image of Titan's surface, taken on the Cassini flyby mission in 2006, the lakes look lavender, but that's because NASA assigned that color to the Cassini photographs to make them easier to identify.

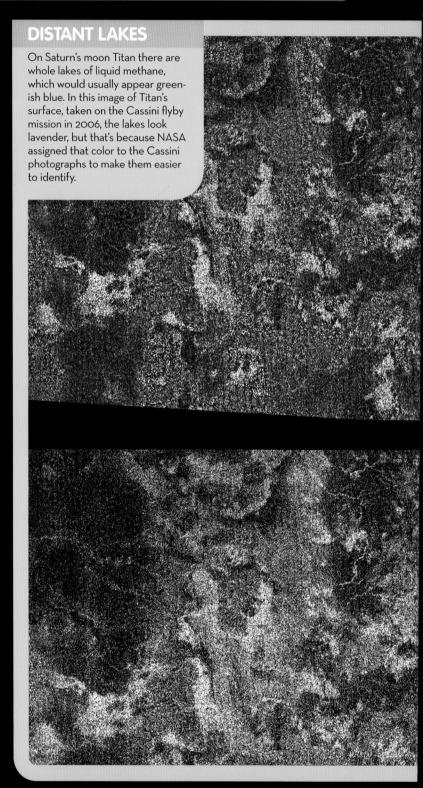

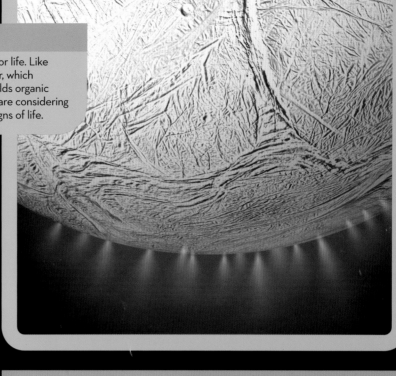

GREAT GEYSERS

Enceladus, another of Saturn's moons, is also a good candidate for life. Like Europa, it has an ocean of liquid water beneath its ice. This water, which regularly sprays into space from cracks in the moon's surface, holds organic chemicals such as methane. Both NASA and private companies are considering sending spacecraft to fly through these watery jets to look for signs of life.

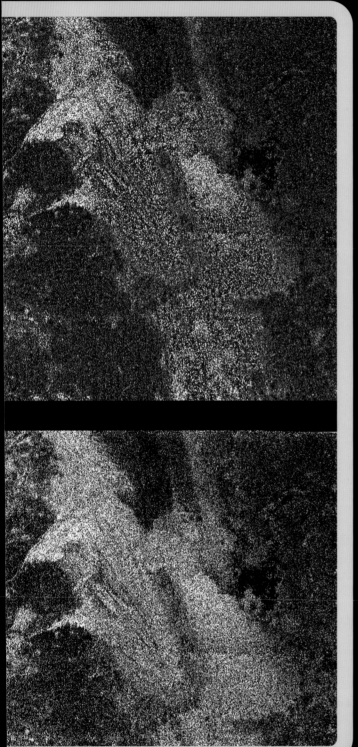

EUROPA'S OCEANS

After drilling through almost half a mile (0.8 km) of ice, a futuristic hydrobot (art right) probes Europa's dark waters. Surface temperatures are frigid here, but the gravitational pull of Jupiter and possible volcanic activity on the ocean floor may keep the deeper water from freezing.

FUN FACT

Jupiter's big moon Ganymede also has an ocean, but it's hard to get to: It's buried deep under 95 miles (150 km) of icy crust.

179

ARE THERE OTHER INTELLIGENT BEINGS?

The possibility that intelligent beings exist out there on other worlds is something humans have imagined for a long, long time. Though there may be some forms of life on Jupiter's or Saturn's moons, there's probably no other intelligent life in the solar system.

To find intelligent life, we have to look elsewhere. Astronomers have discovered more than 3,800 planets circling nearby stars, with more being found all the time. Many of them are giant worlds, either very hot or very cold. Some have properties similar to Earth's.

Scientists are pretty certain we won't find intelligent life on the big, hot or cold worlds. However, the small, Earthlike planets are more promising.

There are two theories about the source of intelligent life beyond Earth. Many scientists believe intelligent life is a natural part of evolution and is common throughout the universe.

Another group believes intelligent life is rare and begins in one place, then spreads to other worlds. In other words, one species ends up colonizing many other worlds.

For more than 50 years, organizations have been listening for radio messages sent by other intelligent civilizations. So far, no ETs (extraterrestrials) have sent us a text or left a return address. But there are billions of cosmic bodies to try to listen to. NASA hopes to narrow the list of those bodies in the next few years.

In 2009, NASA launched the Kepler mission. The spacecraft's telescope studies more than 100,000 stars in our galaxy, identifying those with potential Earthlike planets circling them. Kepler and ground-based telescopes have so far discovered dozens of planets that are near-Earth size and in the habitable zone of their star. In the next 10 years, we could find our first intelligent, alien civilization.

SETI@HOME

You could be the first person to discover a signal from intelligent aliens. In 1999, scientists at the University of California, Berkeley, set up a volunteer computing project called SETI@home. (SETI stands for Search for ExtraTerrestrial Intelligence.) The scientists were searching for meaningful radio signals from space—but there was too much information for any one computer to handle. So they came up with software that could be installed on anyone's home computer and, now, even on smartphones. When the computer is not otherwise in use, the software analyzes radio signals collected by telescopes such as the Arecibo Observatory in Puerto Rico (above). Every time the software detects a suspicious signal, it sends it to a SETI database. Millions of people take part in SETI@home. So far, they've detected millions of unusual signals. Probably almost all of them are not significant—but users are optimistic that one day soon, they'll hear from a real ET.

THE DRAKE EQUATION

$$N = R_* \times f_P \times n_e \times f_e \times f_i \times f_c \times L$$

More than 50 years ago, astronomer Frank Drake came up with this equation to figure out how many intelligent civilizations might exist in our galaxy. He considered the possible number of civilizations that might be capable of communicating, the fraction of stars with planets, average number of planets and how many could support life, how many would have intelligent beings who wanted to communicate, and how long those civilizations might last. Based on his assumptions and today's knowledge, there could be a few thousand alien civilizations somewhere out there among the hundreds of billions of stars in our galaxy.

FUN FACT

People sometimes say that our TV transmissions would reach aliens in space, but in reality the TV signals are too weak and not aimed at outer space. However, aliens might pick up radar signals from military early warning systems or the signals from our power grid.

NOT LIKE US

On this imagined distant world (art below), alien technology is advanced and similar to our own. But the aliens, shown in the foreground, don't resemble us at all.

ALIEN LIFE:
NOT WHAT WE ARE USED TO

The aliens in Hollywood are created so people will buy movie tickets, not to be examples of the weirdness of biology. What really lives out there may be beyond anything we can imagine, let alone deal with. There could be two-foot (0.6-m)-long green garden slugs that communicate using odors and see only in x-ray wavelengths of light. There have been some rather strange creatures here on our own world, too. If Earth hadn't had a run-in with an asteroid 65 million years ago, there might be some even stranger ones walking around today—and we wouldn't be one of them.

Before the asteroid hit, there was an Earth creature with two arms, two legs, and a head with two eyes. It stood upright and was about 6.5 feet (2 m) tall. Its name was *Troodon formosus,* and it was a dinosaur. After the asteroid hit and the climate changed, this contender was knocked out of the race. Earth didn't become a planet of Dinopeople.

On other worlds, alien senses and anatomies may be so different that we won't even begin to be able to relate to them. They certainly won't look and talk like the aliens on *Star Trek.* If there were just slight changes in some of the physical conditions we take for granted here on Earth, life might follow some very odd pathways. If a planet had less gravity than Earth, life might grow taller and thinner. On a high-gravity world, body shapes might be shorter and more muscular. On a world with a thinner atmosphere, lungs might be larger and ears much bigger to pick up faint sounds. On freezing worlds or ocean planets, new shapes and adaptations would certainly appear. And what about life that looks nothing like anything we've ever seen? The creatures imagined in Hollywood may not look nearly as strange as the ones designed by nature.

FUN FACT
Carl Sagan and a co-author wrote that Jupiter could in theory support aliens that look like huge gas-bags, floating in herds in the planet's atmosphere.

LIFE ON AN OCEAN WORLD

This artwork imagines a planet that was mostly covered by oceans until very late in its history. The intelligent creatures here (top) quickly moved from the sea to the emerging volcanoes. There, the creatures rapidly discovered the use of fire, electricity, and nuclear fusion, and they made fast advances in technology.

LIFE ON A STEAM WORLD

This hot, humid imaginary world (art below) is a little too close to its own sun. Its odd creatures stand almost nine feet (2.7 m) tall and move slowly away when approached. The upper, baggy part of their bodies is filled with helium, like a party balloon. They pose no threat to visitors, and they seem to communicate by using electrical impulses.

SUPER STARS

Carl Sagan (1934-1996) was the first modern astronomer to also become a popular author and television star. He grew up in Brooklyn, New York, U.S.A., loved reading science fiction, and was greatly impressed by a visit to the 1939 World's Fair, which had exhibits on the world of tomorrow. After earning a Ph.D. in astronomy, Sagan became a well-known scholar in planetary science. He also started studying the possibilities of extraterrestrial life and became famous for his astronomy series on TV, *Cosmos*.

In 1972, NASA was planning to launch the Pioneer 10 and Pioneer 11 spacecraft, the first to fly past Jupiter and onward out of the solar system. At the last minute, NASA decided to attach metal plaques to each spacecraft as a message to any aliens the craft might meet. Sagan and astronomer Frank Drake (see page 180) decided that science and math were universal languages. They designed plaques that show the solar system and distances from the sun to the center of the Milky Way and to the center of 14 different pulsars, rapidly rotating neutron stars. The plaques also show an image of a hydrogen atom, and the figures of a man and a woman. Both spacecraft have long since stopped communicating with Earth. We don't know if any aliens have spotted them yet on their trip into the galaxy.

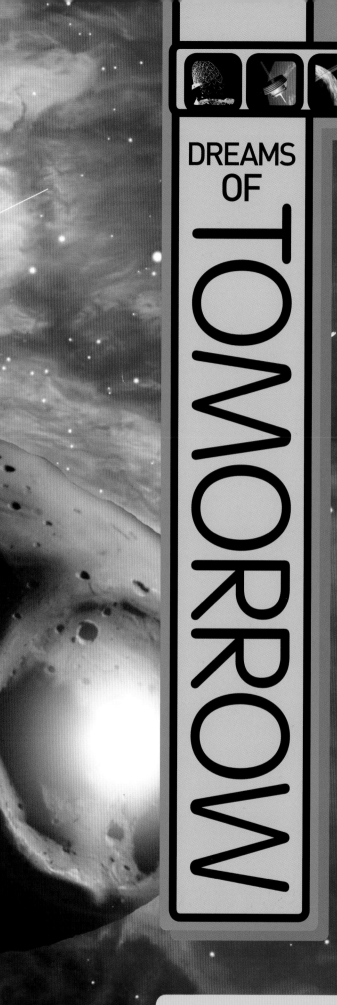

DREAMS OF TOMORROW

In the future, small supply ships and spaceships made from hollowed-out asteroids could service space stations.

SPACE ENGINEERING

O ur close neighbors in space—the moon and nearby asteroids—could give us new resources and new homes for our engineering projects. These resources will help us continue our exploration of the stars. Here are a few ways we might use the moon and asteroids in the future.

A Telescope on the Moon

Airless, cold, and dead quiet, the moon is not a garden spot. It could be the ideal place for gazing into space, however. Radio telescopes could be placed there first, to capture radio waves from distant stars and planets. Placing the telescopes on the far side of the moon would shield them from interfering radio waves from Earth.

Next to be built might be a liquid mirror telescope (LMT). The light-collecting surface of an LMT could be made of a salty liquid that doesn't freeze at lunar temperatures. Astronomers say that an LMT could be built at either of the moon's poles. Since the moon has no air, clouds, or city lights to get in the way, an LMT there might allow us to see farther than ever before.

Asteroid Treasures

As people begin to colonize the inner solar system, they'll need to build homes and labs, space stations and hotels. The raw materials for these buildings may well come from asteroids. Thousands of these chunks of rock, ice, and metal orbit close to Earth. Many are rich in iron and nickel; some contain platinum and gold. They also hold "rare-earth" metals that are valuable for batteries and lasers. The ice in asteroids could be used for water, oxygen, and rocket fuel.

Asteroid miners could be humans or robots. They would dig the metal and ice out of the asteroid and ship it out on space freighters.

SKY-WATCHER
NAMING ASTEROIDS

You don't have to be a professional astronomer to discover asteroids as in this NASA artist's view of an asteroid belt around the bright star Vega. Many amateur sky-watchers with good backyard telescopes and cameras have found them. When you discover an asteroid, you get to name it. At first, the Minor Planet Center will give it a temporary name that includes the year it was discovered, such as 2019 VB12. Then you (the discoverer) can suggest a formal name. It should be no more than 16 characters long, be pronounceable, and not be offensive. Asteroid names include Camelot, James Bond, Purple Mountain, and David Aguilar—the artist for this book!

LUNAR SCOPES

Two radio telescopes (art right), part of a larger group, could look toward space from the moon's surface. These telescopes would pick up radio waves, not visible light, from all kinds of objects: stars, nebulae, galaxies, even planets. Signals picked up by a group of telescopes can be combined into one big image.

ASTEROIDS

Asteroid miners, both humans and robots, could carry metals and ice from an asteroid to a space freighter (art below). Scientists on the spacecraft would break down the ice into oxygen and hydrogen for fuel, and the asteroid's metal would be flown where it was needed.

TYPES OF ASTEROIDS

C-type	Contain a lot of water and carbon
S-type	Contain metals such as iron, nickel, cobalt, gold, and platinum
M-type	Contain mostly iron and nickel

SPACE HOTEL

The space taxi is waiting. Mars-bound astronauts climb into the little craft, buckle up, and lift off from Earth. Soon they see their next stop: a huge spaceship soaring past in the dark. Their pilot pulls alongside, carefully bringing the taxi's speed to 13,000 miles an hour (21,000 km/h) to match the big craft's. With a few more delicate maneuvers, the pilot docks the taxi, and the astronauts enter their new home away from home: the moving Mars hotel.

Traveling to Mars on a regular spacecraft has some serious problems: The journey would require a huge amount of expensive fuel, and being weightless for a long time can badly weaken human bones and muscles. But "space hotels," also called cyclers, that ride the solar system's gravitational forces in a never ending loop between Mars and Earth wouldn't require much fuel, and each one would spin to create a kind of artificial gravity for the travelers inside. Cycler hotels could be the healthiest, cheapest, and most comfortable way to visit our planetary neighbor.

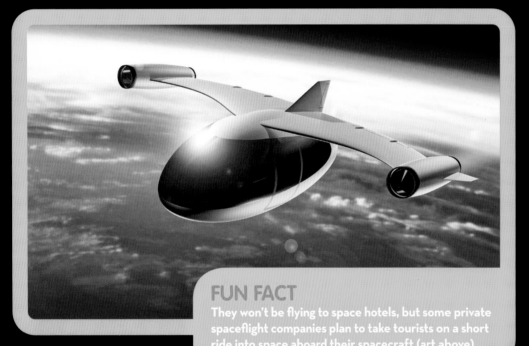

FUN FACT

They won't be flying to space hotels, but some private spaceflight companies plan to take tourists on a short ride into space aboard their spacecraft (art above).

SUPER STARS

Long trips through outer space need expert planning. Who better to do that than an astronaut who is also a doctor and an engineer? Mae Jemison (b. 1956) is all of those things. Raised in Chicago, she is a doctor who worked with the Peace Corps in Africa. She has a degree in chemical engineering and has studied computer science. (She also speaks Russian, Japanese, and Swahili as well as English.) In 1992, Jemison flew on the space shuttle *Endeavor* as a science specialist. After she left NASA, she worked on improving health care in Africa. But that's not all, she also turned to a more futuristic project: heading up the 100 Year Starship, a research group that studies what would be needed to send humans on extended voyages through space. Dr. Jemison points out that as we solve the problems of long-distance space travel, we will solve problems that people face on our own planet as well. Just as on a spacecraft, we need to keep the environment healthy and self-sustaining on spaceship Earth.

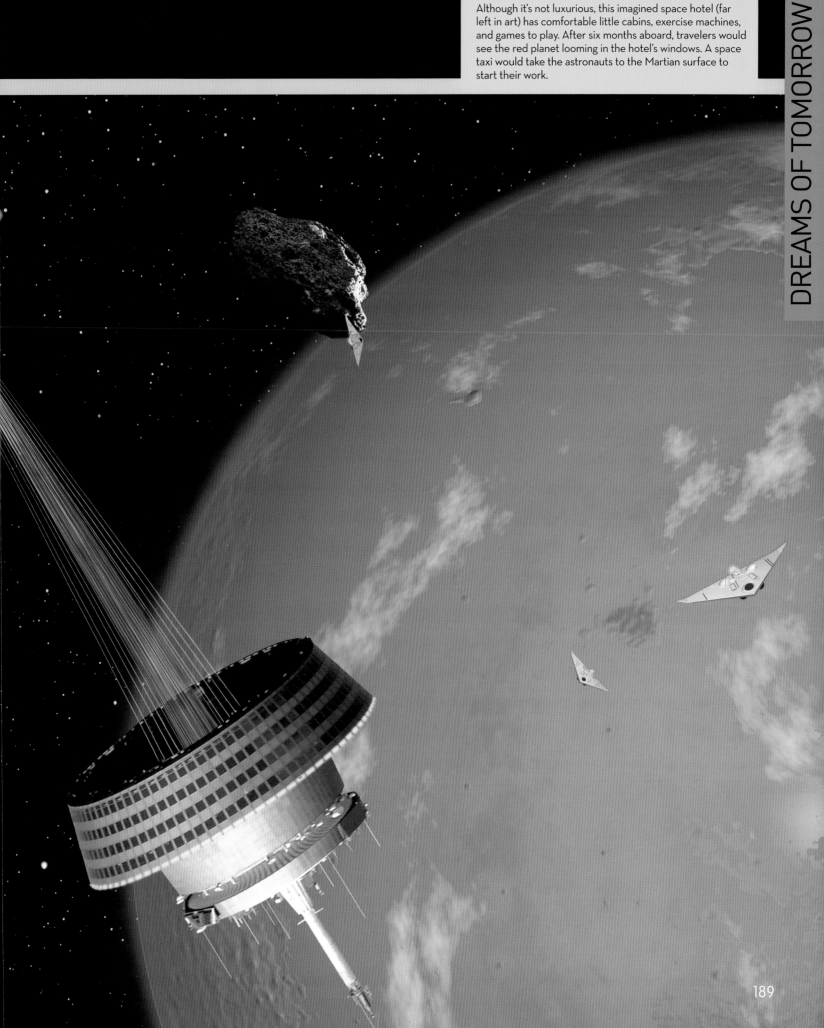

AN EASY TRIP

Although it's not luxurious, this imagined space hotel (far left in art) has comfortable little cabins, exercise machines, and games to play. After six months aboard, travelers would see the red planet looming in the hotel's windows. A space taxi would take the astronauts to the Martian surface to start their work.

THE FIRST HUMANS TO live and work on Mars will face many challenges. They will have to wear high-tech space suits in order to breathe and to block dangerous radiation. They'll live in domed habitats and drive bulky rovers across the rough Martian surface. They will build greenhouses to grow their own food, and will need to extract water from Martian ice. In time, though, settlers can build a self-supporting colony and become citizens of Mars.

TURNING MARS GREEN

Mars is a frigid desert with thin, unbreathable air. But some scientists believe the planet could be transformed into a warm, green, Earthlike home by "terraforming" it. Terraforming means to change something to make it like Earth. Terraforming Mars would be a huge project, taking hundreds or even thousands of years. The first step would be to make the Martian atmosphere warmer and thicker. This might be done by putting huge mirrors in orbit around the planet. The mirrors would focus the sun's rays on Mars's south pole and turn the carbon dioxide trapped in the polar ice into gas. Once in the atmosphere, the carbon dioxide would help hold heat next to the planet's surface.

This warmer atmosphere would melt the water ice now frozen in the soil, creating oceans and rivers. Then green plants could be grown to take in carbon dioxide and give off oxygen, which humans need to breathe. It would take a long time, but one day, people might be able to stroll around on Mars among green trees rustling in the wind.

1 MARS TODAY

A cold and rocky desert, the red planet can't support human life. Its red tint in this photograph (left) comes from the iron in its soil. The planet stays chill under an average temperature of minus 80°F (-62°C). The atmosphere is 95 percent carbon dioxide and 100 times thinner than Earth's.

TERRAFORMING MARS STEP-BY-STEP

YEAR 1

The first crews come and go. They live in shelters that were put in place by earlier, robotic missions. These first astronauts do research, add to the shelters, and set up factories that will give off greenhouse gases.

YEAR 100

Orbiting mirrors focus sunlight onto the planet's surface. The heat melts subsurface ice and releases carbon dioxide into the atmosphere. The air begins to thicken and get warmer. Humans start to live in permanent indoor colonies, walking outside only with the help of space suits.

YEAR 200

Rain begins to fall. Tiny plants such as algae begin to grow and turn parts of the planet green.

YEAR 600

Larger green plants and trees spread across the surface. The atmosphere gets warmer and wetter. Lakes and rivers fill in deeper areas.

YEAR 1,000

Oxygen is still low, but humans can walk on the green surface with simple oxygen masks or other breathing gear. Fusion-powered cities hold thousands of Martian citizens. The planet is green and blue, with some high areas, including mountaintops and high plateaus, still dry and red.

2 GOING GREEN

After creating a thicker atmosphere by melting ice from Mars's poles, scientists could bring in specially engineered plants from Earth. Grown in the warmest regions of Mars, the plants would take in carbon dioxide and give off breathable oxygen.

FUN FACT

Some plans for terraforming Mars include hitting the planet with asteroids. The heat from the impacts would heat up spots on the planet. Ammonia on some asteroids is a greenhouse gas, and it could help warm up the atmosphere as well.

3 BLUE MARS

Under a thicker, warmer atmosphere fed by green plants, ice at Mars's poles and under the planet's surface would melt. Rivers would flow again on the surface and fill in ancient basins, creating oceans (below).

SOLAR SAILING

We don't always need rocket fuel to travel through space. Sometimes, a big sail is enough.

Two solar sailers have launched into space in the past decade, one from the United States, called NanoSail-D, and the other from Japan. The Japanese solar sail, IKAROS, launched in March 2010 and flew past Venus in December 2010. By 2013, it was traveling at close to 900 miles an hour (1,450 km/h). It was still in orbit around the sun in 2015.

The idea behind solar sailing is pretty simple. Light is made of extremely tiny particles called photons. When photons bounce off objects, they push on those objects just a little bit. On Earth, we don't notice this because other forces, like friction in the air, are so much stronger. But in space, where there is no air to get in the way, the gentle pressure of photons from the sun is enough to move a lightweight object.

Sunlight bouncing off a solar sail moves it—and the spacecraft attached to it—very slowly at first. Over time, the solar sailer picks up speed, moving faster and faster. By the time the sailer passes the outer planets, it can be traveling at 45,000 miles an hour (72,000 km/h).

SOLAR SAILING
TRAVEL TIME FROM EARTH

Venus	0.5 year
Mars	1.1 years
Mercury	1.6 years
Jupiter	2 years
Saturn	3.3 years
Uranus	5.8 years
Neptune	8.5 years

LOL!

Q: What did the solar sailer tell the ray of light?

A: Don't be so pushy!

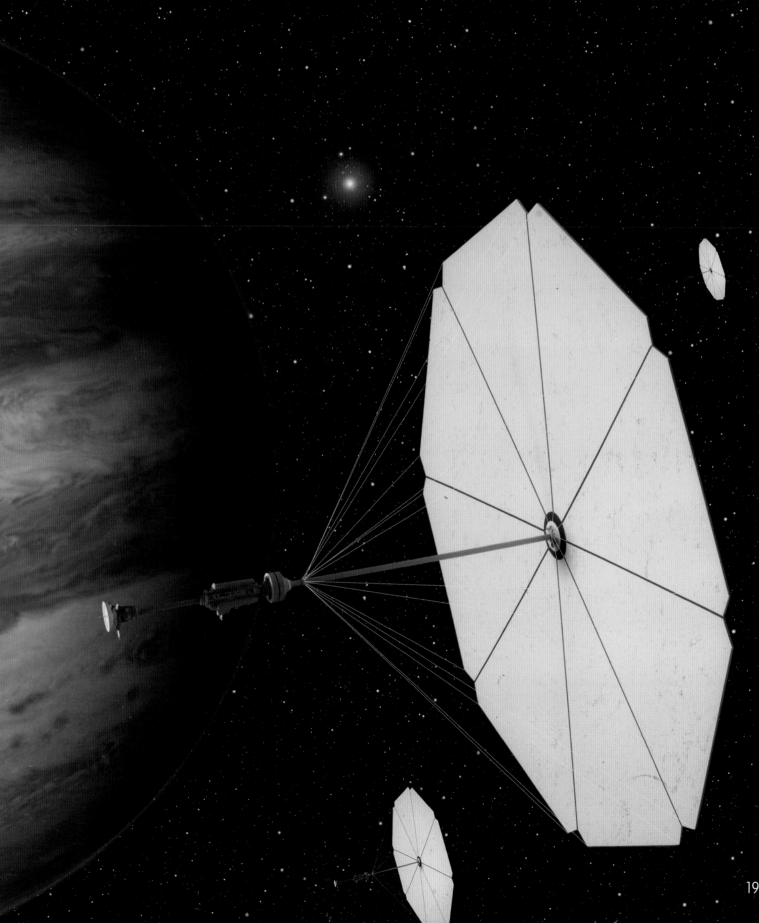

FUN FACT

Some scientists want to launch a swarm of tiny, chip-size spacecraft to other solar systems to learn more about them. Each one would be powered by a solar sail a few feet across. Laser beams from Earth would speed them on their way.

WINGS IN SPACE

Solar sails can be made of shiny metallic cloth thinner than a butterfly's wing. They are also large. The U.S. solar sail NanoSail-D, measuring 100 square feet (9.3 sq m), was one-fourth the size of a football field.

EXPLORING THE UNIVERSE

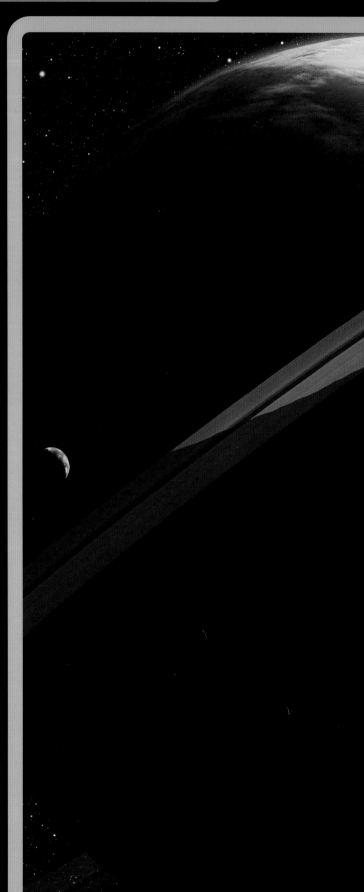

Human exploration will not be limited to our solar system. Now that we know that planets are common around other stars, we will have to visit them. And where better to start than with the closest neighbor to our solar system, Proxima Centauri?

Proxima Centauri, also known as Alpha Centauri C, is a red dwarf star. Along with Alpha Centauri A and Alpha Centauri B, it is part of a triple star system. In 2013, tiny wobbles in the motion of the star told astronomers that an Earth-size planet was orbiting it. The planet, known as Proxima Centauri b, is rocky, like Earth, and seems to be a little larger than our planet. It orbits very close to its parent star, but because that star is cool and small, the planet is still inside the habitable zone that could make life possible. Solar flares from the star might have turned it into a desert. However, if it has a thick atmosphere or a strong magnetic field, any life there could be protected from that threat.

As stellar distances go, Proxima Centauri b is right next door. If we send a probe, what will we find there? A bright blue and green world, like our own Earth? New forms of life? When we look at Proxima Centauri b, what will look back at us?

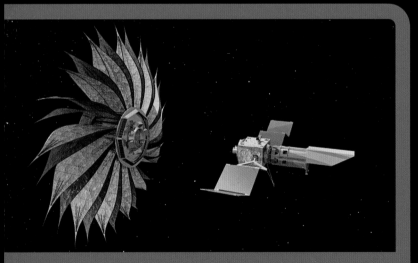

SKY-WATCHER
STARSHADES

A few dozen planets so far have been discovered by direct imaging: that is, by seeing the planet directly in our telescopes. Spotting these distant worlds against the light of their suns is really hard. It's like seeing a speck of dust in the glare of a huge spotlight. So NASA scientists are designing a starshade to help out. Shaped like a huge sunflower blossom, the starshade would float in space between a space telescope and the distant sun it is observing. Almost as wide as a baseball diamond, it would block the sun's glare and allow the telescope to spot the exoplanet.

MOST EARTHLIKE EXOPLANETS

Exoplanet	Distance from Earth	Mass (Earth = 1)
Proxima Centauri b	4.2 light-years	1.3
TRAPPIST-1f	39 light-years	0.7
Kepler 186-f	558 light-years	1.4
Kepler 442-b	1,120 light-years	2.3
Kepler 62-f	1,200 light-years	2.8

TERRA II

After a journey lasting nearly 30 years, the starship Columbus, launched by the inhabitants of Earth, 4.2 light-years away, arrives at the blue-green ringed world Terra II orbiting the dwarf star Proxima Centauri. Terra II is the first planet to be explored for life beyond our own solar system.

GLOSSARY

ASTEROID A rocky body, measuring from less than one mile to 600 miles (1.6–966 km) in diameter, in orbit around a sun. Most asteroids in our solar system are found between the orbits of Mars and Jupiter.

ASTRONOMICAL UNIT (AU) A unit of measurement that is about the average distance between Earth and the sun: specifically, 92,955,807.3 miles (149,597,870.7 km)

ATMOSPHERE The gases surrounding a planet, star, or satellite

AURORA Glowing lights in a planet's atmosphere, caused by atoms moving through the planet's magnetic field

AXIS A straight line around which a body, such as a planet, rotates

BIG BANG A sudden expansion of space that scientists believe was the initial event in the formation of the universe

BLACK DWARF The cooling remains of a dwarf star that has used up its nuclear fuel

BLACK HOLE Thought to form when a massive star collapses. Black holes are extremely dense objects of such strong gravitational force that nothing passing within a certain distance can escape them, not even light.

BROWN DWARF A faintly glowing body too small to sustain a nuclear fusion reaction and become a star

COMET A body of rock, dust, and gaseous ice in an elongated orbit around the sun. Near the sun, heat diffuses gas and dust to form a streaming "tail" around the comet's nucleus.

CONSTELLATION A pattern of stars identified with an ancient god, goddess, or animal; also, an area of sky with one of these star patterns

CORONA The outermost layer of gases in the sun's atmosphere

COSMOLOGY The study of the beginning, end, and structure of the whole universe

CRATER A circular depression in the surface of a planet, caused by a meteorite impact or by volcanic action

DARK ENERGY A mysterious form of energy that seems to be speeding up the expansion of the universe

DARK MATTER An unknown substance that is detectable only by the gravity it exerts. It makes up 27 percent of the universe.

DENSITY A measurement of how much mass an object has within a certain amount of space: its mass divided by its volume

DIAMETER The distance through the center of an object from one side to the other: an object's width. In planets, the equatorial diameter is the planet's width at its equator.

DWARF GALAXY A small, dim galaxy that holds anywhere from about tens of millions to a few billion stars

DWARF PLANET A spherical or nearly spherical rocky body in orbit around the sun and not the satellite of another body; smaller than most of the other planets in our solar system

ECLIPSE An event caused by the passage of one astronomical body between an observer and another astronomical body, briefly blocking light from the farther astronomical body

EXTRASOLAR Outside of our solar system. Extrasolar planets, also called exoplanets, are planets orbiting another star.

FISSION The breakdown of atomic nuclei into the nuclei of lighter elements, releasing energy

FUSION The combining of the nuclei of two atoms to form one heavier nucleus, a process that releases energy

GALAXY A grouping of stars, gas, and dust bound together by gravity. Galaxies sometimes have many billions of stars.

GAMMA-RAY BURST A brief, intense burst of gamma radiation. These are the brightest explosions in the universe and come from sources outside our galaxy.

GAS GIANT A large planet made mostly of gases such as hydrogen and helium. In our solar system, Jupiter, Saturn, Uranus, and Neptune are gas giants.

GRAVITATIONAL ASSIST The use of the gravity of a body, such as a planet or star, to change a spacecraft's path and speed

GRAVITY The force that pulls objects toward each other. Everything with mass has gravity.

HABITABLE ZONE The region around a star in which a planet could have liquid water and possibly support life

INTERSTELLAR Existing or traveling between the stars

KUIPER BELT A reservoir of comets encircling an area just beyond the orbit of Neptune

LIGHT-YEAR Equals six trillion miles (10 trillion km), the distance light can travel in one Earth year

MAGNETIC FIELD The space around a body where magnetic forces can be felt. Many planets and stars have magnetic fields.

MAGNIFICATION The larger appearance of an object seen through a telescope or binoculars; also called power. A magnification of 10x means an object looks 10 times bigger than it would to the naked eye.

MAGNITUDE A number measuring an astronomical body's brightness in relation to other luminous objects

MASS The total quantity of material in an object, determining its gravity and resistance to movement

METEOR A small object from space that appears as a streak of light when it passes through Earth's atmosphere. A meteorite is the remains of a meteor found on Earth. A meteoroid is a rocky or metallic object in orbit around the sun that has the potential to become a meteor.

NEAR-EARTH OBJECT An asteroid or comet whose orbit is close to the Earth's. Abbreviated as NEO.

NEBULA A glowing interstellar cloud of gas and dust

NEUTRON STAR A body of densely packed neutrons formed after the explosion of a supernova. A neutron star only 10 miles (16 km) in diameter could have more mass than three sun-size stars.

OBSERVATORY A building with instruments for studying the sky

OORT CLOUD A reservoir of comets surrounding our solar system

ORBIT The regular path a celestial body follows as it revolves around another body

PLANET A spherical object larger than 600 miles (966 km) in diameter that orbits a star and has cleared its neighborhood of other like-size objects

PLANETARY NEBULA The glowing cloud of gas resulting from a supernova explosion

PLANETESIMAL A small rocky body in orbit around a star, which may become a planet by drawing in more material

PLASMA A collection of electrons and ions that is like a gas but is able to carry electricity. Plasma is the most common form of matter in the universe.

PRIMORDIAL Existing from the beginning of time

PROPULSION The force that moves something forward. In a spacecraft, the way the craft is propelled, such as by a chemical rocket or ion drive.

PULSAR Thought to be a spinning neutron star that sends out bursts of electromagnetic radiation with clockwork regularity

QUASAR A very bright object at the center of a galaxy, possibly energy given off by a massive black hole

RADIATION Energy that is given off in the form of waves or particles. Visible light, x-rays, and gamma rays are forms of radiation.

RED GIANT A cool, aging low-mass star that has fused most of its core hydrogen and expanded greatly from its previous size

REVOLVE To move in an orbit, as when a planet revolves around a star

RING A band of material around a planet, formed of dust-to-boulder-size pieces

ROTATE To spin around an axis

SATELLITE A natural or human-made object orbiting a planet

SOLAR (STELLAR) WIND A stream of charged particles radiating outward from the sun or another star

SOLSTICE The time of year when the sun is farthest north (in summer) or the farthest south (in winter) of Earth's Equator

SPECTRUM The range of radiation wavelengths from long radio waves to short gamma rays. The visible portion can be seen as colors when the radiation (light) is passed through a prism.

SUPERCLUSTER A group of galaxy clusters, bound together by gravity

SUPERGIANT A very massive, luminous star with a relatively short life span

SUPERNOVA The violent, luminous explosion at the end of a massive star's life

TERRESTRIAL Relating to, or similar to, Earth

VARIABLE STAR A star whose brightness changes back and forth over time

WHITE DWARF The small, dense core of a once larger star that has fused all the helium in its core

INDEX

INDEX

INDEX

ABOUT THE AUTHORS

DAVID A. AGUILAR is an internationally recognized astrono-mer whose expertise lies in heightening the fascinating connection between the universe, nature, and ourselves. Recognized for his spirited ability to open minds to the future of space science explora-tion and 21st-century wondrous worlds of discoveries, he tours, lectures, and contributes to some of today's best science exploration programs. He is the author and space artist for nine National Geo-graphic and three Random House award-winning books, inclúding *Seven Wonders of the Milky Way*, a lively galactic journey through our home in the cosmos, followed by *Luna: The Science and Stories of Our Moon*, in time for the 50th anniversary of man's walk on the moon. He is an on-screen contributor and space artist for the History Channel's *The Universe* series, the Science Channel's *NASA's Unexplained Files*, and NHK's (Japan's national television company) *Cosmic Front* series, and a featured contributor in *Chesley Bonestell: A Brush With the Future*, an award-winning documentary about the Father of Space Art. David is former Direc-tor of Science Information and Public Outreach at the Harvard-Smithsonian Center for Astrophysics (CfA), in Cambridge,

Massachusetts, the world's largest astronomical research organiza-tion. In 2015 he joined NASA's New Horizons Mission Team as part of the historic Pluto flyby mission, and in 2018-19 as part of the Ultima Thule Kuiper Belt (KBO) flyby mission. In 2010, Asteroid 1990DA was named to honor his exceptional decades-long work to advance science education outreach. He also leads world study tours for Harvard University and the Smithsonian Institution. For more, see his website at www.aspenskies.com.

CHRISTINE PULLIAM, contributing writer (*To the Stars & Beyond*), is the news director for the Space Telescope Institute in Baltimore, Maryland, and a freelance science writer. She earned her B.S. degree in physics and her M.A. degree in astronomy from the University of Texas at Austin.

PATRICIA DANIELS, contributing writer, has written more than two dozen science and history titles for adults and children, including *The New Solar System* and *Constellations: My First Pocket Guide*. She lives in State College, Pennsylvania.

ILLUSTRATIONS

ADDITIONAL READING

Aguilar, David. *Luna: The Science and Stories of Our Moon.* National Geographic Children's Books, 2019.

Aldrin, Buzz, and Marianne Dyson. *Welcome to Mars: Making a Home on the Red Planet.* National Geographic Children's Books, 2015.

Baumann, Mary K., Will Hopkins, Loralee Nolletti, and Michael Soluri. *What's Out There: Images From Here to the Edge of the Universe.* Duncan Baird, 2006.

Consolmagno, Guy, and Dan M. Davis. *Turn Left at Orion: Hundreds of Night Sky Objects to See in a Home Telescope—and How to Find Them.* 5th edition. Cambridge University Press, 2019.

Croswell, Ken. *Ten Worlds: Everything That Orbits the Sun.* Boyds Mills Press, 2006.

Dickinson, Terence. *Hubble's Universe: Greatest Discoveries and Latest Images.* 2nd edition. Firefly Books, 2017.

Dickinson, Terence. *Nightwatch: A Practical Guide to Viewing the Universe.* 4th edition. Firefly Books, 2006.

Dinwiddie, Robert, et al. *Universe: The Definitive Visual Guide.* Revised edition. Dorling Kindersley, 2012.

Goldberg, Dave, and Jeff Blomquist. *A User's Guide to the Universe: Surviving the Perils of Black Holes, Time Paradoxes, and Quantum Uncertainty.* Wiley, 2010.

Jenkins, Martin. *Exploring Space: From Galileo to the Mars Rover and Beyond.* Candlewick, 2017.

Shetterly, Margot Lee. *Hidden Figures: Young Readers' Edition.* HarperCollins, 2016.

Skurzynski, Gloria. *Are We Alone? Scientists Search for Life in Space.* National Geographic Children's Books, 2004.

Trefil, James. *Space Atlas: Mapping the Universe and Beyond.* 2nd edition. National Geographic Partners, 2018.

WEBSITES

To learn more about space and astronomy, check out these websites.

Ask an Astronomer: curious.astro.cornell.edu

The Astronomy Café: sten.astronomycafe.net/the-astronomy-cafe

Astronomy Picture of the Day: apod.nasa.gov/apod/astropix.html

European Space Agency for Kids: www.esa.int/kids/en/home

Goddard Space Flight Center: nasa.gov/goddard

Hubblesite: hubblesite.org

International Astronomical Union: iau.org

Jet Propulsion Laboratory: jpl.nasa.gov/edu

NASA Astronauts: nasa.gov/astronauts

NASA Kids' Club: nasa.gov/kidsclub/index.html

NASA Science Solar System Exploration: solarsystem.nasa.gov

NASA StarChild: starchild.gsfc.nasa.gov/docs/StarChild/StarChild.html

National Air and Space Museum: airandspace.si.edu

National Geographic Kids Passport to Space: kids.nationalgeographic.com/explore/space/passport-to-space

National Geographic Space: nationalgeographic.com/science/space

Space.com: space.com

This Week's Sky at a Glance: skyandtelescope.com/observing/sky-at-a-glance

First Edition 2013 © National Geographic Society
Art 2013 & 2020 © David A. Aguilar
Second Edition 2020 © National Geographic Partners, LLC

Since 1888, the National Geographic Society has funded more than 12,000 research, exploration, and preservation projects around the world. The Society receives funds from National Geographic Partners, LLC, funded in part by your purchase. A portion of the proceeds from this book supports this vital work. To learn more, visit natgeo.com/info.

For more information, visit nationalgeographic.com, call 1-877-873-6846, or write to the following address:

National Geographic Partners
1145 17th Street N.W.
Washington, DC 20036-4688 U.S.A.

Visit us online at nationalgeographic.com/books

For librarians and teachers: nationalgeographic.com/books/librarians-and-educators

**More for kids from National Geographic:
natgeokids.com**

National Geographic Kids magazine inspires children to explore their world with fun yet educational articles on animals, science, nature, and more. Using fresh storytelling and amazing photography, *Nat Geo Kids* shows kids ages 6 to 14 the fascinating truth about the world—and why they should care.
kids.nationalgeographic.com/subscribe

For rights or permissions inquiries, please contact National Geographic Books Subsidiary Rights: bookrights@natgeo.com

Designed by Callie Broaddus and Carol Farrar Norton

National Geographic supports K–12 educators with ELA Common Core Resources. Visit natgeoed.org/commoncore for more information.

Trade hardcover ISBN: 978-1-4263-3856-4
Reinforced library binding ISBN: 978-1-4263-3857-1

Acknowledgments
The publisher would like to thank the book team: Priyanka Lamichhane and Libby Romero, senior editors; Kathryn Robbins, senior designer; Lori Epstein, photo director; Joan Gossett, production editorial manager; Anne LeongSon and Gus Tello, design production assistants; and the project team at Potomac Global Media: Kevin Mulroy, Barbara Brownell Grogan, Carol Farrar Norton, Pat Daniels, Uliana Bazar, Robert Burnham, Jane Sunderland, and Tim Griffin.

Printed in Hong Kong
20/PPHK/1

This book is dedicated to
James Gordon Irving, illustrator of *Stars*
and other Golden Nature Guide books,
who first inspired me to try oil painting the
solar system while in junior high school;
to Chesley Bonestell, mentor, friend,
and visionary of the future conquest of space;
to Arthur C. Clarke, Isaac Asimov, and
Carl Sagan, who enlightened and lit the fires
of imagination with their beautifully written
books about space and science fiction.
Lastly, this book would not have been
possible without the loving insights, laughter,
and support of my wife, Shirley, "Queen of
the Asteroids," and the unwavering drive
and monumentally gifted artistic talents
of David M. Seager, the book's art director.
Their passions for the beauty and
mysteries of space are in every piece of
artwork found in this book.
David A. Aguilar

To all the girls in love with science
Patricia Daniels